WITCH'S SHADOW

THE HEMLOCK CHRONICLES BOOK 1

EMMA L. ADAMS

This book was written, produced and edited in the UK, where some spelling, grammar and word usage will vary from US English.

Copyright © 2018 Emma L. Adams
All rights reserved.

To be notified when Emma L. Adams's next novel is released, sign up to her author newsletter.

1

If the Hemlock Coven had taught me one thing, it was not to trust the past to remain buried.

Of course, as a necromancer, re-burying things was in my job description, along with skulking around creepy warehouses on what was supposed to be my day off.

"There are no zombies here, Jas," said Lloyd, his voice echoing creepily back at me through the darkness.

"You sound like someone stole your birthday present," I told my friend and ghost-hunting partner. "No zombies is good news."

"Not if there's worse." He inched forward into the gloom, his pocket torch lighting the way. "The guild wouldn't have sent us here on a false alarm."

"If you say so." My footsteps crunched in what I sincerely hoped wasn't human remains. Even in the populated areas of Edinburgh, abandoned places swiftly fell prey to wild fae. Our job was to take care of undead, ghosts and poltergeists, not faeries, but the pair of mercenaries who'd run screaming out of this warehouse an hour ago had sworn that whatever had attacked them hadn't been alive.

Lucky for us.

The creepy old warehouse was prime zombie territory—isolated enough that nobody would be able to smell their stench—but smelled more like a witch's brew. I shone my torchlight over the ground in search of broken bones, but saw only dirt and used condoms. Ugh. "Of all the places to bump uglies, why pick this dump?"

"At least they're practising safe sex," said Lloyd.

"If they're not the ghosts we're hunting."

No dead bodies had yet to materialise, reanimated or otherwise, but ghosts were generally tied to the place they'd died in. That made us suckers for walking right into their lair. There's a reason the necromancers' job description might as well contain the small print: 'first person to die in a horror movie'.

Being able to see and sense ghosts was often a swift ticket to joining them.

I held the spirit sensor in my other hand, following the intermittent beeping noise. The guild's devices were only ten percent accurate, but it was better than nothing, and certainly better than walking in without a plan. As Lady Montgomery's assistant, it was on me to set a good example for my laid-back partner. Banish the dead, try not to get killed. Simple.

Lloyd halted, his torchlight casting long shadows in the gloom. "Is it just me, or does this place smell like the witches' market?"

"It does a bit," I admitted. I could barely make out his lanky frame next to me, tall and dark-skinned, with locs that occasionally brushed against my face when I stumbled over the edge of my cloak. The necromancer dress code made us look like clones of the Grim Reaper, minus the scythe. Just one perk of the job, along with the appreciation for a well-timed zombie pun. "Maybe some humans were screwing around with magic in here."

"Even humans wouldn't be *that* stupid."

"I wouldn't underestimate them. Look at those mercenaries."

"Point taken," he said. "By the way, you might want to look into getting that cloak of yours trimmed if you don't want to see what the floor tastes like up close."

I rolled my eyes at him. "All right, no need to rub it in."

I was a foot shorter than him, under five feet. I'd hoped my growth spurt wasn't over when I'd arrived here in Edinburgh at sixteen and that I'd grow into the uniform, but no such luck. You didn't necessarily have to look intimidating to do the job, but it helped to be taken seriously. I got most of my clout at the guild for being Lady Montgomery's assistant. I was more 'cute' than scary, with dyed jet-black hair, a lip piercing, and the sort of complexion that managed to get sunburned even here in Scotland. The piercing made faeries think twice about punching me in the face, but I didn't go out of my way to antagonise anyone. Not the living, anyway.

As I crept forwards, the faint sound of rustling came from ahead, while the pungent smell of herbs grew stronger. Maybe a witch had been hanging out in here after all, but not our ghost. Performing witch magic required three things: a functioning brain, which zombies didn't have; the ability to touch things, which ghosts were sorely lacking; and a certain amount of magical talent, which witches lost the moment they passed over the veil.

Lloyd took a step backwards. "What the bloody hell is that?"

His torchlight caught on some leaves lying on top of a dark stain on the floor, encased in a chalked symbol.

My mouth went dry. Chalk symbols meant witchcraft, and ominous stains meant trouble. But despite being the expert of the two of us on all things witchy, I didn't have a clue what the symbol actually meant. Ghosts' magic disappeared when they died. Usually.

Oh, boy.

A jet of icy air slammed into me, as though someone had switched on a high-powered fan right in front of my face. I stumbled backwards, catching myself against Lloyd's arm. "That'd be our spirit." But the blast of air hadn't felt like necromantic energy alone. *Please, please don't let that ghost be what I think it is.*

Another wave of icy air blasted into us, along with a helping of snowflakes. Not my lucky day, then. Spirits were harmless. Poltergeists were a nuisance. But what we had here was a half-faerie ghost: the magic of the living fused with the persistence of the dead.

"Show yourself," I said into the empty air. "We're necromancers. You can't hide from us."

The space in front of us flickered like the screen of an old TV, and the transparent figure of a young man appeared, hovering above the chalked symbol. Bright blue eyes glowed with magic, and his silver hair gleamed dimly with the light of the spirit world.

"Wasn't so hard, was it?" I said. "Now if you come with me, you'll leave limbo behind."

Magic crackled between his fingertips, chilling the air. Faerie magic wasn't normally visible to humans like me, but he'd removed the glamour so I'd see every second of his attack in full technicolour glory.

"Nobody likes a show-off," I told the ghost. "Put the magic away and we can talk. I might even introduce you to my supervisors."

"I don't care."

He clearly hadn't met Lady Montgomery, the fearsome leader of Edinburgh's necromancer guild and the person who'd have my head on a platter if I didn't stop this ghost before he caused criminal damage.

"That's not very polite," I said. "Look, you're no longer one of the living. You're dead. Deceased. No magical tantrums will change that."

Half-faeries were by and large terrified of death, probably because their Sidhe parents were undying. Born with a Sidhe's magic but a human's mortality, half-faeries turned into the worst kind of poltergeist. I wouldn't lie, I'd rather trip over a pair of wannabe witches screwing one another in the dirt than face a poltergeist's faerie magic.

The ghost gave me an accusing stare. "You're still alive, but you look… ghostly."

"I'm a necromancer. Did the uniform not give you a clue?"

Blue light exploded from the ghost's fingertips, brushing past my cheek and leaving a painful sting in its wake. *Oh damn.* Necromancy, unlike other types of magic, wasn't designed for use in combat. It was possibly the most impractical magical type in existence, requiring props and incantations and hours of preparation. We didn't *have* hours. More like a minute. If the ghost realised he could blast the doors of the warehouse clean off and wrap the city in a blizzard, then we'd be in real trouble. The presence of the weird chalk symbol made me all the more certain this guy hadn't died here alone.

"Cover for me," I muttered to Lloyd, and dug in my pocket for my set of necromantic candles.

While Lloyd moved in to block the spirit's path, I ran backwards out of range, dropping to a crouch and laying out the candles. We'd done the same routine in worse conditions than pitch-black darkness: he distracted the ghost, I laid the trap. But today was different. My gaze kept drifting towards the chalk symbol as I laid down each candle. *Dark magic... blood magic.*

A whisper traced the back of my neck, a shiver stirring in my blood. Like a faint trace of magic called to something inside me. A part of me long forgotten.

A part of me I wanted to forget.

Twelve candles, set in a circle, would give our ghost an express ticket into the afterlife. They remained unlit until my command, after which any ghost trapped between them would be dragged to the other side of the veil, never to bother anyone again.

I looked up, ready to lure our ghost into the trap—but he wasn't there.

Lloyd swore. "The bloody ghost vanished."

"Shit." I spun around on the spot. "Get back here!"

The candles weren't lit, so the ghost wouldn't spot them until it was too late. One small problem: in order to avoid clueing him in, neither of us would be able to expose the candles, either.

Lloyd stepped to my side. "I suppose it's too much to hope that he hopped over the veil of his own accord?"

"He's a faerie. He wouldn't cross the veil if you paid him."

"Not much you can pay a ghost," he said quietly. "Especially one using blood magic."

"That's not blood magic," I said automatically. Lloyd talked a big game about knowing all the deepest and darkest secrets of necromancy, but to most of us, those areas were out of bounds. Even to me, and I was the one entrusted with staffing the archives in the necromancer guild's library in my free time. Too many necromancers had gone bad to risk that information ending up in the hands of novices.

"Blood, check. Chalk lines, check. Weird herbal concoction, check. If that's not blood magic, I'm a unicorn."

"Lloyd," I hissed. "Get down."

"The blood magic is on the ground."

I grabbed the back of his coat. "And the ghost is right above you. Don't knock over the candles."

As the ghost descended in a shower of icy snowflakes, I yanked Lloyd to the floor along with me. The ghost's attack smashed into the place where we'd been standing, stinging the back of my neck. *Ow.*

Lloyd groaned beneath me. "You're crushing me."

"You're welcome." I climbed off Lloyd, swearing. I'd dropped my torch, and the light had gone out. "Get out here, you cowardly little shit."

The ghost flung another handful of magic across the floor. I dodged, then dropped into a fighting stance. I might not have the range of fancy tricks a faerie did, but if he wanted to thwack me with necromantic magic, I'd return the favour.

"Come and hit me," I said, my voice ringing in the darkness. "I'm wearing iron."

"That's not going to work," Lloyd hissed in my ear. "If it was, I'd have thrown my spell at him."

I twisted to stare at him. "Since when did you even have an iron charm?"

"Why? It won't work."

"*He* doesn't know that. He's a faerie. Being dead isn't quite computing for him yet. He'll see the iron barrier, panic…"

And run right into the candles.

Lloyd went silent. "Yes. Where are the—?"

"Ten metres behind us, give or take," I said in a low voice. "Not sure. I lost track when I knocked you over."

"Yeah, I'm covered in some kind of crap I don't really want to know about. One iron spell, coming right up."

Greyish light flashed before us, lighting up the gloom. The iron barrier looped around both of us, covering our section of floor.

"Come and get us!" Lloyd shouted.

Nothing stirred, but a faint breeze lifted the leaves surrounded by chalk lines. Blood magic or not, I couldn't leave a dubious magical trap lying around. The boss would kill me.

Oh, screw it.

I stepped out of the iron circle towards the dimly lit chalk lines.

"Jas?" he hissed. "What are you doing?"

"Taking down his little piece of witchery." I scuffed the chalk symbol with my toe. That ought to do it.

A whisper feathered over the back of my neck.

"Hey there," I told the ghost. "Ready to play nice?"

I stepped away from the witchy trap, towards Lloyd's faintly lit form. If our pesky ghost wanted to avoid the iron, it would be forced right into the candles.

The ghost appeared before us, silvery hair aglow. I wished I hadn't dropped my torch, but Lloyd turned his onto the highest setting, illuminating the iron spell. A circle of grey light surrounded us all—including the ghost.

"You trapped me!" the ghost screamed. "Get it off—get me out!"

The iron wasn't harming him—it had no effect on the dead—but he wailed and screamed like he'd been tossed into a vat of acid. Screeching, he slipped over the edge of the candle circle—

"Lights." I snapped my fingers, and the candles switched on in an instant. The ghost shrieked again, trapped in a web of twelve criss-crossing lights. A cheap trick, but it worked like a witch charm.

Grey fog filled the room, and everything vanished except for Lloyd, me, and the screaming faerie ghost, still encased in candlelight.

"Welcome," I said. "This is your own personal afterlife. Please proceed directly to the gates."

"And no littering," added Lloyd. "C'mon, hurry up. Hades doesn't like to be kept waiting."

The ghost, his magic sealed and his spirit bound for death, stared at us and the sudden greyness which had replaced the warehouse. As necromancers, we were the only type of supernatural who could cross into the spirit realm without dying ourselves.

"Hades?" said the ghost. "Is that what's behind the gates?"

"Wait and see," Lloyd said. "Necromancer's privilege to know. Your personal coach along the River Styx is waiting for you. Say hi to Charon for me, and don't screw with the archangel at the pearly gates."

"Didn't we already have words about mixing up your mythology?" I gave him an eye-roll. To the ghost, I said, "Just relax and float towards the gates. You'll be on the other side in a second. It's painless. Honest."

The ghost did not start floating towards the gates, but remained where he was. The candle lights grew dimmer.

"You know," he said, "I don't feel like playing nice."

Magic exploded from his hands, right at us. I dodged, my heart sinking. *How* could he still use magic? That symbol... had it been some kind of magical amplifier? It'd been a long time since I'd learned those symbols, but a distant memory stirred, and even here in Death, the faint smell of herbs filtered in.

"Calm down," I warned.

The ghost grinned, raised his hands once more, and blasted us with necromantic power. Lloyd howled, stumbling backwards, until the fog buried him from sight—leaving me alone with a ghost dead set on staying put. If we weren't careful, we'd be the ones taking a swift and brutal trip through the not-so-pearly gates.

"Look, it's not worth kicking up a fuss. You're still dead." I raised my hands, but my own necromantic power paled in comparison to a full-powered poltergeist. They could keep going for hours when pushed.

I *did* have a way to swiftly end this... but playing my best card was risky.

I never knew what might happen when my *other* magic came out to play.

A rush of power welled inside me, from somewhere deep within, a bottomless pit I'd never looked too closely at. My hands tingled, my body reverberating with a humming sensation that seemed to come from deep below the earth—but we weren't *on* earth. Not even close.

The ghost screamed.

"Go," whispered a voice that wasn't mine, though it came from my mouth.

The ghost bolted. His transparent form floated away, towards the gates of death. They appeared—long, endless gates stretching across the horizon as far as the eye could see—but while ghosts became more transparent the closer they got to the gates, my body glowed with magic. Power rolled beneath my skin like a tidal wave.

A shadow in the corner of my eye warned me of another ghost within my personal space.

I whipped my head to the side, and a voice whispered in my ear, "Hemlock."

I recoiled, and abruptly, my senses came back. I sucked in a breath as my body returned to consciousness, and shook my numb fingers to get some sensation back into them.

"You in there, Jas?" Lloyd peered into my eyes.

I stepped backwards, my legs trembling slightly. "Yeah. The ghost's gone. I told him to screw off and I guess I scared him more than I thought."

He laughed. "Go, you. The bastard shut me straight out of the afterlife."

"I saw. What gave him that power?" I didn't expect an answer. Nor did I like deceiving my closest friend, but it was safer for nobody to know that sometimes, when I fought against the dead, I wasn't me at all.

"Haven't a clue." He handed me my torch, which I switched back on. "Your voice goes all posh when you're scared. It's hilarious."

"I'm glad I entertain you," I said, feeling my face heat up. I couldn't hide *all* the signs that I'd spent my teenage years living with a branch of high society English mages, but I did my best. I barely classed as a mage by adoption, and the fact that half my family were a mix of witches, mages and necromancers didn't help. I got by just fine using my necromancer talent, the only type of magic I'd ever have. And as long as it stayed that way, the word 'hemlock' would remain buried deeper than the dead.

I crouched down to retrieve the candles while he put the iron spell away. "That cute ghost was haunting me again last night," he said. "Reckon she'll be impressed with our iron strategy."

"You're not going to tell her it was your idea?" I pulled a face. "You should just ask why she's hanging around."

"Because she's lonely and wants someone to talk to?"

I slipped two candles into my cloak's fathomless pocket. "She can have all that and more in the afterlife, free of charge. Come on, you know I'm not supposed to enable this shit."

"You're not my boss," he said, which was technically true.

"I'm boss enough to tell you to stop making out with ghosts and get on with the job."

"Yes, O wise one."

I rolled my eyes and reached for more candles. Lloyd was bi with a slight preference for dudes. I was straight with a significant preference for dudes who had a heartbeat. You wouldn't think the latter part would need stating, and yet. Necromancers got creative. Especially when, given enough practise, the spirit realm started to feel as real as the everyday one.

Candles retrieved, I cast one last look at the remains of the witch's circle. By now, I was sure that's what it was. It sure as hell wasn't necromancy. But while I might have the dubious honour of calling myself a Hemlock witch, I had zero talent to back it up, and no formal training to speak of. With the perpetrators gone, a scuffed chalk symbol and a weird stain wouldn't qualify as reliable evidence. Not to mention, I'd have to answer questions about how I'd come by that knowledge to begin with—which would make a creepy whispering ghost the least of my concerns.

Hemlock.

There was little of my birth coven left. I had no real ties to them, since I didn't have any witchy talent to speak of, but that didn't make it any less weird that the ghost had spoken the name.

"Jas? You're spacing out. You okay?"

I took in a long, slow breath. The poltergeist was gone and wouldn't bother us anymore. That's all that mattered. Why I'd heard that voice say *hemlock*... I must have imagined it. There was no reason for a disembodied spirit to know that name. The Hemlocks had erased themselves from all public record. For all intents and purposes, they had never existed.

"Yeah." I hitched on a smile. "Let's go and report in."

2

Lady Montgomery regarded me across her desk with her steely gaze. "You didn't interrogate the ghost about the props?"

"He wasn't in the mood for conversation," I responded. "Also, he was a faerie. They can't use witch magic, and certainly not when dead."

"Tell me what you saw again." She didn't ask, she ordered. That's what happened when a woman who'd gone into battle with the Sidhe in the faerie invasion took charge. Shit got done. A stern-faced woman with her greying hair pulled into a bun and her necromancer robes adorned with medals of honour from her accomplishments in battle, she was every inch as formidable as she'd been during the war between the faeries and the other supernaturals twenty-something years earlier.

Unfortunately, she wasn't the expert in this case. Not as far as faerie magic and witch rituals were concerned, anyway. I'd described the scene six times already and that wasn't including the written report, which I had to hand in before the necromancer summit tonight.

"Are you absolutely positive you don't know what the witch's symbol meant?" She drummed her fingers on the desk, which she always kept impeccably tidy, every book and paper neatly tucked away. The only human touches to the spartan decor were a few photographs of her son, River, on a shelf above the desk. The cute pictures of the blond half-faerie went a long way towards making her look less scary, though nobody said so to her face.

"I honestly don't know," I said. "Rituals and spells are not my area of expertise. It's not like I know the local covens, either."

Introducing myself would have been too risky even if I'd possessed the barest hint of talent. Eventually, someone would have asked the wrong question about my background, and then they'd be next on the hit list of the Hemlock Coven's enemies.

"The stain might have been blood," I admitted. "As for the symbol, I don't remember what it looked like, but any coven would kick you out if you walked up to them waving a symbol of potential dark magic."

"I planned on a subtler approach, Jas." She gave me an expectant look.

"Does it involve me knocking on coven doors and asking awkward questions? Because I'd have to at least claim to be a witch to get in."

I was not a spectacular liar. Lady Montgomery had seen through my deception the instant I'd walked through the doors seven years ago, as a frightened teenager who'd fled across half a country to escape her own coven. But she'd let me take on an apprenticeship with her all the same. I had the perfect cover, and I wasn't about to let an amateur occultist ruin it.

"I'm aware of your dilemma," she said, "but you're one of us. If there's a danger to the guild, we need to do everything we can to stop it."

"I have no idea what that spell was, if it was one," I said honestly. "I'd tell you if I did."

She paused for a long moment before saying, "If you have anything more to add, do come and speak to me, Jas. And don't forget the summit tonight."

"Haven't forgotten," I said, in an attempt at a cheery voice. "Let me know if you need anything else."

Translation: *please let me go and change out of my cloak.* Whatever had been on that warehouse floor when I'd tackled Lloyd to the ground wasn't sanitary in the slightest.

She gave me a nod of dismissal, and I left her office with relief. Lloyd himself stood with his hands in his pockets, wearing jeans and a fresh T-shirt. Arse. He'd had time to shower and change while I'd been answering Lady Montgomery's million and a half questions. Lloyd didn't really understand why I willingly spent so much time around the boss, but he didn't probe too far into the reasons why I'd seek out an apprenticeship that put me in a position usually reserved for senior necromancers. If people thought I was more talented than I actually was, I'd be less likely to invite questioning about my… *other* heritage.

Lloyd himself, born into a human family who'd discovered the spirit sight independently by accident, could at least relate to my outsider status. But while it was more common than it used to be for otherwise ordinary humans to discover an affinity for witchcraft or necromancy, other types of skill were less common even in supernaturals.

"Didn't keep you long, did she?" He made a point of stepping out of the way of my dirt-covered, trailing cloak.

"I'm not off the hook for tonight's summit, either. Guess near-death experiences aren't an excuse when we're near death every waking moment."

He pulled a face. "I forgot they're making you take notes at the summit. Hopefully, this one won't be interrupted by a zombie plague."

"Got to have realistic expectations." I made my way down the corridor leading into the locker room and showers next to the necromancers' gymnasium. "I'm going to change. Don't start the movie without me."

After each mission, Lloyd and I had a well-rehearsed routine: we'd watch a terrible zombie movie and order takeout. It gave us the illusion of stability in an unstable job, and we'd established the tradition from when we'd first joined the guild. Lloyd's dedication to seeking out obscure monster movies from the world before the faerie invasion was admirable, if nothing else, but watching zombified actors in makeup staggering around had the added bonus of making our real missions seem less scary.

Seven years. I hadn't expected to stay this long, but the guild was a safe haven for outsiders and I'd taken to necromancy better than I'd expected. The spirit sight was easy enough to develop, even for someone who had the barest hint of the gift, and more to the point, humans tended to favour one kind of magic over the others if they had ancestry from two or more types of supernatural. Nobody would have reason to question why I only used necromancy even if they somehow found out I had mage and witch ancestry, too.

I shoved all thoughts of witchcraft aside and headed for the shower. I had a zombie movie marathon to prepare for, followed by a stint in the cemetery taking notes for Lady Montgomery. No rest for the wicked—or the dead.

Necromancer summits were about as cheerful as you'd expect from a gathering of the dead and the living. I'd lost all sensation in my feet by the end of the first hour of sitting on a cold stone wall in one of Edinburgh's many cemeteries, while the senior necromancers spoke to their ancestors.

By the second hour, I was blowing on my hands to warm them up in between taking notes. The frigid November air didn't help my concentration levels, but Lady Montgomery kept coming to check up on my note-taking so I couldn't sneak away somewhere warm for a bit. I was the only non-senior member allowed in, which would have been an honour if it didn't involve catching my not-literal death of cold.

"Boo," said a soft voice, and I jolted upright, my head smacking into Lloyd's chin. "Ow."

"You're not supposed to be here." I turned around, squinting at his lanky figure behind the wall. "If the boss spots you—"

"Relax." He rubbed his chin, a paper cup in his other hand. "She's too interested in what that boring old ghost has to say. I brought you hot chocolate. Thought you'd appreciate the warmth."

"Thanks," I whispered, taking the cup from him. "You really shouldn't be on senior necromancer territory, not with…"

Faerie ghosts working with someone who used witchcraft? Spirits who knew my coven's name?

"With what?" He cocked a brow.

"Weirdness in the spirit realm."

"There hasn't been a single day since I signed up at the guild where there hasn't been weirdness in the spirit realm, Jas."

He had a point. Since the faerie invasion, the barriers between life and death had been fragile to say the least. All sorts of weird crap rose from beyond the grave. What'd happened today wasn't so unusual at all.

"Also," he added, "were you drawing faeries?"

I shushed him and pulled down the page of my notepad. "Not according to Lady Montgomery."

Drawing calmed my nerves and kept me from seeing shadowy figures where they didn't exist, so I'd been sketching a picture of the faerie ghost we'd seen, and resisting the impulse to draw the chalk symbol to see if it jogged my memory. Even without any witchy talent, copying occult symbols was a great way to invite trouble.

"Watch she doesn't stick you on cleaning duty again," said Lloyd.

"She can't criticise me for entertaining myself while she's over there chatting with ghosts. Besides, she said I'm the best assistant she's had since her son."

River Montgomery, who only vaguely resembled the

blond kid in the photos in his mother's office, currently occupied the predominant position in the meeting, along with his girlfriend Ilsa. Lloyd and I had accidentally arrested her as a potential rogue when she'd first shown up in the city with off-the-grid necromancy skills a couple of months ago, but she didn't hold it against us. Since she and River had helped save the city from a swarm of wraiths, they'd been elevated to the highest level.

"They're really into it tonight." Lloyd jerked his head in the direction of the senior necromancers. "Must be something big happening."

"Nah, the ancient ghosts like to gossip. Nobody else will stand there for three hours and listen to them."

Generally, I thought necromancy was actually a pretty cool type of magic to have, but I had no ambitions to join the upper echelons if it meant spending endless hours listening to the woes of the former necromancers. The dreary night made me want to curl up and go to sleep, not converse with ghosts. I blew on the hot chocolate to cool it down, and took a sip. It had a weird aftertaste.

"And they say the dead have a quiet existence." Lloyd shuffled backwards. "Don't tell her where you got that."

I took another sip of hot chocolate. "Where *did* you get it?"

"Market stall. I should head off before they toss me out for ruining their séance."

"Yeah. Watch your back walking home, okay?" The weird taste persisted. I gagged. Hemlock.

The cup slipped from my hands, spilling all over my notes. My vision blurred, and I slipped off the wall onto my knees.

Lloyd's stricken face swam above me. Voices shouted.

Hemlock...

I was dying. At a necromancer summit. Almost as ironic as being poisoned by the symbol of my own coven.

Blackness descended.

Death brought me directly into the spirit realm. I imagined it'd come as a shock to non-necromancers to see what awaited after death, but I barely blinked at the sight of thousands of transparent figures floating in an endless grey fog. "Hey," I said, to several ghosts I passed. "Nice to join you. Please proceed directly to the gates."

What a way to go. There was no point in kicking up a fuss, though—my time had come, as per the necromancer rulebook. If I threw a tantrum and played poltergeist, it was my former colleagues who'd have to deal with the fallout. I had to maintain some level of professionalism.

And the real kick in the face was that I hadn't reached a high enough level to train as a necromancer Guardian afterwards. Not that I particularly wanted to spend an eternity guarding Death's gates, but it'd have been nice to hang on for long enough to say goodbye to my friends. And my family.

A pang hit my heart. Lloyd's face floated before me. *He didn't know... someone tried to kill me.*

Warn him.

I halted, sensing another ghost behind me.

"You shouldn't be here." The voice was male and flat, with a hint of violence. I jerked backwards—or rather, floated—and turned to face the speaker.

The outline of a person faced me. I stared into the

empty space, confused. Usually spirits looked like a more transparent version of their living self. This guy—if he hadn't spoken aloud, I wouldn't have thought him a ghost at all. More like a shadow shaped like a person.

"Yes, I should be here," I said. "I'm Jas Lyons, a necromancer. I'm also dead. What are you?"

He raised a hand. "Begone, shade."

"What the…?"

With an abrupt jolt, I fell backwards. The ground gave way beneath me, except it couldn't have done, because there *was* no ground in the spirit realm—

And then my lungs drew breath.

3

I coughed, my body shuddering. Trees crowded overhead, their interlocking branches blocking out the ceiling of the... cave.

Why am I in a cave?

Soft moss cushioned my back. I still wore my necromancer cloak, and the soil beneath my hands felt real enough. Trees curved around the walls, blocking out all the natural light aside from the luminescent glow from the web-like glyphs sprawled on the walls. Symbols of an ancient magic, keeping the cave hidden. Tree roots crisscrossed the floor, while their trunks had grown into the stalactites and stalagmites connecting floor and ceiling. A huge stone sculpture formed a mass in the cave's centre, vaguely human in shape.

My heart jumped into my throat.

I was dreaming. This couldn't be real. I hadn't been in a cave within a forest in years. Not since—

The rock sculpture moved, and a face peered at me, a

face with pits for eyes and lines of years beyond reckoning carved into the stone.

"Cordelia," I whispered.

Cordelia Hemlock blinked, her face meshed with the bark, her body fused into the tree. She'd been that way since before I was born, and so had her fellow Hemlock witches. Their bodies and minds were locked into rock and tree and stone, deep within a forest which didn't entirely belong in this world. Other faces appeared in the walls, and their eyes stared at me with judgemental intensity.

So much for running away.

"How?" I whispered. "How am I here? I left."

"You did," said Cordelia. "You abandoned your coven."

"And am I banished to hell as my punishment?" I didn't think so. I hadn't even passed through the gates of death before I'd been yanked back into the land of the living.

Okay, 'living' was a stretch. However old the Hemlock witches had been when their magic had trapped them here in the forest, they were no longer alive in the technical sense, but also unable to die. It wasn't a lie when I claimed to be the only living Hemlock witch remaining, not really. And if I'd been born with any magical talent, I would have suffered the same fate as they did. I'd be stuck in this forest for the rest of my life.

"I'm dead," I said. "Aren't I? I can't be immortal like you, because I don't have any magic."

But judging by the throbbing pain in my head, I wasn't in Death. Ghosts didn't feel pain, no more than echoes. They left all physical injuries behind.

"You have magic," said the leader of the Hemlock Coven. "I see you've been making use of it."

I took a step backwards, my foot catching on a tree root. "Look, not that it isn't nice to see you, but I really don't understand how I'm still alive, or how I got here in the first place."

"You're here because an ally of ours brought you here to save your life," said Cordelia. "Aren't you going to ask me how the coven has survived without you?"

"Survived?" I held back a comment about how being trapped in a tree was stretching the definition a little. "Perfectly fine, I imagine, considering the last time you saw me, you said I had less magical talent than a garden gnome."

And she wondered why I hadn't come back to say hi? Aside from the fact that the forest was supposed to be several hundred miles from Edinburgh, so my being here at all was supposed to be impossible.

"You don't have magic," she said. "But *she* does. And she's finally awakened."

Something in the way she said *she* chilled my blood. "Who?"

"I think you know who I mean."

I shook my head slowly. "No. I really don't." If you weren't born with magic, nobody else could give it to you. It was one of the basic rules of the supernatural world. No exceptions. Not even Cordelia would be able to manipulate her way around that one, right?

"You didn't inherit the gift," she said. "But your spirit is bound to someone who did. Have you ever heard of a shade?"

I shook my head automatically. My mind was whirling, and a cold pit opened inside me as denial dug its heels in. There was no way—*no way* I wouldn't know—

"A shade is a spirit that inhabits the body of one of the living while that person is still alive," said Cordelia.

"What?" My voice was barely a whisper. "It's not possible, not when I'm still living and breathing and walking around. There's no spirit inside me except my own."

"Wrong," said Cordelia. "I'd be surprised if you'd never felt her presence, being a necromancer, but the shade is so close to you that I doubt anyone would have noticed you weren't the same person. After all, she has been dormant most of your life."

"You can't have two spirits in one body," I said. "It's one of the standard rules of necromancy. It's possible for someone to be temporarily possessed, but not permanently."

"This is no possession," she said. "Her spirit is attached to yours. And that means her magic is yours, too."

My cloak caught against the cave wall as I backed away from her stare. "You're being absurd. Who even is this... shade?"

"Her name is Evelyn Hemlock. Since your parents are dead, and no other living heirs remain but you—"

"Sorry, but I've spent the last seven years living in the same building as experts who would swear point-blank that it's absolutely impossible for a spirit to survive inside another person's body." Even if it *was* possible, possession was dealt with in one way: by kicking the offending spirit right into the afterlife.

"Most spirits aren't strong enough to survive it," she said. "But we Hemlocks are stronger than most people."

Because *that* wasn't egotistical at all. Witches weren't typically big-headed or ambitious, certainly not compared to the mages, and I'd gathered that said big-headedness had been responsible for the Hemlock witches ending up stuck in a cave for all eternity. They never had volunteered the details of how it'd happened. Maybe I didn't want to know.

Speaking of things no sane person would want to know...

"How did this... *Evelyn Hemlock* person end up being bound to me in the first place?" I asked.

"Because there was no heir," Cordelia growled. "There needs to be one. You had no magic, but you're of the bloodline. The spell would have been performed the instant she died, which made the transfer smooth. You were a baby. You won't have felt it."

I was fairly sure I was going to throw up. "So it was... a sacrificial ritual? That's what you're saying? She gave her life to be bound to me on purpose?"

"To continue the bloodline. Yes."

My fingers dug into stone as I steadied myself against the wall. "That is sick. It's also against magical law."

Did it explain how I'd survived the poisoning? Yes. It also explained how I'd survived a fair few other almost-fatal accidents over the years. Two spirits in one body made both stronger.

"We didn't have a choice," said Cordelia. "We need an heir. It's necessary for the survival of the coven, and should I die, it is you who will take my place."

"Lucky you're not about to expire anytime soon, right?" I said, folding my arms to hide my trembling hands. "Just don't do anything too rash."

"Flippancy won't serve you well."

"Neither will dragging me into your cave, telling me

I'm possessed by another person, and practically ordering me to take your place. No thanks."

"You will come to understand in time, Jacinda Hemlock."

The cave vanished, leaving me alone on a forest path.

"Oh, come on." I stared around at the crowding trees, the endless paths leading into shadow. The forest had no clear boundaries, since it didn't belong to a dimension that made any sense. Which meant I was stuck here until the Hemlock witches said otherwise.

I felt in my pocket for my phone and pulled it out. The time had stuck at 9 o'clock in the evening. From the light streaming through the trees, it was daytime, but the forest didn't even subscribe to the usual laws of time and place. Let alone anything else.

I'm... possessed.

I ran a hand over my face. Everything was where it should be, down to the lip piercing. I was alive. I'd survived death by hemlock poison and walked right into a life sentence.

No. I'd find a way out of it, once I got home. If the forest had brought me here, surely it could take me back to Edinburgh, too.

I stopped walking mid-step. The spirit realm... I'd been half dead when I'd woken up here, which meant I should be able to access the spirit realm from here. If so, I could run a test on whether or not Cordelia was right about there being another person living inside me. There'd certainly been enough moments when I'd tapped into that realm of power, a source I couldn't explain, and spoken with a voice that didn't belong to me at all. Had I been channelling the other spirit the whole time?

"This is batshit." Unfortunately, it all made sense. Whatever the faerie ghost had seen when he'd looked at me had been enough to send him screaming through the gates of death, but it wasn't as though I could take a look in a mirror and see what, exactly, had frightened him so much. Ghosts didn't have reflections.

Witch or not, there was zero chance I'd be giving up my apprenticeship anytime soon. After all, necromancy wasn't simply concerned with raising the dead, but also banishing it. Unwanted shades included. As Lady Montgomery's assistant, I was one step away from the guild's top-secret archives, and if anywhere contained a clue about how to get rid of the second spirit, it was there. If I ever got out of this forest.

I tapped into the spirit realm, and grey fog swirled around me. It was risky going into Death without candles for backup, but I hadn't brought any with me to the summit, and I was a whole world away from the guild. Besides, I'd survived worse as a guild employee—falling into the river, being flung into walls by poltergeists, and even being stabbed by a fae intruder a few months ago. Lloyd sometimes joked that I had nine lives. Should have figured my luck had a limit somewhere.

Death looked the same from this angle as it ever did, since the spirit world didn't overlap directly with the mortal realm. The view looked identical wherever you stood geographically—grey fog, and the distant shape of a set of endless gates. Whatever lay beyond those gates was off-limits to everyone but the highest necromancer Guardians. You needed to be permanently dead to get there. And if this Evelyn Hemlock's spirit had been lurking around my whole life, I doubted detaching from my body and floating over to the gates would encourage her to hop out of my body without a fuss.

Besides... maybe that wasn't the answer. After all, if she disappeared, so would the last of the Hemlock magic. There must be a way to separate her spirit from mine without either of us dying. Right?

"You again," said a cold voice.

The shadowy male who'd spoken to me before towered over me. I squinted, trying to make out his features. *He's not a shade? Is he?* I had no idea what the spirit possessing me actually *looked* like. But he'd said *begone, shade...*

"Who are you?" I asked.

"Someone intrigued to know why a shade is wandering around the spirit realm, unchecked."

My heart thudded, a reminder of my mortal skin. "What if I came here of my own accord?"

"Then you're a fool."

"Wow, you sure know how to flatter a girl. Care to explain what *you* are?" I vaguely gestured to his shadowy form.

"No, I don't think that's something you need to know."

Not a ghost. Was he some other form of necromancer? "Are you stalking me?"

"I'm afraid I have no idea where you are, if you're still one of the living. Shade or not."

"Stalking still counts as stalking if you don't have a body." Was he the person who'd whispered *hemlock* in my ear? It was hard to recall the voice, but something about him seemed familiar to me all the same.

"How do you know I don't have one?" His gaze skimmed over me, and though I couldn't actually see his eyes, his stare was penetrating enough to make heat rise to my cheeks. Could ghosts blush? Yes, apparently.

"Educated guess. I'm a necromancer." He must have had training from someone in the know to be able to tell I was a shade. He also hadn't run screaming in terror, so maybe I wasn't wearing my shade guise this time around. But nobody except for the Hemlocks could access the forest, so how had he managed to reach me here? He had some seriously powerful spiritual powers... which made him a fellow necromancer. Not a guild one, surely. I might not have spoken to every member, but I'd met most of the senior ones, and he was way too cocky to be a novice.

"You seem too intelligent to be a guild lackey," he observed.

That answered that question, then. "What does that make you?"

He stilled, his gaze shifting past me. "There's something here that shouldn't be."

"Yeah. I'm looking at it." Not that I could actually see him, but if you spent enough time in the spirit realm, you learned to recognise when there was someone close by even if you couldn't see their face. The spirit sight was a sixth sense of sorts, and right now, it told me there was something inhuman nearby.

A greyish mass appeared at our feet, trailing white smoke. Wisps—faerie spirits—weren't supposed to appear in the spirit realm. By travelling into Death in the forest, I must have brought them with me.

"Shoo." I waved a hand at the wisps. "Go away."

"Is there any reason faerie spirits are tailing you, Jas Lyons?"

"How do you know my name?"

"Don't you remember telling me?"

Of course I had. The wisps swirled around me, growing brighter. Their usual trick was to lead humans through the forest to their deaths, which wouldn't do much good here in the spirit realm. "I can't banish these little shits through the gates."

"Then you'll have to scare them off."

Scare them. Like the faerie ghost. Simple, yet... did I really want this stranger—a stranger who was only partially here, and had powers I couldn't begin to understand—to see what I could do?

Magic hummed in my fingertips. The same power I felt in the forest, multiplied several times over.

Guess I don't get a say after all.

The wisps recoiled away from me as my hands continued to glow with the strange, alien power. I lifted my head, and a faint glow permeated my entire body. "Go," whispered a voice, quiet yet commanding. It came from my mouth.

Evelyn?

The wisps vanished, leaving me alone with the strange shadowy man.

"Tell me where you are, Jas Lyons," he said. "Tell me what magic you're using."

"I won't."

My mouth moved, but the voice wasn't mine, and neither was the alien, terrifying power, roaring through my veins.

Hey. Stop that. I'd completely crossed over into Death, leaving my body behind. If I'd stayed too long, even an extra soul might not save me from being trapped in the spirit realm with this dangerous stranger. I closed my eyes, ignoring the relentless glow enveloping my body, and willed my spirit to return to the waking world.

The grey fog, and the stranger, vanished, leaving nothing but darkness.

I blinked awake. I lay on my back on a soft, warm bed, under a ceiling painted in white. The walls were faintly stained with what might have been blood. The modest room contained a few bookshelves and little else. *I'm not at the guild.*

My head pounded, and a thin layer of ice covered my skin when I moved. I hadn't spent that long in Death in a while. If I'd stayed much longer—

No. Maybe I wouldn't have died. After all, to the witches, I was a precious commodity, thanks to the other person sharing my mind.

Speaking of whom, they'd apparently booted me out of their forest after all. But where was I? The window showed only a rain-soaked brick yard. I tried to open it, but it was locked tight. So was the oak door opposite the bed.

I reached in my pocket for my phone and found the clock had started running again. I also had a few dozen missed calls. After tugging on the door once again, to no avail, I called Lloyd.

"Jas!" he yelled into the phone. "Where in hell are you? Are you dead?"

"Do you think I'd be able to use the phone if I was a ghost, Lloyd?"

"How the bloody hell should I know?" he said. "I watched you *die.* Then these people—people wearing cloaks, but not necromancers—took you away, right in front of the boss's eyes. Where in the world are you?"

"Locked in a room. No clue where. I'm gonna try to break the door down, but I thought I'd let you know I'm alive first. Who—who took me away?" I already knew it must be a witch—someone sent by the Hemlocks—but the bombshell they'd dropped on me had made me forget to ask who they'd had spying on me for the last seven years.

"I don't know, they wouldn't let me near you." His voice broke. "I didn't know there was poison in that drink, Jas. I bought it at the market. This is my fault."

The market. Panic bubbled up in my throat. "You mean the witchcraft market?"

"What other market would I be talking about?"

Oh gods. Someone from another coven tried to kill me. And they know who my best friend is. "Lloyd, who sold it to you?"

"Haven't a clue. It was dark and I was freezing, and I knew you would be too. I didn't check."

I swallowed hard, my heart hammering a mile a minute. "It's not your fault, Lloyd. The witches... gods, this is *not* how I wanted to have this conversation."

"What conversation?"

"The part where I tell you I'm a witch. A rare one. And I think another witch tried to have me killed."

"What?" His voice rose to a high pitch. "Is this some kind of—"

"Hemlock," I said. "That's my coven. It's also the poison they used. I have zero magical skill, that's how I wound up a necromancer. But I'm Hemlock by birth."

"What?" He sounded about as bewildered as I'd

expected. "What do you mean, by birth? I thought anyone could start a coven in their own back yard."

"They can. My coven... their magic is different. It runs through the bloodlines, and I'm the last of them."

"You're joking."

"Look, I'm not even in Edinburgh. I'm almost certain I'm in the middle of England, which is where my coven came from in the first place. I can't even get out of this room."

"The middle of England? How? Do you have a secret teleporting ability? Because let me tell you, if you've been keeping it from me, we should have words, Jas."

Not a secret teleporting ability. More like psychotic relatives who won't take no for an answer.

"No, I travelled via a creepy forest which exists outside of space-time." I rested my heel against the door and wondered if it was worth risking a broken foot to get out of this room. The place didn't *look* like it belonged to someone out to do me harm, but then again, neither did the forest, at first glance.

"Jas, please cut the bullshit. I've been awake all night and Lady Montgomery is demanding answers."

"We hunt ghosts for a living. Surely a magical forest isn't that much of a stretch. Look, I have no idea how I got here, but as soon as I get out of here, I'll be on my way. It might take a little while, though."

It'd taken a day and a half for me to reach Edinburgh seven years ago because the faeries had wrecked most of the major motorways during the invasion. But between that and the forest, there was no contest.

"If I tell *her* that, she'll put me on cleaning duty for the next six years," Lloyd said. "I'm in the shit for coming to that meeting to begin with. Why not *tell* me?" His light tone was tinged with the slightest hint of bitterness.

"Would you have believed me?" I asked. "I didn't want you to end up targeted by association. And now… whoever sold that poison to you knew we were friends. They might be watching you, too."

"That is *not* cool."

I screwed up my forehead. "I'm sorry. I thought nobody in the whole of Scotland had even heard of the Hemlock Coven. We're a forgotten legend even in England."

"Next you'll be telling me you're secretly royalty."

"More like the pariahs of the supernatural world. The Hemlock witches don't have a high survival rate." Unless being eternally trapped in wood and stone counted as 'survival'.

Witches' gifts varied even more than the mages' did, limited only by their own imaginations. Give a witch a handful of herbs and there was nothing they couldn't accomplish. But the Hemlocks? Their power was off-the-charts, dangerous enough to take command over nature entirely. That forest was no natural creation. It was pure magic, not bound to this world or any other. And the power I'd felt when I'd tapped into the shade's magic in the spirit realm was barely a fraction of that strength. If I went back into the forest and put myself at the Hemlocks' mercy, they could easily trap me in that place for the rest of my life.

"That," said Lloyd, "would make a hell of a story. Should I call the papers?"

"If you do, I'll kill you."

"You know that threat means nothing to a necromancer, right? I'm perfectly capable of spending the next few decades haunting you."

"That sounds almost as terrifying as the fact that I got kidnapped by my own relatives and yanked halfway across the country. Believe me, I'd rather be listening to a diatribe from Lady Montgomery."

"They're that bad?"

I thought of Cordelia's remorseless gaze as she'd sealed my fate. "You have no idea. Anyway, wish me luck."

"Good luck, Jas. Let me know if you need me to exorcise someone."

Exorcise. *Hmm.* "I might just take you up on that, once we're back in the same city."

I hung up the phone. Never mind the coven, the mages, or anyone else—I needed to get back to Edinburgh, before the person who'd tried to kill me targeted everyone I knew.

I stepped back from the door, drew back, and kicked it as hard as I could. Pain shot through my toes, and the door rattled against a lock someone had obviously put on the outside. I gritted my teeth and kicked with the other foot—

And found myself face to face with the second scariest thing I'd seen that day: Lady Harper, retired mage, and the Hemlock Coven's only living human ambassador.

Today just got better and better.

4

I overbalanced, catching myself against the edge of a cupboard. Lady Harper looked me up and down as though contemplating something the cat had dragged in and smeared all over the floor. A fearsome eighty-something woman who'd famously killed two Sidhe in person, she rested one hand on her carved cane and the other on the door frame, blocking my escape. While her neat button-down shirt and long skirt made her look like a retired head-teacher, her mage talent involved tossing people through windows without lifting a finger. Or breaking into their minds.

"Er... hello, Lady Harper."

I didn't know you were still alive wasn't a polite way to greet a woman who'd served on the West Midlands council of mages twice, but it wasn't like she couldn't have got in touch with me if she wanted to. She was a former Mage Lord, and probably had Lady Montgomery's phone number.

By way of a greeting, she said, "What in the name of the Sidhe did you do to your hair?"

It's nice to see you, too.

"I dyed it." I ran a hand over the rumpled edges. "What... what are you doing here?"

"I should be asking you the same question." She scrutinised me with her intense stare, and made me acutely aware of every speck of dirt on me and every hair out of place. She hated anything dirty or sloppy. I'd been on the receiving end of her ire pretty much non-stop ever since she'd plucked me out of the witch orphanage and tried to drag some magic out of me by sheer force. While she was distantly related to the coven, she had no witch magic to speak of, and she was the only person who'd ever worked for the Hemlocks who wasn't confined to that creepy forest.

"I have no idea how I got here," I said. "I was in the Hemlocks' forest. Where am I?"

"You're in the home of one of the witches."

"You don't mean the Edinburgh witches, do you?" I knew her answer before she spoke. Somehow, that forest had transported me from Scotland all the way to the outskirts of south Birmingham.

She gave a sniff. "No, of course not. The covens and I don't get along."

That's because you don't get along with anyone. "I need to get back home. I take it one of your people brought me into the forest in the first place?"

"Naturally," she said. "I suspected your cover story would be a flimsy one, so I took precautions. I told the Briar Coven to look out for you."

My nails cut into my palms. "You told people what I am. And you wonder how *assassins* found me?"

"I bound the witches I ordered to watch you to a confidentiality agreement, Jas. They've known for years."

"That's even worse," I said. "What's the point in telling an entire coven I'm the heir to the Hemlock legacy if they couldn't stop an assassin from sneaking into their own market? And the killer's still at large, so I need to go home and pass on the warning to everyone who's ever come into contact with me. Cheers."

"Obviously, I didn't tell them about Evelyn," she said. "Which you'd do well to be grateful for."

Goosebumps crawled across my skin. "You knew about her, too? Did everyone?"

"Just myself and your fellow Hemlocks. If others had known, they might not have turned a blind eye to your ill-advised plan to flee the country."

"It was going perfectly fine until tonight—last night." How much time had even passed when I'd been in the forest? "It's not like I had 'get poisoned' on my agenda. I already dealt with a deranged ghost yesterday, and I was hoping I'd get to skip the summit and watch zombie movies, actually."

"And there I was, hoping your attitude might have improved during your stint at the guild," she said.

"Oh, I'm not ditching my apprenticeship," I said. "I'll say that much. Look, you and I both know I have no more witchcraft than your average piskie. I can't be their heir."

She studied my face. "Believe me, the circumstances aren't ideal, but you're the only one from the bloodline."

"And someone tried to kill me for it," I said. "Someone sold the poison to my best friend—who, by the way, had no idea about any of this until about ten minutes ago. So if you don't mind, I'd like to take the Creepy Forest Express back home and tell my boss that I'm not deceased after all."

"No, I think not," she said. "You claim not to have used witchcraft, but it's dormant in you, and I think we can pull it out."

"There is no 'we'. Did you not hear the part about the assassins and the boss—"

"Yes, I think we can." She snapped her fingers. "I have someone here who may be able to help you."

Two other women appeared behind Lady Harper. On the left was a pale woman of average height with a sword strapped to her waist. Her brown hair was swept into a ponytail, her leather jacket hugged her muscular shoulders, and she cast a glance at Lady Harper that conveyed an impressive amount of disdain. The woman on the right, on the other hand, smiled at me. She looked more like I'd expect a witch to—bright clothing, flowers woven in her curly hair, hints of chalk marks on her warm brown skin, and the faint aroma of herbs hovering around her.

"Hey, I'm Isabel," she said. "This is Ivy."

Her sword-wielding companion scanned my face. "I know you."

"You're... Ivy Lane?" I said.

Ivy snapped her fingers. "You were at the council meeting in Edinburgh. How'd you get all the way here?"

"Witchcraft," I said. "It's nice to meet you, but I'm kind of in a hurry."

"Did you say witchcraft?" asked Isabel. "You're Jas, right? Hemlock?"

"Does the entire *planet* know?"

"She's the one?" asked Ivy.

"Unfortunately," said Lady Harper, limping past me. "You take care of her."

Ivy sidestepped her cane as the old mage shoved her way out the door. "We didn't sign up for this."

"I'm the leader of the Laurel Coven," Isabel said to me.

"You're related to the creepy tree people?"

"You've met them, too?" I asked. "They used their magic to bring me here through the forest, but I need to get back to Edinburgh. Someone up there tried to kill me."

Ivy's brows rose. "I didn't know you could use the forest to cross the country."

"Pretty sure only Hemlock witches can," I admitted. "But I don't have any of their magic. I'm a professional necromancer working for Edinburgh's guild and my boss is probably planning my funeral as we speak."

"Tricky," said Ivy, with a glance at Isabel. "Is Lady Harper kidnapping people now? You know, that doesn't surprise me."

"You must know what she's like," I said to both of them. "She's a manipulator. She wants me to serve as heir even if it gets me killed in the process—which is what an assassin tried to do to me, at any rate, so—"

There was a tremendous crash from behind the door.

"Did anything follow you here?" Isabel asked Ivy.

"I don't *think* so—"

Isabel rolled her eyes at Ivy and turned into the hallway, while Ivy drew her blade from its sheath. It was a seriously nice sword, not like most of the bulky metal blades in the guild's weapons room. I got on better with knives than swords, but I had none with me. I hated feeling defenceless.

Ivy ran into the hallway, and there was a shout, followed by a splattering noise. By the time I caught up to Isabel in the hall, the remains of some kind of faerie creature lay in a heap on the doormat.

"Bloody menaces," said Ivy, scattering blood droplets everywhere. "Ah, shit, I wrecked the wallpaper again."

"Don't worry," said Isabel. "At this point, you might as well just leave it there."

Ivy surveyed the blood splatter on the white plaster. "It's an aesthetic. Nice of Lady Harper to leave the door open."

"What, she's gone?" I asked.

Isabel nodded. "She doesn't like hanging around here. She had an argument with my Second the other week."

"And Third," Ivy put in. "I don't think there's a coven member she *hasn't* argued with."

"Sounds like her," I said, eyeing the faerie monster. "Do those things come after you a lot?"

"All the time," said Isabel. "We were a week overdue for an assassination attempt."

"That can't have been aimed at me," I said. "Nobody should even know I'm here." Were the assassins pursuing me across two countries now? Despite Lady Harper's assertion that she hadn't revealed my identity, witches were notorious gossips and anyone might have let the name slip in the last seven years.

"Did you grow up here?" Ivy kicked the front door open and heaving the monster's body over her shoulder. "You have the accent."

"I was raised in an orphanage," I said. "At least until

Lady Harper pulled me out. She knew I was from the bloodline and took me under her wing. Kind of."

"You grew up with the mages?" asked Ivy.

"For a few years. Only because I'm the Hemlocks' heir." Not that anyone aside from Lady Harper actually knew that. She'd been on the front lines when the Sidhe had attacked and targeted the forest, nearly destroying it, which was why I'd been raised as far away from it as possible. But there was little point in training a Hemlock heir without magic. My extra soul went a long way to explaining why she hadn't just dropped me back at the orphanage again when I'd failed to manifest any kind of power other than the ability to annoy the crap out of her. "Not to be rude, but I don't get why she asked you two to watch me."

"Who even knows what she's thinking?" said Ivy. "I'm going to take our dead monster here to Larsen. I'm sure he'll appreciate it."

"I'm going… for a walk," I said. "I can leave, right?"

"Technically, no," said Ivy.

"But we never saw you," added Isabel, with a wink.

I gave her a smile, and once Ivy had got her faerie corpse over the threshold, I went after her into the garden.

The red brick house was unobtrusive enough from the outside, with flowery curtains and herbs growing on the windowsill marking it as a witch's abode. Lady Harper must have used her magic to bring me here, or strong-armed one of the other mages into helping. Despite only being vaguely related to the Hemlocks, she possessed their strong-willed attitude and complete and utter self-centredness. The quicker I got away from their influence, the better.

I crossed the road, looking around to get my bearings. I'd been around the witches' district before, but it was far from the polished world of the mages I'd spent my teenage years in, let alone the regimented existence of the guild. Similarly to Edinburgh, supernaturals didn't live entirely separate lives from one another in this area of town—witches mingled with shifters, and even the odd necromancer or two. I debated asking one for directions, but the necromancers here didn't have a reputation for being friendly, and had no ties to Edinburgh's guild.

I stopped, looking at the shop I'd just passed. A sign in the window said, *Property of the Society of Ley Hunters.*

That's new.

I scanned the empty room within, which appeared to be under construction. 'Ley Hunters' probably referred to the Ley Line, the main spirit line that went through the middle of the UK. Necromancers got the most use out of the spirit lines, but particularly strong ones gave any sort of magic a boost. Nothing aside from the sign in the window indicated whether it was a supernatural establishment or otherwise.

"You again," murmured a male voice from behind me.

I spun around, taking a step away from the speaker. A tall man whose hood obscured his face had appeared behind me, unnoticed, and his voice… it was the same as the shadowy man I'd run into in the spirit realm.

He *was* a real person.

"Did you want to look?" I smoothly stepped away from the window. "Feel free."

"Human Ley Hunters." He gave the sign a nod, but

didn't take his eyes off me. "Interesting, but irrelevant. I rather think you're the one who has what I'm looking for."

So much for feigning ignorance. I stood with my legs slightly apart, ready to fight or run. "I think the question is, what are *you?*"

"Does it matter?" He stepped closer. "What matters is that you're going to give me what I want. And what I want is the property of the Hemlock Coven."

5

"I'm not their *property*," I told the stranger. "I'm nobody's, least of all yours."

I wished I'd scoured the witch's house for spells or at least a weapon, but I wasn't without my own set of tricks. He moved, as though intending to grab me, and I brought my fist up into his nose.

His hood fell back, revealing blood dripping down his chin. "Ouch," he deadpanned.

I frowned at him. Something about his voice didn't quite match his grizzled appearance. It sounded like it belonged to someone younger than the guy in front of me. His hair was flecked with grey, his chin rough with stubble... and he wasn't breathing.

In fact, I was pretty sure I'd just punched a dead man.

Dead people don't bleed, Jas. I shook the thought off. "Are you the assassin? How'd you travel halfway across the country?"

If he was the person who'd tried to poison me, it made no sense for him to be here, but who else would want to kidnap the Hemlock Coven's heir? *Aside from everyone else who wants to kill me?*

"Aren't you going to show me what else you can do?" The man spoke, but his lips didn't move.

Oh... my god. What is he?

Despite myself, I took a brief second to check the spirit world. His voice was definitely the same, but he didn't look like a ghost. Ghosts weren't solid. He *sounded* like the shadowy man I'd seen, but in the spirit world, where the man's ghost should be, nobody was there at all.

He moved, and I blocked his grab with my forearm. "What are you? You're dead, but not a ghost or zombie."

Blood continued to roll off his chin in droplets. "Vampire is the technical term."

"Vampires don't exist." What the hell?

"Do you hear yourself?" he asked, softly. "You're a Hemlock witch, and unfortunately, you're standing between me and what I want. Tell me where your coven is hiding."

"Yeah, no thanks." I clenched my fist, and punched him with necromantic power. I might not have as much as a poltergeist, being alive, but no wonder I could hit so hard in the spirit realm. There was someone else's spiritual presence alongside me the whole time.

His head snapped back, and grey fog momentarily surrounded us again, showing me his shadowy outline. I'd thought he looked less substantial than a ghost, but it wasn't true. He was like darkness shaped like a person, and if I wasn't careful, that same darkness would swallow me whole.

But the shadowy creature didn't remotely look like the man I fought. As Death faded a little, the fog turning transparent, threads of blue light became visible, connecting the shadowy figure with the man in the waking world.

The man had no spirit, but in its place, threads of blue magic spiralled from his body. Necromantic power... like reanimation.

Or possession.

Holy shit. The vampire was possessing a dead body. A body that had recently been alive, if the blood streaming from his nose was any indication.

Clever. If anyone who wasn't a necromancer had run into the man bleeding in front of me, they'd have taken him for a living person, not an undead. And if they fought, they could have taken the man's body to pieces and they'd never have found the real culprit. The vampire must be within the city limits to be exerting control over the dead body, right? But I'd seen him in the spirit realm hundreds of miles away.

All right. Let's deal with this. I readied an attack, but he caught my fist in his. An icy sensation spread through my body, creeping down my spine. Bone-chilling cold pierced me to the core, and threads of blue light streamed from me to him. His shadowy form loomed over me, the darkness growing, threatening to drown me.

He was draining the very essence from me.

Oh. So that's why they call them vampires.

"Stop..." My voice was faint. I didn't know for sure how much my spirit could take before it gave up the ghost (sorry), but I didn't want to find out the hard way.

"Take me to your coven, Jas," he whispered. "And I'll let you go."

"I'll take you to them," I gasped, improvising. "Let go of me and we can talk somewhere more civilised."

If I knew the local covens, I'd be able to think of a plan, but the only coven I knew of was the one run by Isabel. As a fellow coven leader, she'd have access to powerful magic I could only dream of. And her coven's headquarters was just down the road. She wouldn't thank me for dumping a vampire on her doorstep, but what choice did I have? Not to mention the house was covered in wards and also contained Ivy Lane and her sword. I was pretty sure even this half-dead guy wouldn't keep walking if decapitated.

Whatever he wanted with the Hemlock Coven, he didn't know where they lived. That could definitely work in my favour.

The dead man kept a tight grip on my upper arms as I retraced my steps down the road leading to the witch's house. *I hope Ivy doesn't decapitate me for leading a vampire to their doorstep.* But the icy sensation pressing against my neck told me I was in serious danger of joining this one in the afterlife.

Wards shone from the walls of the house. If they were standard security wards, the vampire wouldn't be able to get inside, and I'd be in a position to mount a counterattack. I knocked on the door, and the vampire reached and *pushed* with a blast of kinetic energy that sent me pitching forwards. He caught my arm before I fell on my face... and followed me inside.

Crap. This isn't how it was meant to go.

Isabel appeared in the doorway to one of the rooms, frowning at us. "Jas? I thought you left. Who's that?"

"Hey there," I said. "Apparently I'm a hostage."

Her brows shot up. "Seriously?"

The vampire didn't move, doubtless scheming, but his grip on my arms tightened even further.

"Who is he?" she asked. Not being a necromancer, she wouldn't see the total absence of a soul.

"A zombie, basically," I said. "I hoped your wards would take him down."

"Huh. They should have done."

"What is this?" growled the vampire.

I rammed my head backwards, smashing him in the face. Wrenching my arms free, I jabbed my elbow into his throat, knocking him into the already blood-splattered wall. He came upright, and I swept his legs out from underneath him. Isabel ran back into the hall, holding a handful of rubber bands. *I hope those are spells, not stationary.*

The man caught my leg in a claw-like grip and unbalanced me, causing my head to hit the wall. In a surge, he was on his feet, grasping my arms behind my back once again.

Ow. Jesus. No zombie should be this strong. The necromancer's power must be through the roof. How was he keeping this thing going?

I stomped on his foot, hard, then drove my heel into his shin. As his grip broke, Isabel threw one of the rubber bands. There was a bang and a flash of light, and the vampire let go of me, hitting the wall so hard it rattled.

Isabel dusted off her hands. "I think he's out cold."

"Thanks." I stepped away from the body. "What kind of spell was that?"

"I haven't named it yet. It's a cross between a knockout spell and a shield. I guess that counts as a successful test run."

I could see how she'd ended up as a coven leader. Spells came with so much potential for error that even fully trained witches often stuck with the safe, mass-produced ones instead of experimenting with their own. "You're saying that's the first time you've used it?"

Isabel walked over to the man's limp body. "It's ninety percent similar to my other spells with the same base ingredient set, so there's a certain degree of certainty. Since he's not really alive, I figured it wouldn't hurt him."

"Need a hand?" I moved to the dead man's side. "Watch he doesn't wake up."

"I have a trapping spell in there." She indicated the partly open door she'd come out of, then lifted the man's shoulders. Isabel was stronger than she looked, doing most of the work as we carried him through the door. The room within was laid out like a workshop, containing shelves against each wall and a large number of chalk circles and herbs spread across the floor. We deposited the vampire in a crumpled heap, while Isabel grabbed one of the bands she'd left on the sideboard, and threw it over him. The band expanded to contain the vampire in a circle of red light, forming criss-crossing lines over his body. A trapping spell, but more advanced than a market version.

"Are all those spells hand-crafted?" I asked, fascinated despite myself. I'd always liked drawing the chalk circles and patterns, even if I couldn't make anything magical materialise out of them.

"Yes," she said. "I've been making my own brand for years. It's easier than working with the limited range on the market."

I nodded in understanding. While I possessed no

talent for crafting spells myself, everyone used them, even humans. Witch spells used to be confined to the supernatural community, but after the faerie invasion, demand had skyrocketed, particularly for spells to fix the damage the faeries had done and heal magic-related injuries. Market healing spells were expensive to buy unless you personally knew a witch—and these days, almost everyone did.

"So you're the Laurel Coven's leader?" I asked, keeping one eye on the vampire in case he made an unexpected recovery. "You mentioned working with Ivy… she's not a witch."

"No," said Isabel. "Ivy and I have run our own business since before I was coven leader. She works for the mages now, too, but we still take on independent cases, and we do pretty well. We have a few other mercenaries helping out now. Mostly, we deal with faerie-related trouble. It's her specialist area."

"And yours is magical explosions?"

"That was more of a mild blast than an explosion. You should see the state of our old flat." She dropped to her knees beside the vampire. "You're right. How is he walking and not breathing?"

"Haven't a clue," I said. "I have a whole bunch of necromancer contacts up in Edinburgh, but I can't exactly take him with me even if Lady Harper and the Hemlock witches let me go back. Which they don't seem inclined to do at the moment."

"Why would a vampire attack you to begin with?" she asked.

"Because I have a target on my back, thanks to my being the Hemlocks' heir," I said. "Someone sent him to find the coven, but I don't think he knows they're in the forest. I thought the wards would destroy him."

"They should have, but I guess they got confused about whether he's dead or living. Undead-proof charms are kind of essential around here."

"So who do you test them on? Vampires don't walk in here every day."

She grinned. "Usually I test them on myself, otherwise Ivy volunteers herself, and then I end up with the Mage Lord hovering over my shoulder."

"I can see that. Wait, did you say the Mage Lord?"

At that moment, Ivy herself walked in, her sword back in its sheath and her clothes lightly splattered with faerie blood. She raised an eyebrow at the vampire. "Another dead body, Isabel?"

"He attacked Jas." She moved to the other side of the circle. "He's a vampire, apparently. Yes, they exist."

Ivy barely blinked. "Not the weirdest thing I've heard all day. Is it dead?"

"No… well, that guy is, but he was dead before the vampire got him." God, this was confusing. "The vampire was puppeteering his body. Like a zombie, but more coordinated. When I checked into the spirit realm, it had no spirit. The only life in there was whoever was controlling it. The vampire. And he *spoke* through it."

Ivy's brow furrowed. "Weird. I've heard talk of vampires, but I tend to assume people met a bloodsucking fae of some kind and got confused."

"Necromancy must be keeping him going," I said. "That's the only magic I see on him. Unless you see anything different?" Ivy's abilities were unique, I'd heard, but I didn't know the details.

"No," she said. "I can only see faerie magic, and he doesn't have any. That's... bizarre."

I stepped around the inert body. "He was looking for the Hemlock Coven. Lucky he didn't know where they actually are."

"So Lady Harper *wasn't* being paranoid?" said Ivy. "That's a first."

"Yes, it is," said Isabel, picking up more rubber bands. "If we destroy the vampire's body, it should break the connection. Do you want to warn the Hemlocks, Jas?"

I'd rather have three more rounds with the vampire than another conversation with Cordelia.

"Maybe throwing a vampire at them would be an incentive to make them let me go home through their forest," I said.

Ivy and Isabel exchanged glances. "Lady Harper said your powers were untrained," said Isabel. "When she asked me to help you, I didn't know the Hemlocks brought you here against your will. Lady Harper told me they saved your life."

"I guess they did," I relented. *Or Evelyn Hemlock did, anyway.* "But my magic... it's more than untrained, I've never even used it before. And I don't know why everyone suddenly wants me dead for it, either."

"You've never used magic?" asked Isabel.

"I'm a necromancer," I said. "Technically, I'm part mage, part witch, part necromancer, but I've only ever been able to use the spirit sight, so I'm not much use as a coven heir. They're wasting their time trying to recruit me. Not that I'm ungrateful for the offer of help, but I left my friends up in Edinburgh, and whoever tried to kill me is still up there, too."

Isabel chewed on her lower lip. "Hmm. Lady Harper insisted you need guidance, for your own safety. I'm not sure how open to persuasion the Hemlocks will be, but I can come with you and help you plead your case."

"Are you sure?" I had my doubts they'd be any more responsive if I had another witch with me, but it'd be nice to have some moral support.

"I'll tell Lady Harper you left," Ivy said to me. "I'm already on her bad side, so this is nothing. Isabel… what do you want to do? You're the one assigned to train her."

"Lady Harper said nothing against taking a detour," she said. "Hmm. I never did get a look at the market during the summit at Edinburgh."

Ivy grinned a little. "You should go with her. It'll be a nice holiday, and it's not like Lady Harper can breathe down your neck all the way up there."

"I wouldn't put anything past her," I warned. "Seriously."

A hint of steel appeared in Isabel's expression. "Oh, she can try. It'll take my mind off Rick the Dick, too."

"Who?" I said blankly.

Ivy snorted. "Her ex. Necromancer, and Grade A Twat. Maybe you'll meet someone on your travels."

"I can set you up with one of my friends, but they're all necromancers, too," I said. "Also, you know. Distance. Unless you want to spend all your time in the Hemlocks' forest. We'll be lucky if they don't take great offence and kick us out."

"They won't object to you going home if I come with you, Jas," said Isabel. "How's that for a compromise?"

I smiled. "That works. But I think we should get rid of the vampire's dead body first."

6

With Isabel at my side, I had fewer reservations about entering the forest again. Even the Hemlock witches wouldn't smack around another coven's leader.

Ivy kept her sword out, and cast distrusting glances around every so often as we walked down the road leading to the forest. Then without warning, she lunged, swiping at the hedge. A bunch of redcaps jumped out, fleeing into the trees with yowling screeches. The forest was right next to half-faerie territory on this side, which meant Unseelie faeries made their homes on the outskirts. While the Seelie faeries weren't exactly angels either, the Unseelie had more of a reputation for preying on humans —if not in a literal sense, then by leading them to their death in the woods.

Most humans avoided this part of the city. I wasn't old enough to remember what it'd looked like before the faerie invasion, but rumour said that the forest had appeared from nowhere around the same time, as though the influx of faerie magic had dragged it into existence. Considering the forest sat on a liminal space where the spirit lines crossed, I could believe it.

Speaking of spirit lines, I never did find out what that 'Ley Hunters' shop was. But if anyone tried poking this particular spirit line, the forest would eat them alive.

There was no actual path into the forest that didn't run directly through half-blood territory, so Ivy improvised by cutting a sizeable hole in the back of the hedge so we could climb in. The forest closed around us as soon as we did. Not a single bird sang, while eerie silence shrouded the thick trees. Even knowing that the witches were watching our every step didn't make me feel any safer. Sure, the Hemlocks could destroy anything that attacked us, but they were capable of devising some seriously nasty traps for trespassers, human or otherwise. Their magic was tied into the forest to the degree that they could instantly sense if anyone entered and whether they posed a threat or not, and react accordingly.

Now I had to hope Cordelia was in a forgiving mood, and that I hadn't messed things up too badly when I'd inadvertently shown my magic to a vampire.

"I never asked," I said to Isabel. "Who carried me to the house? Lady Harper?"

"You've got it," she said. "No idea how she knew where to find you, but she often goes walking in the woods."

"She has a death wish." Actually, I suspected the woman would fight Death itself when it came down to it. "Cordelia might not like me that much, but at least she didn't leave me unconscious on half-blood territory."

While half-faeries obeyed the humans' laws for the most part—significantly, the 'don't kill or eat people' ones

—there were never any guarantees their fae pets would behave themselves. Redcaps, goblins, trolls and kelpies all had a taste for human flesh.

"The half-faerie Chief's on the brink of losing his crown... again," said Ivy. "He's clinging to power by a thread, and things are on edge. Nothing new really, and the witches won't allow fights to break out in the forest."

"You know the Hemlock witches personally?" I asked, surprised. They'd put me under a geas so powerful that I hadn't even been able to tell Lady Harper what they'd told or shown me during that last fateful meeting in the forest seven years ago. That's why running had been the smartest option.

"They're not my biggest fans," Ivy admitted. "Despite the fact that I saved their lives."

"You did?"

Apparently that story would have to wait, because the forest chose that moment to plunge us into total darkness.

"Not again," Ivy muttered. "We've done this before. Can we skip this part?"

She waved her sword, and its blue glow lit up the path enough that we could see one another.

"The forest punishes trespassers," I said. "Er, I thought you said you've been here before."

"We have," said Ivy. "They're just messing with us. They know who you are, right?"

"Unfortunately. What I don't get is how you two know who *they* are." I inched forwards a few steps. "They told me—when I came in here as a teenager, they said even Lady Harper didn't know their location. They put out the rumour that they were extinct."

"Yeah," said Isabel. "I used to think they were a legend.

When I was the second-in-command of the Laurel Coven, Francine—the last leader—told me about them, but she made it sound like they'd died out a long time ago."

"What changed?" I asked.

"An attempt on their lives," said Ivy. "Several. I guess that's why they decided to contact their heir."

It would be nice if said heir had had a choice in the matter.

After the Hemlocks had made us stumble around in the dark for a bit, we reached a wooden door stretched between two trees. On the door was a symbol. I didn't know its meaning, but the magic in me hummed in resonance as the door opened, revealing the Hemlocks' cave. It looked exactly the same as before, down to the glyphs on the wall and Cordelia's judgemental face staring from the stone sculpture in the centre.

"I don't remember asking you to bring friends," she said.

"You asked Isabel to train me," I pointed out. "And Ivy came along... for protection. I want to request to use the forest's magic to get back home."

"You wish to abandon us once more?" asked Cordelia. "And you have the audacity to ask for our help?"

"You said yourself the magic is dormant inside me," I said. "I should be able to learn it just as well in Edinburgh as anywhere else."

Not bloody likely, I added silently, but I had no intention of ever setting foot in this place after I was home.

"Tell me your reasoning," croaked Cordelia. "Or be prepared never to set foot in the mortal realm again until you've learned some humility."

Oh, now we'd reached the threatening stage. Wonderful.

"There's an assassin out there who tried to kill me," I said. "And they got to my friend in order to do it. Aren't you a little curious about why someone at Edinburgh's market might know who the Hemlock witches are, much less want to kill me for it?"

"Not enough to allow you to seek them out in person."

I looked her dead in the eyes. "Okay, first of all, you have no power over me. Second, you haven't exactly looked out for my well-being in the past. And thirdly, I was attacked by a vampire today, who's trying to get into this forest as we speak. You might want to look into that."

"Vampire?" hissed Cordelia. "There's no such—"

"You're a witch who's eternally stuck in a tree," I said to her. "You're not seriously trying to tell me you don't believe in vampires? They can suck the life out of you with a touch, and can possess dead bodies miles away. He found me in the spirit realm, even in here."

There was a long pause. "Impossible."

"Nope," I said. "He doesn't know where you are, but he's close. He can reach anyone, anywhere, and I've never even met him in person. I'm certainly not strong enough to kill him as a ghost, but if I find him in the real world—"

"And what if he kills the only heir to the Hemlock Coven?" she enquired.

"I have the entire necromancer guild at my back," I said. "Besides, he didn't try to kill me before." *Probably because he needs me to find you,* I didn't add. He might be the enemy, but who needed to employ poison when you could suck out someone's soul? Of course, if he wasn't the poisoner, that meant there were at least two people who wanted me dead, but I'd handle that part later.

Cordelia studied me, her eyes like pits of shadow. "I

see. In that case, you are to use your resources to find this... vampire, and take care that he perishes without ever learning the location of the Hemlock Coven. Was it he who poisoned you?"

"Maybe. I don't know." With the necromantic power he possessed, it would be much easier for him to use those powers to drain my soul instead—or my *other* soul. *Hmm.*

"I can train her," added Isabel. "It's pretty clear there's someone in Edinburgh plotting against the Hemlock Coven. Isn't it more logical for us to work together to take them down rather than hiding?"

"You make a good point," said Cordelia. "Isabel, do see to it that she never leaves your sight. The future of our entire existence depends on it."

Ivy made a disparaging noise under her breath. Guess I wasn't the only one who thought the coven needed to tone it down.

I led the way out of the cave, returning to the forest. The resonant humming sensation of the glyphs forming webbing between the trees called to my magic, like hearing the lyrics of a semi-familiar song.

"Jesus, talk about overdramatic," Ivy muttered.

"They're drama queens," I said. "I didn't lie—I don't have magic. I certainly can't be their saviour."

But I knew who did.

Nope. I'd find the first necromancer with the ability to exorcise a spirit and send my ancestor off to deal with this herself. Okay, I'd never heard of a spirit being exorcised from a living person she'd been attached to for *years* before, but I couldn't be the first. Certain spells were forbidden, but in order for them to be banned, someone must have used them and had something go horribly wrong.

And where did vampires come into it?

"We'll see," Isabel said. "I can give you some basic lessons, just to placate her. It won't do any harm."

"I should go," said Ivy. "I reckon their magical travel methods only work on witches, and I don't want to get lost in here for hours. Isabel, text me, let me know when you're coming home. The witches should let you use the forest to come back."

"I don't see why not," I said. "Isabel's the only one of us who didn't sass them."

"Ha," said Ivy. "You're not wrong. See you around, Jas."

"Bye."

Isabel waved at her, then turned to me. "I don't suppose you know where the path to Edinburgh is?"

"No, but it's part of the Hemlocks' mystique that they never tell you about anything before dumping you headfirst into it. If we keep walking, they'll—"

The sky fell on top of us. Trees tumbled, and my magic flared up in alarm as the world spun like a merry-go-round.

The next second, we lay on our backs. Not on a soft surface, either, judging by the metal slats digging into my spine.

"And on cue..." I sat up, wincing. We'd landed on the disused rail tracks near Edinburgh's abandoned train station. The spirit lines moved around a lot, but I hadn't known there was one here. "I guess the witches wouldn't have cared if they threw us into a nest of fire imps."

The ruins of the station were filled with wild fae despite the Mage Lords' and the necromancer guild's best efforts to keep it clean, so they'd fenced off the whole place. Isabel and I picked our way over the tracks, past the decaying shell of a train half-off the rails, until we found the path back to Waverley Bridge.

"The necromancer guild is that way." I pointed at the houses on the other side of the bridge in the direction of Edinburgh's Old Town. "I guess you know where the mages' guild is. I've only been there at the summit."

"What're you going to do now?" she asked. "We can arrange a meeting point, so you can tell your friends you're still alive and not have to answer questions about the coven. Does anyone know?"

"My best friend, Lloyd," I said hesitantly. "He knows... I don't know how much of it he took in, but I told him I'm a witch, and a little about the forest and their magic. And that I'm possessed, but I think he flat-out disbelieved that part. I'm not sure how far the Hemlocks' confidentiality agreement goes. I'm surprised I was able to tell him anything at all. With the geas they put on me, I couldn't even tell people my full name when I moved here."

"Makes sense," she said. "I have a few witches I'd like to check in with. I can ask some questions while I do that. Is there a safe place for us to meet up later, after you've reported to the guild?"

"Cassandra's Café." I named a popular café for supernaturals. "Meet you there at six? Unless she puts me on the night shift, I should be free then. It's fairly close to the guild."

"Sounds good," she said.

"Perfect," I said. "I'd offer to introduce you to Lady Montgomery, but she's probably going to flay me alive for not telling her I *was* alive, so... wish me luck."

"Good luck," said Isabel. "I'll be at the market."

"Are you sure? I'm pretty sure the person who tried to kill me came from the market."

"Don't worry," she said. "Being a coven leader comes with its own useful protective magic."

Interesting. So far, *my* coven leader status came with no benefits other than a price on my head. Unless the Hemlock witches had withheld the other benefits from me on purpose. But having protection meant having magic, and it wasn't a surprise I was lacking both.

Let's get this over with.

Edinburgh's Guild of Necromancers had been hidden before the faeries came, and now it lay in the middle of the busy tourist district between restaurants, bars and cafés. Humans didn't generally get too close, though they liked watching us from afar. Its bricks were the same faded brown as its neighbours, but iron had been built into the walls in thick grey streaks, while the solid metal doors pretty much said 'No Sidhe allowed in here'. Wards covered the walls, too, and my skin tingled when the glyphs flashed, as though I was suddenly weirdly attuned to every form of witchcraft possible. I'd have a job and a half explaining where I'd been for the last… however long I'd been gone. It was daytime, but when I checked my phone's clock, it appeared to be afternoon. Time passed differently in the forest, which meant I'd been gone almost a full day.

Nothing to do but gather my excuses as I walked to the gallows—or rather, Lady Montgomery's office. Cloaked necromancers milled around in the entryway, and I walked past them quickly with my best 'mission face' on to avoid being waylaid. I didn't see Lloyd, so I assumed he was on a mission. I climbed the stairs, strode down the corridor, and knocked on the boss's door.

"Come in."

I took in a deep breath, then entered.

"Jas," said Lady Montgomery. "So nice of you to join us again."

"Hi." I closed the door and swiftly walked over to her desk. "I'm sorry I disappeared. I… got summoned by my blood coven. Long story. They saved my life."

"Really, now," she said. "Who exactly tried to kill my assistant?"

I shook my head. "Haven't a clue, but they sold poisoned hot chocolate. To Lloyd. You haven't punished him, have you?"

"No. He's been filling in for you in the archives while you've been gone. He told me this morning that you called him."

I'd bet he'd been 'accidentally' added to the rota. "He thought I was dead. I guess everyone else did, too."

"Considering being poisoned with hemlock has a low survival rate… yes," she said. "I'm glad you made it back, Jas. I was concerned when you were removed from the summit with no warning."

Well, well. Maybe I was more than a useful assistant after all. After dealing with Lady Harper for so long, I had trouble trusting supernatural authority figures to have my best interests at heart, and part of me had expected to come back to find I'd been kicked out, permanently.

"Now, where have you been all day?" she asked. "I was perturbed at how difficult it was for the guild to track down who took you."

"Um, they came from a local coven. I was unconscious for a while." I'd never met anyone from the Briar Coven, though hopefully Isabel would be able to find out more. "I'm a witch, so... they helped me." A faint humming sensation permeated my words. That'd be the geas at work. The most I could tell anyone was that I was a witch and belonged to a coven. As soon as I tried to say more, I'd find myself changing the subject whether I wanted to or not. Lady Montgomery wouldn't be pleased if I started telling blatant lies, so I added, "Anyway, I should find Lloyd. He was seriously worried about me."

"Tell him he can leave the archives early," she said. "And do decide if you'd like to tell me how you survived being poisoned and pronounced dead."

Ah. "Sorry. It wasn't planned, believe me."

What was I supposed to say? If I so much as hinted that there was a shade hitching a ride in my body, I'd be booted from the supernatural world at large and locked in a cell for the rest of my life. Possession wasn't legal, while letting a dangerous supernatural take up real estate in one's body fell into the category of 'highly forbidden necromancy', even more than blood magic. And that was assuming I could tell her at all. I didn't know how I'd managed to tell Lloyd, but every word the coven spoke to me was supposed to be kept secret on pain of death. I hoped I hadn't put his life in any more danger by confiding in him.

I made my way to the archives, rehearsing a dozen conversations in my head. It wasn't fair of me to keep the boss in the dark, especially about my vampire stalker, but the guild could only help me protect myself from the dead, not the living.

Lloyd sat at the desk in the archives, his head resting against the back of the seat and his eyes closed.

"Napping on duty again?" I asked.

His eyes snapped open, and he jumped up and tackle-hugged me. Unprepared, I caught the desk with the edge of my hand before I fell over.

"You're alive! I've spent the last few hours thinking a ghost called me on the phone and pretended to be Jas."

"Have you ever seen a ghost use a phone?" I retrieved my cloak from where I'd dropped it. "No, it's really me. I'm alive. I made it back."

He pushed a loc out of his face. "You mean all that shit about a magical forest and creepy witch assassins was a joke?"

"Do you seriously think I'd lie about something like that? I used the forest to get back here, on the condition that I find the bastard who tried to kill me. Can you remember what they looked like?"

His mouth turned down at the corners. "No. Sorry, Jas. He kept his hood up and it was dark."

"It's okay. You wouldn't have known to look out for sneaky witch assassins." What worried me was that the killer knew we were friends. Maybe that ghost we'd dealt with the same day had told everyone he knew… but faerie ghosts weren't friends with the witches. Half-faeries in general didn't tend to mingle with other supernaturals, and he'd seemed too freaked out at being dead to be capable of sharing my deepest secrets.

No… there was one person who'd known I was a Hemlock witch—not to mention a shade—and he was likely hiding somewhere within this city. Maybe behind another undead-like host. Creepy bastard.

"Want to grab something to eat after my shift?" Lloyd asked.

"Brilliant idea. I asked Isabel to meet me at the café—she's kind of my new mentor."

His eyes bulged. "You disappeared for a day and came back with a mentor and an extra soul. I have questions."

"Keep it down," I hissed. "Not a word to anyone else. Yes, that includes Ilsa and Morgan Lynn, *and* the boss's son. I know they have a basket of secrets of their own, but this is different."

He blinked. "You haven't even told the boss?"

"Not all of it," I said. "Think *faerie vow* levels of secrecy. Can't say a word. Not sure why I managed to tell you about the extra person hitching a ride in my head, but maybe that's not a coven secret."

That, or the witches didn't mind other people finding out I wasn't alone in my own mind. I had my sincere doubts. The sooner I figured out how to get that spirit out of me, the better.

7

Lloyd and I picked a table outside Cassandra's Café despite the cold, in order to avoid anyone overhearing our conversation. I'd ditched my cloak and changed into jeans and a plain jacket to hide that I was a necromancer, but even being around other supernaturals made me edgy. I wished I'd picked a human café instead, though the food here was to die for. I'd worked up an appetite during my brush with death, and chewed my way through half a double cheeseburger before coming up for air.

"Is your friend coming here?" Lloyd asked, biting into his own burger.

"Any minute now." I wiped grease from my fingers on a napkin. "So we can get to work on tracking down the person who tried to bump me off."

"Didn't you say she was your mentor?"

"Kind of. She has her own reasons for being here, but she had to tell the Hemlocks she'd train me, otherwise they wouldn't have let me come back. She's a powerful coven leader in her own right, which qualifies her to train the Hemlocks' heir."

"That's bonkers," he said. "You mean to say that because you're a Hemlock witch, you *have* to work for them? I thought working for a coven was voluntary."

"The Hemlocks aren't what you'd call conventional." I chewed another mouthful of burger. "I have to learn their magic, which means playing nice with the witch whose soul they bound to mine. Isabel's here to help with that, but what she's *really* here for is to help me track down that vampire."

He blinked. "Vampire? They don't—"

"Yes, they do." I summarised the encounter with the dead man in Isabel's house. By the time I'd finished, Lloyd's jaw was on the floor and he'd forgotten all about the food. "You're being stalked by a vampire. Holy shit. I don't think even Lady Montgomery has enough necromantic power to possess people *that* far away."

I put down the remains of my burger. "She *might,* but she's definitely not given to using the recently-dead as puppets. Anyway, he tried to suck out my soul and force me to take him to the forest. Isabel saved my life."

"You weren't doing such a bad job yourself," Isabel herself said from behind my seat. Lloyd jumped.

"Hi," he said. "Er, when she said coven leader, I thought she meant someone Lady Montgomery's age."

"Age is no guarantee of wisdom," I said, as Isabel pulled out a chair next to me. "Look at my ancestors. Stuck in a forest for thirty-odd years and they think they're justified in shackling their descendants to a lifetime of service. This is Lloyd, by the way. Lloyd, Isabel."

"Hey," said Isabel. "Nice to meet you. Jas and I just met,

but she seems to think you're trustworthy enough to let in on her secret."

"I am *absolutely* trustworthy," said Lloyd in a mock-solemn voice. "No, really. Jas's secrets are mine, too. Let's face it, we all knew she was a bit off."

I elbowed him in the ribs under the table. "Cut the crap, Lloyd. This is serious."

"You're damn right it's serious. Someone tried to murder you, someone else tried to kidnap you—and did we skip the part where the assassin knew we were friends?"

"I'm trying to work out why that is," I said, glancing at Isabel. "I've definitely never ticked anyone off lately... except the ghosts. That's where it started. After we banished that half-faerie spirit, someone in the spirit realm whispered *hemlock* at me. Not sure if it was the same guy I ran into afterwards, but..."

"Who, the vampire?" asked Lloyd. "He's the assassin?"

"Possibly," I said. "We destroyed the vampire's spare body, right, Isabel?"

She nodded. "Yep. He was already dead, so once I knocked him out, it must have broken the connection. I'm not a necromancer, so I'm not the expert here."

"His connection to that body was way stronger than the average necromancer's control over an undead," I said. "Otherwise, necromancy doesn't tend to do well in combat. All you can really do is thwack people with kinetic energy, and usually the ghosts have more of that than the living do."

"And faerie magic," Lloyd put in. "This vampire wasn't a faerie, right?"

"Nope," I said. "More like an undead, but under one

person's control, so deeply that it's like he *became* him. You know undead, they're usually as uncoordinated as baby kittens."

"Minus the cute," added Lloyd. "Yeah. So aside from the ability to control undead on a high necromancy level… what was the deal with the life energy thing?"

"I don't know. It's like he sucked the spirit out of me, or tried to. I know it's creepy and horrible, but I can think of scenarios where that might come in handy."

Lloyd's eyes lit up with understanding. "Don't you have a second soul you want rid of?"

"We'll get to that later," I said, in a low voice. "For now, Isabel… I should probably fill you in on the latest."

I quickly explained how the poisoning had happened, giving a rundown of my role at the guild for good measure. Lady Montgomery had let me get away without an interrogation for now, but her leniency wouldn't last, and I didn't know *how* to explain what the witches had done when I was still supposed to be under a confidentiality agreement. To say nothing of the fact that binding a spirit to mine had violated supernatural laws.

"When did you first meet the Hemlocks?" asked Isabel, after she'd gone into the café to order some food. "Did they teach you magic?"

"Lady Harper tried." I tossed a handful of fries into my mouth. "I lived in a witch orphanage for the first few years of my life, until Lady Harper found me and took me in. I don't know if she knew I was the Hemlocks' heir beforehand, or found out later. What about you?"

"My parents were killed in the invasion," said Isabel. "Afterwards, I went to live in one of the witch orphanages, too. Then I applied to join the Laurel Coven as soon as I was old enough."

"And met Ivy."

"That was a couple of years later," she said. "I'd been custom-making spells for a while then, and Ivy was *always* injuring herself on mercenary missions. I made it one of my goals to find a way to stop her doing that, but I'm not sure I was very successful at it."

I grinned. "Lucky you won't have to do that for me. I have a second soul who can take the damage for me. It's how I survived the poisoning."

She lifted a brow. "Seriously? Wow. I've never heard of that before. I mean, I got the protective spells when the leadership of the Laurel Coven passed onto me, but even that can't protect me against everything."

"I have no protective spells," I admitted. "I'm not a coven leader, but whatever Lady Harper told you to do, you really don't have to."

"Oh, she didn't," said Isabel. "I mean, she did ask me to train you, but I accepted out of curiosity. I've never met a living Hemlock witch, and it sounded like she forced you into the role. You said something about… a spirit? Who is it?"

"Evelyn Hemlock," I said quietly. "She was bound to me when I was a baby, but obviously, I don't remember."

"That is *messed up*," Lloyd pronounced. "Am I the only person who thinks forcing someone to live in another person's body should be illegal?"

"The supernatural laws agree," I said. "Keep it down. God only knows how the Hemlocks got away with it, considering they used to be involved with the supernatural council before the invasion, but they've been stuck in that forest long enough to have lost what's left of their marbles."

"Well, the other covens definitely aren't in on the secret," said Isabel. "But I do know people on the council. It's sort of complicated with the witches at the moment, because the covens are so insular and geographically separate, compared to the mages. But if you need the council's input, I can probably help."

I winced inwardly at the idea of the most powerful supernaturals in the UK having an inkling that my coven had broken the law by binding another person's spirit to mine. "Not that I don't appreciate the offer, but the Hemlocks' confidentiality agreement will probably stop me from telling anyone anything useful. I don't know why they let me tell you, Lloyd."

"Maybe because I'm magical and important." He grinned, then shook his head. "Actually, it's probably because I've seen it. Her."

"You have?" I frowned.

"In the spirit world, I've often felt like you weren't quite... you, if you know what I mean. Since I sort of already knew it, maybe that's why you told me. I overheard the Lynns talking about faerie vows once, and they work in kind of the same way. Or Ilsa's Gatekeeper's powers. She couldn't tell anyone about them until we witnessed her using her magic."

That sounded familiar. Ilsa Lynn had actually sensed something was odd about the way I used necromancy and had offered to help me if I needed it, but that was before I knew I was possessed by a spirit. She might have magic which had gained her the title of the Gatekeeper of Death, but I doubted either she or her psychic brother could pull the evil spirit out of my body.

No... my best bet was to go directly to the vampire who'd been the first to notice, and find out why he was dead set on meeting my coven. Oh, and get him back for trying to suck out my soul.

"Vow or none, the magic is yours," said Isabel. "I can't imagine Lady Harper was a nice mentor, but I can teach you a few tricks. Have you ever used your witch power? At all?"

"I tapped into it when I met the vampire," I said, crumpling a napkin in my hand. "That's how he knew what I was. But I've never managed to brew up a potion in my life."

"Let's give it a go," said Isabel. "Not here. Do you have a place we can safely train?"

"Sure," I said. "I live right above the guild. I can't take any sneaky trips over the veil without being caught, but as long as we don't run into Lady Montgomery, we're probably safe."

As it turned out, Lady Montgomery wasn't the one I needed to worry about.

The necromancers' accommodations were self-contained flats spread across two floors above the guild's headquarters. Most necromancers who lived here would be hanging around the cafeteria at this time, so the place was deserted when Isabel and I made our way to the private staircase leading to the guild's upper levels.

What I hadn't counted on was the one person who was

never where he was supposed to be at any given time: Morgan Lynn. Tall and skinny with a mop of dark brown hair, he wore the vacant expression of a necromancer immersed in the spirit realm and stood in the middle of the corridor like it hadn't occurred to him that other people might live here as well. Luckily, Morgan's level of observance ranged from 'slightly off' to 'you could waltz in with a full-grown elephant and he wouldn't notice'. We were halfway down the corridor when he blinked at us as though we'd popped out of thin air.

"Hey, Morgan," said Lloyd, casually standing in front of Isabel to hide her from view.

He frowned. "Isn't one of you supposed to be dead?"

"Me," I said. "I survived. No harm done."

Morgan squinted at me. "Are you sure? There's something about you that seems... off."

"She's been dealing with zombies," Lloyd said. "Say, have you ever heard of a zombie possessed by a person?"

"Nope," said Morgan, so quickly that it was like he'd been expecting the question. "Absolutely not. Bye."

He sidestepped Lloyd and walked on down the corridor with the slightly unsteady movement of someone either drunk or walking off the aftermath of spending hours in the spirit realm. From what I knew of Morgan, probably both. When Ilsa had brought her older brother to the guild a couple of months ago claiming that he was being haunted, none of us had expected him to turn out to be a genuine psychic sensitive. Psychics were almost as unheard of as vampires.

"He wasn't dealing with vampires, too, was he?" I muttered to Lloyd.

"One way to find out. You and Isabel go ahead." He

followed Morgan down the corridor, while I walked the rest of the way to my flat door. The flats weren't that well spread out and the walls were paper-thin, so we'd have to keep our voices down, but at least I was reasonably confident no vampires would get into my room.

I unlocked my door, letting Isabel in. "Morgan probably wouldn't rat you out to Lady Montgomery. He's broken enough rules himself."

"This is your place?" asked Isabel. "It's... cosy."

"That's one way of putting it. I didn't pack much when I left."

I favoured a minimalist style—to be honest, in case I had to pack up and run again. All the necromancers' flats were built along similar lines. One main room which served as bedroom, study and zombie movie theatre depending on the occasion, with an en-suite bathroom to the side. I'd papered the walls in paintings and sketches in an attempt to make it look like someone actually lived here, but aside from the necromancer gear tossed onto the bed, the handful of clothes on the floor and the small stack of textbooks and Stephen King titles on the bookshelf, I didn't own that much in the way of material possessions. I'd grown up with nothing, after all, and even spending my teenage years with the mages hadn't erased that.

I moved my discarded clothes to the laundry basket and cleared the desk chair so Isabel could sit on it. "If you want to stay here, I can borrow a sleeping bag from Lloyd."

"No need. I did come prepared." She smiled. "There's a local coven who owns a hotel, and they owe me a favour. I didn't expect to be back so soon, but you have somewhere else to practise magic if you like."

"I won't be using necromancy, so we should be fine here," I said. "That is… I don't know what this Evelyn Hemlock is actually capable of, but I'm assuming Lady Harper told you more than she told me."

Isabel nodded. "Let's start with basic witchcraft and go from there." She emptied her pockets. Bands, pencils, pieces of chalk and herbs scattered onto the space I'd cleared on the floor. "You can at least use witch spells someone else has created, right?"

"Yes, but so can anyone with magic." They were designed that way, for at-home use. *Making* the spells required a finesse that even some witches struggled with. Brewing solutions in cauldrons, sketching out chalk circles and symbols… witchery in its modern form could be practised in a thousand ways. Some witches swore by one method or another, others embraced them all. Most witches picked a specialist area, but I'd never met one quite as creative as Isabel. No wonder she'd made coven leader at a fairly young age. Though I hoped Isabel would keep her penchant for magical explosions under wraps, for the sake of everyone else living in this corridor. "You can draw on the carpet with chalk. I have a few cleansing spells and a couple of repair ones, but not enough to fix broken furniture."

She grinned. "Don't worry. You're the one who'll be using magic, not me." She indicated the props she'd laid out on the floor. "Try making a ward."

Wards. Right. "Got a textbook? I'm a little rusty."

"Burdock, tansy, nettles." She pointed out each ingredient. "Use a spell circle for protection. It's the least volatile magic type there is, though, since it's intended to be used for warding off foes."

"Not really necessary here," I said. "The whole building's one of the most secure places in the city. Evil can't get in, through the physical or spirit worlds, and there's enough iron to put off most faeries, too." I picked up the small cauldron I kept next to the kettle for brewing up healing salves in an emergency, and picked out the selected ingredients.

Isabel watched as I sketched out a chalk circle on the carpet, hoping that I wasn't about to blow my chance of getting my security deposit back. Then I mashed the ingredients together in the cauldron and tossed them into the circle, sprinkling salt on top for good measure. Some witches used incantations, but Lady Harper had told me that they were like the words necromancers used for summoning or banishing ghosts. The actual words didn't matter so much as the intent.

If my coven's magic was really so special, I shouldn't need props at all. But as seconds passed and no magic answered my call, I began to doubt Evelyn Hemlock had any intention of making an appearance. The ingredients alone weren't enough, and neither were the chalk symbols. What I needed was a dose of witchy magic, something I lacked at the best of times. Isabel had it in spades. I waved both hands over the circle, but the spirit's magic remained noticeably absent.

I sat back on my heels. "I think I'd have to let her totally take over to let her use magic, and I'm not sure I can. I'm the one who's been in the driving seat my whole life. And I like my body the way it is."

"Maybe if I give her some encouragement?" Isabel

moved to my side and reached out her hands. Holding her left palm over the circle, she took my hand with her right one and whispered something under her breath.

Power hummed in my own skin, too, so sudden and startling that I yanked my hand away from hers, breaking the connection. "Whoa."

Isabel looked up at me, picking up the ingredients, which had fused into a single spell, shaped like a band.

"Which of us did that?" I asked.

"Both of us." She gave me a smile. "Lady Harper said it might take a while for her powers to properly wake up, since they've been dormant for so long. But they're definitely there. I felt them."

"That makes one of us. I thought it was your magic I felt." Not the raw power that had flooded me in the spirit realm, and made my mouth move with a voice that wasn't mine. "Necromancy came easily to me by comparison. Perhaps that's all I have."

"Nah, you've had years of practise with the spirit sight, I'll bet," she said. 'Let's try again."

8

The spirit realm surrounded me, grey fog stretching in every direction. I hovered on the spot, looking around at the pale shapes of the dead drifting towards the faint shape of the gates on the horizon.

The answers are in here. I turned to the left, seeing a familiar shadowy shape. The outline of a person who was half here, half not.

"You again," the vampire said. His voice rumbled with anger.

Oh, boy. I'd really ticked him off when I'd destroyed his pet. Not that I could see his face, or the rest of him for that matter.

"Me," I said to him. "Sorry I broke your vampire."

"The word is *vessel,* and I can always choose another. You, on the other hand, have only the one."

His hand reached out, and icy energy sprang to my fingertips, coursing through me like wildfire.

"Tell me who you are," I demanded. "Or so help me."

"JAS!"

A tremendous crash drove me back into my mortal body with a jolt. My back hit the floor as I rolled over the edge of the bed. Another crash, and the door swung inward. Lloyd stood there, gaping at me.

"Ow." My head felt like it might split in two. I kicked the bedcovers off me and got to my feet. "Lloyd, shut the door. I'd like some privacy, thanks."

"So would the dozen necromancers you just woke up with whatever you did in the spirit realm."

"*Shit.*" I rubbed my forehead. "I don't know how it happened. I've never gone into the spirit realm by accident before, much less while I was sleeping."

"No shit. That's a great way to test our security measures."

My throat went dry. No... the vampire hadn't known where I was. Thank goodness for small mercies. But if he couldn't find me, maybe I couldn't find him, either.

Lloyd folded his arms across his chest. "What did you do to cause that much of a disturbance, Jas?"

I rubbed my forehead. "The vampire tried to attack me while I was sleeping."

"Seriously?" Lloyd swore. "You're lucky the senior necromancers live on a different floor. Better hope they aren't light sleepers, especially Lady Montgomery. As it is, I think you gave Morgan Lynn a hell of a headache. I heard him yelling."

I screwed up my face. "What did he have to say about zombies yesterday, anyway?"

"Not much," said Lloyd. "I think he knows there's something up with you, though. Want to let him in on this?"

"Too many people are already in on it," I said. "I'm not sure even the Lynns know about vampires. I need to track the bastard and deal with him in person." I gathered my bedcovers and threw them back onto the bed.

"So the guy can possess any dead body in the city?" He eyed the remnants of the chalk circle on my floor. "You know, I doubt it'll be that tricky to find him. The two of us attract the dead like a corpse attracts flies. All we have to do is walk out the doors and a horde of zombies will appear to attack us. When they do…"

"I shift into the spirit world and find him? Might work. If I can trick him into letting his location slip. But if we get caught, we'll end up with worse than being put on cleaning duty."

And someone might get hurt. The last thing I wanted was to put Lloyd in harm's way, but the longer I let that vampire roam free, the more people he could tell I was a Hemlock. And what if he wasn't the only vampire around?

"Fair point," Lloyd said. "Okay, I'll steal the candles, and you—"

"You know we're both technically on the rota, right?" I said. "There's nobody stopping us from taking on a voluntary extra mission."

He grinned. "I like the way you think. I'll go and *borrow* the candles. You work your magic with the rota."

"Not magic. Just a few years gaining the boss's trust." Lloyd had jokingly called me a suck-up and I didn't have many other close friends because they thought I'd snitch on them to the boss, but being trusted with access to spaces usually reserved for senior necromancers sure came in handy. I just hoped some of that trust would still be left when this was over.

Ten minutes later, I stood in a circle of candles in an alley, about to indulge in a bit of off-the-grid necromancy.

Lloyd stood guard at the alley entrance, wearing his necromancer cloak so nobody would question what we were doing here. I'd texted Isabel but received no reply, so I assumed she was busy with her witch contacts. It was before eight in the morning, and most people who didn't work early hours would be asleep.

The spirit world unfolded, grey and uniform. With the candles surrounding me, I could spend as long as I liked on the other side without making it permanent. I didn't plan to spend long there, anyway. Just long enough to find the vampire, ask some pointed questions, and pay him back for nearly sucking the life out of me.

Come on. I know you're here somewhere.

A shimmer caught my eye, a patch of darkness that didn't belong to a spirit. *Gotcha.* I moved closer. The outline was shaped like a person, though closer than he'd been the last time I'd seen him in the spirit realm. There he was.

The shadow split in two.

Huh?

I blinked hard, half convinced I was seeing double, but the spirit sight didn't lie. Two vampires faced me, each a man-shaped shadow. But while the vampires looked almost identical in their faceless shadowed forms, instinct told me that neither was the man who'd attacked me this morning.

One of the vampires raised a hand and a blast of kinetic energy slammed into me, flinging me backwards through the spirit realm. I flipped over, thankful for the lack of gravity, and raised my hand to attack. Necromantic energy poured from my own hand, smacking him into his neighbour. *Wait. How do you kill a vampire?* Could they be banished the same way as ghosts, or were they like necromancers? Considering they were still alive, maybe they couldn't be destroyed unless we found their real bodies. Which might be anywhere.

"Jas!" Lloyd's voice cut through the fog of the spirit realm. "Jas, give me a hand here!"

I blinked, back in my body. In front of me, Lloyd stood with a blade buried in a zombie's chest. As I watched, it tumbled backwards and fell to the floor. "Bloody thing crept up on me when I was watching the circle."

"Lloyd, back up—there's two vampires, and they might have any number of zombies."

He jumped backwards as the zombie lurched to its feet again, despite the gaping hole in his chest. "Oh, bugger. This is one of those vampire vessels?"

"Yes." I grabbed the nearest candle, holding it like a shield. "Don't touch either of us, zombie. Take us to the one controlling you."

Lloyd kicked the undead hard in the shin, sending him toppling once again. "Creep."

"Hang on. I have an idea." I reached past Lloyd and grabbed the zombie by the scruff of his neck, calling on all the power I could muster. Prodigy, I was not, but every novice necromancer knew how to pilot a zombie.

The man kicked and flailed, but I held firm and focused on the thin ray of blue light connecting the zombie to whoever held him in the spirit realm. The candle was an amplifier, but knowing I had twice the power with two spirits in my body was enough of a confidence boost on its own. I opened my mouth to speak the words that would grant me power over the zombie, then recalled last night's witchcraft lessons. The words weren't strictly needed at all, if you had enough power.

Time to see which of us was the better necromancer.

I grabbed the threads of blue light, and pulled, hard—and bounced off an invisible shield. My hand lost its grip, and if not for Lloyd standing at my side, I'd have fallen flat on my face.

"What was that?" Lloyd wanted to know.

I pushed back from the wall, my skin slick with cold sweat. "Ow. I tried to override his zombie control. That's what I get for jumping the gun."

"If he's possessing it, it must be stronger than when a necromancer raises an undead, Jas."

"Yes, but... it's not total possession," I said. "He was fighting me in the spirit realm at the same time—both of them were—so this zombie must have been on autopilot. I get the impression he's controlling a bunch of these things at once. You know if a necromancer does that, it makes them less effective."

The zombie lunged. I caught his fist in mine and pushed back, adding in a blast of necromantic power for good measure. "Tell you what, let's get him in the circle."

"You know, that might just work." Lloyd hit the zombie over the head with the heel of his knife, and I swept his legs out from underneath him. Between us, Lloyd and I kicked him into the candle circle. While Lloyd pinned down the struggling zombie, I moved the last candle back into place, and the lights snapped on again. Candles were more use against ghosts than zombies, but if the person controlling him was anywhere near, the lights would drag them into the circle, too.

At least, I really hoped so.

"There." I brushed sweaty hair from my eyes. "Maybe now our vampire will talk."

The zombie remained mute, as did his undead controller.

Energy burned in my hands as I reached for the threads of light connecting the zombie to its owner. I grabbed the threads of blue magic visible above the zombie's inert body, and pulled with all my might, willing them to surrender control to me. The spirit realm blurred, grey fog becoming distorted, and this time, the blue lines of energy connecting us were mine.

Problem: now I had an unwanted pet zombie and no vampires. There were no shadowy figures in the spirit realm at all.

I blinked back into the waking world. "The bloody vampires ran away. Cowards."

"Did you say vampires, as in, plural?"

"There were two." My hands curled into fists, and the threads of blue light connecting me to the zombie continued to burn. "And now there's zero, and I just took control of a zombie without guild permission."

"But you beat the guy," said Lloyd. "It *was* the same guy, right?"

"No clue," I said. "It's not like I could see him. Unless I used a tracking spell… hmm."

"On the zombie? Good idea. Your mentor can make one, right?"

"I'll ask her." After my disastrous attempts at witchcraft last night, not to mention the way Evelyn had nearly woken up the entire guild retaliating against the vampire this morning, I wasn't about to request help from the spirit.

"You captured a zombie?" asked Isabel, raising her eyebrow at the crumpled heap in the middle of the candle circle.

For want of a better plan, I'd brought her here to the alley, since I couldn't exactly walk a pet zombie all around the city without inviting a few questions. Isabel had picked up on the third call, and had said she'd been neck-deep in a spell since the early hours of the morning.

"Yep," I said to her. "I managed to break the guy's control over her, but the vampires—there were two—disappeared before I could track their location. I thought a spell might work better, but I don't typically keep tracking spells around."

"Scumbags," said Lloyd. "It'd be great if you could get a glimpse of what the guy actually looks like."

"That's what I'm hoping." I prodded the zombie with my toe. "I still have control, but there's no point in expending all my power on this when the vampires aren't even here."

"Right." Isabel pulled a band out of her pocket. She wore several on her wrists, too, in a rainbow pattern.

Lloyd raised an eyebrow. "Rubber bands? Those are your spells?"

"They look harmless," Isabel responded. "Plus it's easier to cover a limited area this way." She tossed the band at the zombie, where it expanded to fill the circle I'd trapped him in. Then she walked up close, leaning into the spell. "Do you want to try, Jas? It might kick-start your witch magic."

I had my doubts, but I couldn't keep being afraid of Evelyn's power. Not when it might well save my life.

I crouched down, extending my hands into the spell's circle.

At once, images snapped through my head—black and white, and upside-down until the world reverted itself. I watched through the zombie's eyes as it climbed to its feet, facing a person. A youngish man stood with his hands splayed in a pose familiar to a necromancer. *So this is our guy.*

The vampire looked more like he owned the voice I'd heard than the old dude he'd used as a vessel. Handsome, I supposed—rough and stubbly with a jawline sharp enough to cut your fingers on. If he hadn't been a soul-sucking vampire, he might have been my type, but that hardly mattered. *I really need to get out more.*

He leaned forwards and spoke to the zombie. Tracking spells only showed images, not sounds, but I read from his lips: "You will obey me."

Power sparked to my hands, my skin tingling with it. I yanked my hands out of the spell circle, and it dissolved, leaving only the candles and the inert form of the zombie.

"Whoa!" said Lloyd. "Isabel, did you see that?"

"Your eyes changed colour," Isabel commented. "They went from bluish grey to sort of… black-grey."

"Damn." I held onto the image of the vampire as it threatened to slip away. "I think my witchy powers might have switched on in self-defence, since the vampire was so close. I saw his face." Grabbing a pen and notepad from my pocket, I started sketching.

Isabel gave me a bemused look. "Did you see where the zombie came from, in the vision?"

"Yeah, but I doubt the vampire stuck around."

"Not if this guy's recently dead," said Lloyd, prodding the zombie with his foot. "Look at him. He's been dead for hours, at most. If we go around asking people if someone they know died this morning—"

"We'll be struck off the rota," I interjected. "You know the rules. We're supposed to get guild permission first, and there's no time. Anyway, what if the vampire killed him? It wouldn't surprise me." I held up the notepad, where I'd sketched a rough likeness of the man's face. "Was this the guy who sold you the poison at the market?"

"Shit, I don't know. He kept his hood up, but he sounded… old. And he had an English accent."

"Oh. The vampire had a Scottish accent. Doesn't mean he wasn't working with the assassins in some way, but I guess he wasn't the one who actually sold you the poison. Maybe they're working together."

"Let me see that." Isabel took the notepad from me. "Did you take drawing lessons?"

"On and off." My apprenticeship didn't leave a ton of time for hobbies, but sketching had become as much a habit as a hobby. "Anyway, I know the picture's not much use if we don't have anything of his we can track him by, but at least I'd know him if we met in person."

"I can't believe he ran away," muttered Lloyd. "What are we supposed to do with this zombie, call the guild and pretend we found it by accident?"

"Wouldn't be the first time," I said. "But there must be

a way to track the vampire's actual location. I get the feeling he skipped out on registering as a necromancer, and if that's the case, he probably didn't leave a paper trail, either."

"If he's outside the guild, he must be a rogue," said Lloyd. "Nobody ought to be able to control zombies from that far away. Hell, most of the guild can't project more than a few metres, except maybe the Lynns and Lady Montgomery."

"He's something else," I said. "He deliberately picks the recently dead to control so nobody can tell they're dead. Even a necromancer would have to work hard to pick them out of a crowd."

But the other two vampires… I'd been so sure neither of them was the same as the man who'd attacked me this morning. Tracking spells didn't lie, though. The first vampire I'd spoken to was the person who'd reanimated this zombie.

Lloyd swore under his breath. "Just what we need."

"I'll use a spell to destroy the body," said Isabel. "That way you won't have to drag the guild into this. Did you see whereabouts he was, in the vision?"

I nodded. "Maybe he left some clues behind. But he probably anticipated us using a tracking spell and set up a trap or three as well."

"Good job I have some dispelling charms," said Isabel, producing a handful of bands from her pocket. "Not quite as fancy as the ones the mages use, but it sounds like this vampire creep needs to get up close and personal with my best work."

"She's not wrong." Lloyd slid the band she handed him onto his wrist. "What do you think, Jas?"

I studied the image of the man's face again. I was sure neither of the two vampires who'd attacked us had been him, but it'd happened way too quickly to be certain. And if not, my fear that the city had a whole underworld of vampires wasn't so far-fetched after all.

The real question: why were they so interested in bumping off the heir to the Hemlock Coven? And if they wanted to snack on my extra soul, surely they wouldn't have tried to poison me.

Right?

———

Five minutes later, we came to the street the tracking spell had shown me. It was mostly empty of humans, probably because of the bitterly cold air and the rumble of thunder that promised an imminent storm. That, or the faint smell of rot that said *zombies*. None of the stone buildings showed any signs that they might belong to someone with a habit of possessing the dead.

"Is there any way to draw him out?" asked Lloyd. "Throw a bunch of magic around? Summon a wailing horde of ghosts?"

"Nah, that'll just draw the humans' attention—not to mention the guild." I kept both eyes out for traps, but despite the three of us carrying the witch equivalent to a battering ram, nothing had materialised yet.

"Maybe one of us should play dead and see if he tries to possess us," said Lloyd.

"Don't joke about that," I said. "For all I know, he *can* possess the living. I never asked." A faint noise drew my attention, and I checked the spirit realm. No ghostly activity, which meant… "Undead, incoming."

Several zombies shuffled out of a nearby alley, faintly glowing. When I checked the spirit realm again, thin rays of blue light connected them to a shadowy form. Shit. Was he possessing the whole lot of them at once?

I grabbed a candle from my pocket and blasted one of the undead with necromantic energy. If they were true undead, they'd keep walking and flailing until we took them to pieces—but with someone exerting control over all of them at once, the quickest way to deal with the zombies was to take out their owner.

Isabel threw a spell. There was a flash of light, and several undead reeled backwards, one of them catching on fire.

"Nice," I said. "Let me guess—your first time using that spell?"

"I've been waiting for the best moment." Isabel advanced on the zombies. "Let's take them down."

She flicked spells on both wrists, and flames blasted into two undead, taking them to pieces. Lloyd drew a knife and went on the attack, while I threw a shielding spell up and dove into Death. Threads of blue light indicated a vampire's presence, or at least a necromancer, but there was no visible sign of him. *Shit. Don't tell me he ran away again.*

"Sorry, guys," I said, waving my knife. "Either our vampire friend has done a runner, or we've run into someone else's zombie patrol."

"Seriously?" Lloyd swore, and a flash of light from Isabel made both of us turn towards her.

Isabel's arms and face lit up with glyphs, which appeared to glow beneath the surface of her skin.

"Whoa," I said, as the glow faded. "What was that?"

"That," she said, "was my coven's defensive magic. And I think something in the spirit world tried to kill me."

Vampire. "Crap. He must be hiding close by."

A zombie hit out at me before I could go into Death to check. Lloyd got there first, cutting its arm off at the wrist. Isabel threw another explosive, causing a zombie's head to cave in. I threw another shielding spell up, and I plunged into the spirit realm once more.

"I know you're in here." I glared at the blue threads, then reached for the nearest, the zombie stirring under my command. I pulled on the threads of light, gripping as hard as I could, then looked deep into the zombie's eyes. *"Take me to your master."*

The zombie turned, slowly, and began to walk. I swayed on the spot, my head pounding like the hangover from hell. Zombies could only obey simple commands and I'd wiped out half my necromantic power, but if it took me to that cowardly bastard of a vampire, it was worth the risk.

"Whoa," said Lloyd. "You got him?"

"Just about." I cut down another zombie, following its brethren's path. The connection to the undead tugged on my spirit, threatening to drag me to join it. *Ow.* Why amateur necromancers raised swarms of zombies for fun was beyond me.

"Are you sure about this, Jas?" asked Isabel.

"Nope. But I've got him. If he's hiding outside the spirit realm, he's about to get a nasty surprise." I gripped Isabel's explosive spell in my hand, ready to use it.

With Lloyd and Isabel at my heels, I followed the zombie's path down an alley that had the definite stench of the dead about it.

"Are you absolutely certain it's him?" asked Lloyd.

I groaned, my head throbbing. "I wouldn't be in this much pain if it wasn't."

Darkness filled the alley, complete with the stench of rot. I hadn't expected somewhere teeming with zombies to smell like a flower shop, but the pungent aroma of dead bodies still made me gag. Pulling my cloak up over my mouth, I hissed to the others, "Okay. There's something really nasty in here. Last chance to back out."

"Lady Harper will kill me if I lose the Hemlock heir," Isabel added. "Just let me know where to throw the explosive."

"Don't blow him up until I've made him tell us why he wants to destroy my coven." It was time to finally clear up the question of why the vampire was so interested in the Hemlock witches.

"Word of advice," whispered a voice in my ears. "Don't look down."

And the ground gave way beneath my feet.

9

I fell into the darkness, dropping both the candle and the witch spell, then tumbled headfirst down a slope. Wincing, I rolled onto my back. The street was barely visible through a sliver of light above, but I saw no way to climb out of this hole. A tunnel extended to my right, disappearing into the gloom.

I'd known Edinburgh was once riddled with underground tunnels and catacombs, but they were considered the domain of the ancient dead, not vampires. That's what I got for not watching my step.

"Wonderful." I climbed to my feet and grabbed the candle and the explosive spell. If that dick of a vampire was hiding in this hole, he'd be sorry he ever met me.

A bone-chilling screech echoed through the tunnel ahead of me, turning my blood to water. *Uh... or maybe not a vampire.*

Magic sprang to my fingertips, and my hands glowed with white light. Not necromancy. Evelyn Hemlock really didn't like whatever had made that noise. My heart thundered in the silence following the cry, then came the faint sound of movement. Someone else stood in the dark, just a few feet away.

Gotcha.

My candle light shone on handsome features and a sharp jawline—the mirror image of the sketch I'd drawn.

"Nice to see you in the flesh, creep," I said. "Give me one reason why I shouldn't use this spell to blast a hole in you."

"Get out," hissed the vampire. "Get out, or it'll follow you."

"I'd need to be able to fly to get up there." I pointed at the slither of light with the hand holding the candle. "I expected you to be hanging out in a luxury apartment, not a hole in the ground. Guess setting zombies on people for kicks doesn't pay well, huh."

"I'm not hiding," he said. "Put that candle away."

"How else am I supposed to see how to get out?" I dropped my voice. "You have some nerve giving me orders after your undead tried to kill me."

"Do I look like I'm in a position to send zombies after anyone?" He shifted to his other foot, and I glimpsed blood streaking his face and a sharp knife clenched in his hand. "I'm flattered that you have so much faith in my multi-tasking skills, but whatever attacked you didn't belong to me."

"Nice try, but your zombie brought me here itself."

He swore under his breath. "I knew I should have left them somewhere else. Thieving scum."

"What, you're saying someone else hijacked your zombie?" I snorted. "Nice try, creep."

"I've been a little preoccupied." He raised his knife. "I'd advise you to stand back."

Before I could throw a spell at him, the vampire disappeared in a flurry of sharp claws.

I gaped at the spot where the vampire had vanished. My candle's light reflected off glassy scales, sharp teeth, and claws longer than my forearms. The vampire, pinned beneath the creature attacking him, stabbed wildly, his knife sinking between two of its scales.

I slipped the candle into my pocket and drew my own knife. I wasn't above leaving him alone with whatever ghastly monster he'd brought after him, but the monster was between me and the way out. Flashes of light revealed red wings edged in black, feathers of the same hue, and eyes as dark as the shadows of Death itself.

Holy shit. I bloody well hoped it was an unknown fae monster and not a new zombie nightmare, because I'd never seen anything like that walk out of a summoning circle before.

The vampire's knife flashed. The beast screeched but kept lashing out at its target. Those talons looked sharp enough to gut a human, but its attention was on the vampire, not me.

I gripped my knife tight, advancing on it from behind. Not that I cared for the vampire's well-being, but it'd be a fine thing if the guy I needed to talk to got mutilated before I could find out who his allies were, and if the person who'd tried to poison me was still out there. He must know. Unless I'd read the situation all wrong, but the one lesson Lady Harper had drilled into me was that it was always best to strike first.

With a quick lunge, I stabbed the creature in the spine.

On most other fae, it'd have been an instant kill, but the beast merely shook me off, releasing another horrible cry. My back hit the wall, knocking the breath from my lungs. *What the hell's it made out of, concrete?*

The vampire swore, freeing his own knife from its chest. "Didn't I tell you to run?"

"You're welcome." I stabbed the creature again, slicing down its back and side as it whirled on me. Its eyes locked with mine—dark and shimmering. I'd have backed up if I had anywhere to go, but its gaze held mine captive. A horrible kind of intelligence shone from within. This was no wild faerie beast, but a creature as smart as a human.

The vampire struck from behind, his blade protruding from the beast's ribs. As its gaze snapped away from mine, I grabbed for my knife, which had remained stuck in its side. "How many times do you have to stab this thing before it dies?" Fae could be resilient, but not like this.

"Don't look it in the eyes," the vampire responded.

The creature whirled on me, emitting another horrible screech. With my knife still stuck in its side, I had no weapons, so I blasted it with kinetic power. The beast didn't even flinch.

"Necromancy doesn't work," the vampire said, giving it another swift stab. He'd brought a spare knife, and I wished I'd had the foresight to do the same. What the hell was immune to necromancy? More to the point, while the injuries would have been fatal on any other beast, it either had incredible pain resistance or was too set on killing both of us to notice it was bleeding out.

I lunged forwards to retrieve my knife, and its eyes locked with mine once more.

Magic sprang to life in my hands, lighting them in a

cool silver glow. I swayed, mesmerised by the power within those pit-like eyes... a power that resonated with mine—

A thread of silver light snapped from my hand like a whip, severing the monster's head.

The vampire stared, mouth half-open, as the monster crumpled. Neither of us spoke for a moment, while I forced my arms to drop to my sides. Moving my body was like wading through mud—sluggish, distant, as though the person who'd momentarily taken control was reluctant to give up—and my legs gave out against the wall.

"You're immune to fury magic?" the vampire asked.

"What magic?" To my relief, the voice that came from my mouth was my own. My head pounded, and dampness from the wall soaked into my jacket.

"Fury magic," he said, reaching a hand out to help me.

Against my better judgement, I let him pull me to my feet. "Thanks," I said. Then it hit me... I was thanking the guy who'd tried to kill me, who'd been driving me out of my skull for the past few days. "So this is what you really look like?" The gloom hid most of his appearance, but I could make out that he was several inches taller than me, with longish dark hair and the sort of muscles one did not develop while sitting around using the dead as puppets.

"You sound disappointed," he remarked, turning the fury's body over with his foot, yanking my knife from its side. I tensed, but he held it out to me, handle-first.

I took the blade warily, ready for any sudden movements, but he made no motion to attack me. In the flesh, he sure as hell didn't look like a shadow. Or a necromancer.

"You aren't like the vampires in the stories," I said to

him. "Pointed teeth. Bursting into flames in sunlight. Unless that's why you're hiding in this hole?"

"I told you I'm not hiding," he said. "These creatures have been leading me around the sewers all day. And most of the stories about us are human nonsense."

I pulled out the candle, and its pale light illuminated his blood-streaked face. No signs of any teeth or claws, but he was easily as dangerous as one of those monsters on his own. After all, he'd nearly sucked out my soul without being anywhere near me.

I shone the candle down the path ahead, which forked into three tunnels. "Care to tell me the way out?"

"This one." He indicated the path on the left. When I didn't move, he shrugged and took the lead. "I wasn't responsible for the zombies that attacked you. I'd like to know which vampire thought it was necessary to steal my vessels. We'll have words."

"Meaning you'll suck out his soul." I walked after him, leaving the fury's rotting carcass behind. "Whether you sent those zombies after me or not, you're still a walking crime against nature."

"Didn't you pilot a zombie yourself, to find me?" he asked, his eyes cutting. "You're two souls in one body, Jas. By all definitions, we're the same."

"We are *not* the same," I snapped.

I was possessed. He was the one doing the possessing. Same creepy factor, but he'd *chosen* to spend his days piloting the dead. Nobody had given me a choice in this at all.

"No need to shout."

"Considering you lured me into a monster's nest, I'd say I have good reason." I walked on through the gloom, wondering if it wasn't worth just leaving him down here to rot. Apparently, he wasn't too concerned I'd attack him from behind, but then again, he was so tuned into the spirit realm, he'd be able to see anything coming.

"I seem to remember warning you *not* to follow me. I'm very interested in hearing how you were able to track me down."

"You know how I found you. I tried using a tracking spell on your zombie, and when that didn't work, I followed the trace you left behind on another zombie when you raised it."

"So casual," he said, his voice soft. "You do realise how few necromancers could attempt such a feat, much less successfully?"

I shrugged. I didn't care how rare the ability was, I cared that the person it was attached to wasn't me at all. Evelyn's magic—raw and untamed—had sliced through that unbreakable monster's skin like it was nothing.

"Modesty? You're full of surprises, Jas."

"No, I'm wondering when you're going to cut the crap and tell me why you tried to kill me."

"I've been tracking the furies all day," he said. "I can show you their bodies, if you don't believe me. I left my zombies on the surface while I was dealing with this little pest problem, and I assume another vampire took them from me and used them to attack you."

"Why would another vampire want me dead?" I queried.

"Power, I would guess." He glanced back at me, his brief gaze penetrating. "Two souls in one would satiate a vampire for quite some time."

"Don't get any ideas." If he'd been a normal necromancer, overpowering him wouldn't be an issue, but who knew what other tricks he might be hiding? He'd nearly sucked out my soul using someone else as a proxy, even if I believed he hadn't been responsible for today's zombie swarm. "Is that why you tried to drain my soul out?"

"I wouldn't have killed you," he said. "To most people, the sensation of being touched by a vampire is... not unpleasant. To your other soul, probably less so."

I nearly stopped walking. Had he been trying to suck out *her* soul, not mine? Surely not. If he had, she'd have retaliated. "She's not *mine*."

"My mistake," he said. "At first I assumed you were one and the same."

"Your vessel still tried to murder me, you scumbag."

Relief flooded me when the tunnel widened into a cave, and a ladder lay against a back wall at a crooked angle. It didn't look sturdy, but I wasn't about to stay down in the dark with the vampire a moment longer.

"After you," he said.

"Why, so you can pull me off the ladder when my back is turned?"

"You think so little of me?"

Well, yes.

He chuckled a little as though he'd heard the words I hadn't spoken aloud. "Fine. Better hope there's nothing else on our tail."

And he gripped the ladder's rungs, pulling himself up. I waited until he was too high up to kick me in the face, then climbed after him. While he was swift and athletic, he moved with neither the quiet grace of a faerie nor the brute force of a shifter. Vampire or not, he looked human.

"Your name?" I asked, climbing into the street behind him. "You know mine."

"Keir," he said.

He might be lying or using an alias. Who knew. In the daylight, against the grey sky and pale stone buildings, he looked less... supernatural. You wouldn't pick him out of a crowd. He wore grey jeans, a plain T-shirt, and had no apparent concern for the cold air or the drops of rain beginning to fall.

"So you can possess any dead body," I said to him. "Can't you just grab your zombies back from the other vampire's control, if there really is one?"

"That's not exactly how it works." He walked back to the hole and grabbed the top of the ladder. "To be more accurate, I can detach parts of my spirit and use them to control vessels." He pulled the ladder out, folding it in two. "The ability drains my own spirit essence, which I must replenish by draining others. Hence the name... vampire."

Sounds almost as much fun as being permanently possessed. "So there's no limit? You can control as many as you like, no matter how far away they are?" I tapped an impatient foot as he folded the ladder again. "Come on, you might as well answer my questions. I did save your life."

"Are you implying you're interested in learning from me?" He finished folding the ladder and straightened upright, his voice dropping suggestively. "If you'd like to embrace your full potential, I can help."

"No, thanks. What would I even do with an army of zombies? I'm not really into that whole world domination thing. Not my style. I prefer chilling out and watching zombie flicks to controlling an army of them."

He picked up the ladder again, balancing it on one shoulder. "A necromancer who likes zombie movies?"

"My friend likes taking them to pieces. The movies, not the zombies—okay, both, but that's not the point."

"No, the point is that you have two souls."

"Says who?" He knew what I was. Never mind whether he wanted me dead or not—all he'd need to do was drop a hint to a necromancer who couldn't keep a secret and the boss would find out. Then I could wave goodbye to my apprenticeship and freedom all in one go. "If you tell anyone, I swear—"

"Relax. I can keep a secret." A smile played on his mouth. "I'm quite good at it, believe it or not. I might even be able to help you. I can't say I've ever mentored a shade before, but I like a challenge."

"I have a mentor. She's the one your zombies tried to kill."

"They're not my zombies." His eyes glazed over for an instant, the vacant expression of someone tapping into the spirit world. "They're gone. I assume your friends destroyed them."

"Well, that's one piece of good news." I took a few steps down the cobbled street. "Aren't you coming to get them?"

"Vessels are no use to me if they're in pieces. As you know well."

"Don't berate me for destroying your pet," I said. "I seem to remember you tried to use him to suck out my soul."

"Not *your* soul." The light came back into his eyes again. "That's what you want, right? Nobody wants a shade. I might just have a way for you to be rid of it."

"An... exorcism?" Crap. I did *not* need this. He was the

person I should least trust with the tricky matter of extracting an extra soul, to say nothing of the fact that the witch's magic had killed that fury without exerting any effort at all.

"As it happens, I may know someone," he said. "I didn't lie when I said I needed something from you. Just take me to your coven, and I'll deal with this… spirit of yours. That's what you need, right? You want your body and soul to be yours again."

Some choice. Sell out my coven or spend an eternity walking around with an evil spirit attached to my own.

An evil spirit who'd saved my life.

"You know," I said, "I'm actually not interested in working with you at all. Have a nice life."

I turned and walked away, hoping I remembered the route. Lloyd and Isabel might think I was dead. Or buried underground. I really hoped they hadn't followed me, but I'd have seen if they had. *What the hell was he doing down there in the first place?*

"Jas," Keir called after me.

I whirled on him. "Did I not tell you to go away?"

"I can help you," he said, catching up to me. "But I need something from you first."

"I'm not letting you get within a mile of the Hemlock Coven, you wannabe assassin creep."

"Assassin?" he echoed. "I can only possess the dead, not the living, and I can't say I've ever assassinated anyone. Nobody living, anyway."

"You want to kill the Hemlock witches. I'd say that fits the definition." What the hell. I was too curious *not* to give him a grilling at this point.

"No," he said. "As a matter of fact, I don't want them dead. I want to ask them a question."

"What?" I folded my arms across my chest. "You stalked me with your creepy vampire vessel so you could ask my coven a *question?* Is that why you poisoned me, too?"

"I'm not the one who poisoned you, Jas," he said. "At first, I thought you and the shade were the same person, but I was wrong."

"Do you want me to thank you?" I turned the corner at the street's end, and he followed.

"I was told shades were unequivocally evil and depraved. But you're clearly neither of those things."

"Oh, I'm so flattered," I said, with an eye-roll. "I barely qualify as a Hemlock witch, so if you want any magic tricks from me, forget it. I'm not part of their coven."

"After what you did in the fight? Don't underplay your talent. I've seen it." His gaze showed an odd kind of hunger. "I felt it. When I set my hands on your soul."

"There isn't a single part of that sentence that wasn't creepy as fuck, Keir."

He broke his gaze from mine. "I apologise for making you uncomfortable. I spend a lot of time in circles where people like me aren't so unusual."

"Are these circles where you can find someone who can perform an exorcism?" I'd put my trust in him when hell froze over, but curiosity about how the vampires managed to keep their pet zombie armies a secret with guild members patrolling everywhere momentarily overrode my wariness.

"Yes, I can," he said. "I can't say I know how it feels to share one's body with another, much less a shade, but I imagine if it's anything like trying to wrest control of an undead from another person… one of you must win, and the other must lose. And given what I saw of that shade, if I were you, I'd be questioning my options."

Well, shit. What he was right? Two spirits shouldn't be contained in one body, according to all the laws, and when she'd fought against that fury, she'd completely pushed me away from the wheel. Even if I discounted the fact that the Hemlocks wanted both of us to be tied to their creepy forest the instant they died out, if Evelyn kept trying to take over, we were bound to come to blows eventually. And she had most of the magic.

If only any person other than an untrustworthy vampire had made the offer.

"That's a nice argument," I said. "But there's nothing in it for you if you help me. How do I know you won't bring a horde of *vessels* with you to attack me?"

"A horde?" he echoed. "I can't control a huge number without effectively reducing them to undead. Not my style."

"You tried to attack me this morning," I said. "That was *after* you saw me in person. You knew I wasn't the shade."

Keir shook his head. "I can't actually see that well through the spirit realm," he said. "Most shades… I can tell you've never met one before, because if you had, you'd understand why I struck first. She doesn't look like you at all."

Considering I'd never actually seen what the spirit looked like, only that she could send half-faerie ghosts screaming into the afterlife just from seeing her face, maybe he was telling the truth. Or maybe he was talking bollocks. Anyone's guess.

I sighed. "What do you want from me? Because I'm not the person to ask about the coven. I want an exorcism, not an interrogation."

"My question isn't about the coven itself," he said. "It happens that someone linked to your coven took something from me. Maybe you can answer the question... do you know the location of the Ancients?"

I blinked. "The ancient what?"

"I suppose not," he said. "In that case, ask your fellow Hemlock witches. If you bring me a satisfactory answer, then I'll take you to my exorcist contact."

Damn. I shouldn't be thinking of actually asking Cordelia and the others. After all, they could fob me off with any excuse they wanted. I knew they weren't looking out for my safety. But it seemed an innocent enough question. And I did have a fair few questions to ask myself, about the nature of the spirit's bond with mine, and how she'd managed to take the wheel so easily after being utterly quiet for most of my life.

"I'll take it under consideration," I said, "but you must know, I'll be breaking guild law by accepting any offer of a black-market exorcism."

"That's your choice to make, Jas," he said.

Yes. It was. Dammit. Why had the Hemlocks decided to force me to break supernatural laws just by existing? "Why does the guild let you carry on as you are?" I asked, unable to help myself. "Don't they notice zombies going missing?"

"For my kind, we're allowed to do as we like," he said. "The guild knows of our existence, certainly. But they don't want our filth corrupting their perfect system."

"You're not a fan of the guild?"

"I think they provide a fine service to the city," he said. "But not to me. And speaking of vampires, it's time I found whoever stole my zombies. If you want to meet with my contact, come to Queen Street, at seven this evening, with an answer to my question."

"Uh-huh." Once I found my friends, I'd check with the guild whether they were aware of the vampires' existence or not. Letting rogues who could suck out souls roam free sure didn't sound like the guild's usual approach, but most supernaturals just wanted to exist without persecution. Maybe they'd struck a deal. It wasn't like necromancers couldn't be deadly when pushed, too.

Besides... I needed to speak to Cordelia Hemlock. She owed *me* answers, and if I got a satisfactory answer to Keir's question, I might be able to free myself from the Hemlock Coven forever.

10

"So he's *not* the bad guy?" asked Lloyd. I'd finally found him and Isabel, who'd been investigating every alley in search of another way into the tunnel. Given that it'd taken a blast of freakishly overpowered witch magic to kill that fury, I was kind of glad they hadn't found their way in.

"Yes, he is, but not the person who tried to kill me," I said. "He wants to talk to the Hemlock witches, but I think I misread him as the villain when he's actually…"

"A rogue," Lloyd said. "I bet Lady Montgomery would promote you if you brought him in."

"Or he'd cause a scene, escape, and land me on her shit list again."

Isabel cleared her throat. "I have no idea what that guy's deal is, but I'm here to protect the Hemlock heir. If you definitely know what you're doing—"

"She doesn't know what *he's* doing," said Lloyd. "Dude's a wild card. I'd say report him."

"Right." I chewed on the inside of my cheek, debating.

"Look, Lady Montgomery is smart. There's not a corner of the city's underworld she doesn't know about. He told me the guild does know vampires exist, so I'll check the records."

"If you say so," said Lloyd. "Are you sure he didn't know the poisoner?"

"Positive," I said. "Isabel, did you get any clues from the market? I never asked."

"Unfortunately not," said Isabel. "I'll keep looking. While you're at the guild, I can ask around to see if anyone has sold hemlock lately."

"Are you sure?" I asked.

"Yep. I've got it covered." She snapped a band on her wrist and transformed into a large red-faced man with a beard.

Lloyd let out a low whistle. "That's one hell of an illusion spell."

"It's what I spent last night doing," said the man, in Isabel's voice. "I switch to a different disguise for each person I speak to. Makes it harder for anyone to track me."

"Good thinking."

Isabel could handle herself... which left it up to me to handle my not-so-fanged vampire friend. The sooner I found out what a vampire was actually capable of, the better.

After a quick detour to my room to change out of my filthy clothes, I made my way to the archives. I'd expected there to be a novice at the desk, but instead, Morgan Lynn sat in my usual seat, feet up on the table, reading a book.

Oh, come on. First I'd blown my perfect record, now Morgan had got muddy footprints all over the archive's notebook I'd left on the desk.

"Hey, Morgan, can you move?" I tugged at the notebook under his feet. "Didn't you know you were on archive duty."

He shifted his feet off the notebook and pushed several overlong strands of hair out of his eyes. "I got temporarily removed from the patrol list for 'excessive use of necromancy'. How the hell does that even work?"

"Depends what you did." If I had to guess, he'd thrown a zombie through someone's window again. I walked to the back shelf and began scanning titles. "Ever met a vampire?"

Morgan looked up from the book he'd balanced on his knees. "Sure. They were everywhere in Glasgow."

"What?" I turned to stare at him. "You know of them? Does Lady Montgomery?" If the entire guild had been aware of vampires' existence, it'd have been nice if someone had clued me in before I ran into one.

"She might," he said. "Catch." He threw the book he'd been reading at me, where it hit me in the side of the head.

"Ow." The book slid to the floor. "What the hell, Morgan?"

"Ah. Sorry. Thought you might be interested in that."

"You're supposed to warn me more than half a second before throwing things at me." I rubbed my head, retrieving the book to check the cover. "Advanced necromancy? Are you even allowed to be reading this?"

He shrugged. *Honestly.* Both Lynns were weird even by guild standards, but I figured he'd spent so long in the spirit world that he'd pretty much forgotten how to act around normal people. Admittedly, calling myself 'normal' was stretching the definition, but still.

"Did the vampires you met drain the life from people with a touch?" I asked, flipping the book over to read the back cover.

"Sure. Nasty fuckers."

"And possess people?"

He removed his feet from the desk, knocking over my carefully arranged paperwork in the process. "How'd you learn about vampires? You're not supposed to know—"

I grabbed the papers before they fell off the desk and put them on the nearest shelf. "You're reading a senior book and you're barely a novice, not to mention you got kicked off a mission for overstepping your boundaries. I don't think I'm the one you should be worried about. Thanks for this."

"Hey, I wasn't finished with that," he said indignantly, as I left the archives with the book tucked under my arm. After the morning I'd had, I didn't have the energy to wrangle answers from Morgan Lynn, and the book was exactly what I'd needed.

Vampires occupied an entire chapter. I slowed down, reading as I walked. The description matched Keir exactly, and it didn't sound like he'd omitted anything important from his description of how vampires worked. I'd need to ask the boss about the current laws on vampirism, though I doubted they were allowed to snatch random people off the street to snack on. The species of fae which did that were delegated to the 'kill on sight' list for not playing nice with humans.

I stopped at the entry on 'shade'. Then I reread the passage, my heart sinking into my shoes.

A shade is a spirit that has taken entire possession of another person, leaving nothing behind but a husk. Shades are created when a soul is transplanted into a different body, by means of a ritual combining elements of witchcraft, necromancy and blood magic. Highly forbidden since the dawn of the supernatural council, there has been no recorded incident of shade possession which has not resulted in both parties dying.

"Oh, god." I whispered.

Keir was right. My coven had done more than break the laws of the council, they'd broken the laws of *nature* to preserve their own magic. The longer the shade stayed in my body... would I eventually disappear for good?

"What exactly is that book?" inquired Lady Montgomery, stepping out of the corridor in front of me.

"Lady Montgomery." I licked my lips, my mind helpfully blanking out. "Uh. I picked it up in the archives." Not a lie, and I didn't even feel like tattling on Morgan. It sounded like he was in enough trouble already.

"I gathered, since you changed the rota. Care to explain?"

"Vampires," I said, intelligently.

She arched a brow. "What about them?"

"You know vampires exist?" I said. "Soul-sucking, zombie possessing... that type of vampire?"

"I've been the leader of this guild for thirty years, Jas. I would be concerned for our safety if I *didn't* know of the vampires' existence. They have their own form of governance and a strict code of rules, guild-approved."

"Oh." If the rulebook had Lady Montgomery's handiwork all over it, the vampires wouldn't be able to grab a zombie without filing a report. "I ran into one when I was looking for clues on who poisoned me, and I assumed he was going behind the guild's back. Guess I was wrong."

"I cannot say I'm on a first-name basis with most of the local vampires," said Lady Montgomery. "We also don't broadcast their existence, the same way we don't allow the public to know of psychics and our other skilled adepts. They're quite strict about their own secrecy."

"And they're allowed to keep their own pet zombies?" I asked.

"There's no rule against necromancers temporarily controlling the recently dead for their own reasons."

"Most of us wouldn't have reason to." How Keir had followed me was underhanded but not illegal. *Dammit.* Sure, it was nice to strike one enemy off the list, but that left me with zero clues about the poisoner. Hopefully Isabel would have better luck.

"Thankfully," said Lady Montgomery. "Jas, do let me know when you're ready to be added to the patrol rota. And please be careful with the vampires."

Only when she was gone did I remember that if Keir had told the truth, there *had* been a vampire or two working against us. The two I'd seen in the spirit realm, who'd stolen his zombies. I hoped he'd managed to track them, because I had bigger problems. The boss might be fine with the vampires' existence, but even she would draw the line at shades. And if the authorities got wind of Evelyn's existence, not even my Hemlock magic would save me.

I texted Lloyd asking him to meet me in the lobby, and he showed up a couple of minutes later.

"Jas," he said. "You look like you saw a—"

"That got old on our first day, Lloyd. I need to go and talk to the witches."

"What, now?"

"Urgently. Can you take care of this for me?" I handed him the book, which he turned over, raising an eyebrow at the cover.

"Advanced necromancy? Isn't this one of Lady Montgomery's?"

"I borrowed it from Morgan Lynn. Turns out he knows about vampires, and so does the boss."

He flipped the book open. "She does? Since when?"

"Longer than me. I guess it's senior necromancer level." That the vampires weren't illegally running a zombie trade made me feel a little better about going off-grid... not so much about seeking an independent exorcist. Guild law aside, it was as advisable as seeking dental care from a false hedge witch.

But the book proved one thing: shades weren't supposed to exist. And if I wasn't careful, the person sharing my body would usurp me forever. I liked being alive too much to hand over control to another person, let alone a witch with terrifying powers.

"Let me know if you need me to hide any bodies," said Lloyd. "I know you can ask the same of anyone in this room, but still."

I rolled my eyes at him. "See you later."

Time for a long overdue conversation with Cordelia Hemlock.

The witches apparently had even less patience for ceremony than I did this time around. The moment I crossed the disused railway tracks to the spot where I'd reappeared the last time I'd left the forest, the world disappeared, and the witches' cave replaced the Edinburgh sky. The faintly glowing glyphs brought a glow to my own hands, and I clenched my fists, tight, willing it to go away.

Cordelia's judgemental frown loomed over me. "Yes?"

"When exactly were you going to tell me you're planning on letting the shade take over my body?" I demanded.

She gave me a long stare, her eyes gleaming like black glass in a manner disturbingly similar to the fury that had attacked Keir and me. My whole body snapped to alertness at the power thrumming beneath my feet, resonating through the ever-present glyphs glowing on the cave's walls.

"Don't be absurd," Cordelia said. "By your own admission, no spirit who has passed into Death can return to the land of the living again."

"You yourself said it was more than necromancy that brought her back," I said. "Dark magic. Blood magic, rituals, evil magic... basically, everything in the earthly realm that's ever been outlawed by the Mage Lords and the supernatural council. And I'm supposed to cooperate with this *thing* you put inside my body, in the hope that she won't displace me and take over completely?"

"What would give you that idea?"

"I read up on shades," I said. "The whole reason they exist is to replace the original soul, but usually, both end up dying. Care to explain?"

"Shades summoned by amateur necromancers are doomed to failure," she croaked. "But you're much more than that. You can use her magic without involving her at all. That's what your training is supposed to involve, if you've allowed your mentor to teach you."

"She has," I said. "I can't even create a simple warding spell."

"According to what the forest tells me, you used her magic to fight the dead, and worse," said the old witch. "If you use her magic, you can create more than simple hedge witch spells. You can do anything at all."

And I'd thought that vampire was full of himself. "In your dreams," I informed her. "Which is all you've got now you're stuck here, I might add, so don't try to live out your twisted power fantasies through me."

"JACINDA HEMLOCK."

Cordelia's booming voice rang through my bones. For an instant, I was convinced I'd been pushed right out of my body. The glyphs on the wall lit up, and my limbs trembled as the whole cave jumped to attention. Then the hum of her voice died down a little, and I released a shaky breath.

"Don't you dare presume to think that you were given those powers lightly," she said. "You are to use them to defend your coven, and by extension, this entire realm."

"I did," I told her. "At the risk of losing control over my own body, over my own *life*. You might be cool with being a garden ornament forever, but I'm not."

"If you learn to adequately use your magic, Jacinda, then you will have no reason to fear being replaced."

"That's not what I'm afraid of." Evelyn stepped in

without a thought, and while her magic had saved my neck, I hadn't been able to access an ounce of her power myself. While Cordelia and the others might be formidable, none of them had experienced having their soul bound to another. How did they know for sure that this wouldn't end badly?

"Learn your magic," ordered Cordelia. "Come back to me when you've made progress, and don't waste my time with ridiculous questions."

"Just one more question," I said. "Have you ever heard of the Ancients?"

Cordelia's piercing gaze pinned me like a butterfly's wing. "That is your purpose," she said. "The Ancients are what we gave up our magic and our lives to keep contained. There are things between the worlds that should never be allowed to escape. Your magic allows you to continue our legacy, and for that reason, you must master it."

"*What* are these Ancients, exactly?" And why would the vampire be interested in the secrets of a coven who had nothing to do with necromancy? He hadn't known I was a shade until he'd seen me.

"Allow me to demonstrate."

The glyphs on the wall folded outwards, revealing a tunnel. At first, I thought I was staring at a magical illusion, or some kind of luminous painting of a giant closed eye, bigger than I was. Above and below the eye was a black tufty substance. Fur. And beyond was… not darkness, but emptiness. So much emptiness, if a person stepped close to the edge, they'd be sucked into the void to join the sleeping monster.

Cold energy roared through my veins, reacting to the

living thing sealed inside a place that quite clearly wasn't earth. Not even close.

They weren't kidding around, then.

I sagged against the wall. "Close the giant eye-hole, Cordelia. I think I've got it."

Namely: their magic was the only thing keeping that creature locked in whatever dimension it lay in.

Tremors ran from my hands to my feet. No wonder they wanted a successor so badly—badly enough to fuse one of their people's souls with a baby who had no say in the matter at all. But whatever magic the spirit possessed—it wasn't enough to stand up to the power keeping that monster contained. No way in hell.

I was hardly aware of leaving the cave, let alone stumbling down the forest path, until I found train tracks beneath my feet instead of tree roots. My whole body trembled with adrenaline.

They're batshit. Totally batshit. And yet, I knew no other magic user with enough power to keep that monster contained. Except maybe the Sidhe, but they had their own terrifying dimension.

Someone stepped onto the tracks in front of me. Magic sprang to my fingertips, an echo of the forest's power.

"Jas!" Isabel held up her hands. "Relax, it's me. I wanted to make sure they let you go."

"Oh, they let me go." Hysterical laughter rose in my throat. "They're out of their goddamned minds, but that apparently doesn't matter as long as they get a willing host."

"I'm lost," said Isabel, frowning. "What happened?"

"You've seen the thing they keep in the forest, right? Please tell me someone else has seen that monster."

Her eyes rounded. "Yes. You've never seen it before?"

"Nope." I wrapped my arms around myself, shivering in the sudden cold. "They told me it's my duty to help protect the world against things like that, and that's why I have to use the Hemlocks' magic." I decided to leave out the part where they seemed to expect me to take their place, because that was far too much. "But you know I can't. *She* can, and I'm not sure she'll let me use her power willingly. What if I fail?"

"You won't," said Isabel. "The Hemlocks… they're tough, but they wouldn't give you an impossible task."

"Their existence is built on the impossible," I said. "And for that matter, I didn't get the impression they've ever bound a soul to another person before. Let's just say the book I found at the guild said this isn't going to end well for me. Two souls can't coexist without one of them dying." And, eventually, both of them.

Isabel swore. "The Hemlocks… damn. Want me to talk to them?"

I shook my head. "I'm going to consult an exorcist," I said. "One of Keir's friends. Maybe it's a mistake, but I can't lie down and let this slide. If I can get the spirit out of my body—not kill her, but find a new host—then there'll still be a Hemlock heir."

Her lips pursed. "Can a necromancer do that?"

"None of the ones I know, but Keir seems to have a firm grasp of the supernatural underworld." Exorcism or not, I dearly wanted to know how a vampire might have possibly encountered that terrifying void monster, if that's really what an 'Ancient' was.

"Are you sure vampires aren't on the 'totally illegal' side of the supernatural law?" Isabel queried. "Because I'm —okay, it's mostly Ivy—not exactly inexperienced with flaunting the rules, but there's a difference between bending laws for the sake of keeping people safe, and well... sucking out souls."

"The guild knows about the vampires," I told her. "Not the ones who attacked us, but Keir was on their tail. I'll give him a good grilling. Trust me."

11

I bounced on the balls of my feet, wishing I'd had the good sense to grab some food before leaving to meet Keir. The smell of coffee and sandwiches from the nearby food cart was highly distracting. I'd learned my lesson about buying strange food or drink, considering someone wanted to poison me, but the vampire was taking his sweet time showing up. I'd paced up and down the street a dozen times, looking for any signs of the living or dead.

I paced back to the spot outside an empty shop, and Keir emerged from a side street, hands in the pockets of a dark jacket he hadn't been wearing earlier, his casual stance not giving any indication that he might secretly be possessing multiple people at once. I couldn't help wondering what he actually did for a living. Did he pilfer the bank accounts of the dead bodies he possessed? It was the sort of thing unscrupulous necromancers did until they were slapped down by the guild. There was a reason our rulebook was so extensive, and for Lady Montgomery to tolerate the vampires' presence in the city, they must abide by guild laws to the letter.

Keir stalled beside the sandwich stall, buying one, and walked to me while eating it.

I raised an eyebrow. "Weren't you warning me about poisoners?"

"Not here. Jarvis is safe. I didn't get to eat anything all day."

"Nor me. All right, I'll be back in a moment."

I went to buy a sandwich of my own, scanning the empty street in case Keir had brought an undead friend. I'd been patrolling around here before and rarely encountered any zombies despite the number of calls we got from concerned locals. If the undead all had owners who disposed of them when they started to decay, no wonder.

"So who's this exorcist friend of yours?" I asked, walking back to Keir's side and taking a bite out of my sandwich.

"Patience. He'll meet us here."

"Hmm." I chewed my mouthful. "It won't hurt, will it?"

He screwed up his empty sandwich wrapper and tilted his head as though to study me. "Are you absolutely certain you want to go through with this? It looked like you got on quite well with the shade's magic during the battle, and her skill far outweighs yours."

I nearly threw my sandwich at him. "You are such an arse. Only the witchcraft is hers, and I don't use it. The rest of it is all me."

He smirked, tossing his sandwich wrapper into the nearest bin. "I didn't mean to offend you—"

"Because that changes everything."

"I meant to say that her skill is more... unconventional. No, being with the guild doesn't count. They hire anyone with the merest hint of magical talent. And my acquaintance will expect reassurance that the witch's magic won't turn against him if you decide to go ahead with the exorcism."

I wouldn't bet on it. Maybe Evelyn would lash out when she found out my plan. But I couldn't just let her hitch a ride in my body forever. Keir had spotted her easily enough, and if she came out during another fight in the spirit realm, and a necromancer saw her... there was only one end for both of us, and it looked like the inside of a cell.

"It's your choice," he said. "That shade won't leave you by itself. They can be... tenacious, especially when bonded to the living for a long time. How long has it been bound to you?"

"None of your business." I tossed my own wrapper into the bin. "Listen, I'll be blunt: I don't trust you any more than I do your lowlife friends. Did you catch the vampire who stole your zombies?"

His jaw tightened. "No. Your friends exterminated all the dead, so I assume the thief left the scene."

"Great." Trusting any vampire was a terrible plan, but short of telling the guild about the shade, there were no other necromancers I could trust not to hand me over to the authorities. I'd heard enough rumours about the dungeon beneath the guild where the few people who did illegal necromancy and survived spent the rest of their days rotting—assuming the mages didn't execute both me and the spirit on the spot. Nobody who broke the magical laws, whatever their reasons, got away with it. Hemlocks included.

"But I do have my own theories about who might have tried to take your life," he added. "Starting with the people who tried to exterminate your coven."

My jaw hit the floor. "Excuse me?"

"I assumed you already knew," he said. "If you're not the last of your kind."

Dammit. Thanks for that one, Cordelia. If they hadn't told me the shade might take my place, of course they wouldn't tell me who their enemies actually were. Aside from the Sidhe, that is.

"Who tried to destroy my coven?" I asked, quietly. "Tell me."

"I heard rumours," he said. "Nothing concrete. Did you get an answer to my question?"

"The Ancients?" I said. "I'll tell you, if you tell me who my coven's enemies are."

"That's your answer," he said.

The image of a giant eye floated before me. *Oh. Maybe they did tell me.* But why would inter-dimensional monsters need to administer poison to wipe me out? And for that matter, how in hell would a vampire know about them?

"You saw what we fought in the tunnel," he added. "The same beasts, and much worse, tried to destroy your coven along with the rest of the world, and they'll take every opportunity to do it again."

I swallowed hard. "That thing in the tunnel wasn't an… Ancient. You called it a fury."

He shrugged, but the casual movement didn't quite hide the hint of tension in his posture. "It's a relation. They're from wherever the Ancients dwell, and someone summoned it, using a ritual known only to a select few—including the Hemlock Coven."

My throat went dry. "Excuse me? You're saying my coven summoned it? Trust me, that is *not* possible. You wanted me to ask them about the Ancients because you think the *Hemlocks* summoned those things?" I nearly laughed, though there was nothing amusing about the situation in the slightest. Powerful though they might be, the Hemlocks remained trapped in their prison.

"If the rumours are true and you're the last living survivor of the coven in this realm, I suppose not," he said. "I wanted confirmation that you weren't the summoner before putting you in touch with my contact."

"Assuming he shows up." I shivered, not just from the cold. "I don't get it. How did you know the Hemlocks existed if you're not one of them? No outsiders are supposed to—"

"A conversation for another day," he said. "Our exorcist is here."

A tall man staggered towards us. He had long shaggy dark hair and wore a long coat. From his unsteady movements, he didn't look capable of removing his own shoes, let alone an evil spirit. Why had I trusted Keir not to screw with me again?

"Hemlock," the man said, in a croaking voice.

What? "You told—"

"No." Keir went very still. "Jas, he's not here. He's—"

"Possessed by another vampire." I grabbed my knife.

The dead man raised both hands, and necromantic power blasted into both of us. The spirit world rose around me, revealing two shadowy outlines behind the dead man.

Two vampires. Crap.

Hands locked around mine, pulling me back into the waking world, and coldness spread through my skin right to my soul.

"Let go." I kicked at the man's shins, but while the zombie overbalanced, the vampire's grip on my spirit remained tenacious. *Shit.*

As greyness filtered in, a shadowy blur collided with the vampire from the side, breaking his hold on me. I barely had chance to gasp out a *thank you*, before the second vampire grabbed for me, this one not even bothering to use a zombie as a proxy.

I blasted him in the face with necromantic energy, shouting the words of banishing at the top of my lungs.

Before I could see if the banishing had worked, the first zombie collided with me, hands flailing. I tried to raise my knife, but my body didn't obey my command.

Instead, threads of white power whipped from my hands, slicing through the zombies, body and spirit both. Keir jumped aside with an alarmed hiss as the magic grazed him.

Hey! Stop that.

"Jas?" he said, looking me in the eyes. "Let her go, shade."

I floated above my body in the spirit realm, threads of blue-white energy glowing in my hands, not so different to piloting a zombie. Except the person being piloted—was me.

If Evelyn can do that, then so can I.

Gritting my teeth, I grabbed those threads of light, and shoved my way back into my body. For a few panicked seconds, I went nowhere fast. Then sensation shot back into my hands so abruptly, I yelped with the shock of coldness. Icy fragments cracked on my knuckles, and I caught my balance before I fell to my knees.

"Jas?" Keir looked me carefully in the eyes. "Good. You're back."

"You seem confident it wasn't me who wanted to kill you," I said shakily. My mind spun in circles. Even reading that book, hearing the Hemlocks' words, part of me hadn't wanted to believe I could forfeit control of my own body that easily. But she hadn't just taken the reins. Pushing her out of my head had been like wresting control of that zombie from someone who absolutely did not want to give it up.

"Are those vampires permanently gone?" he asked.

"You should know if they are." I wasn't going back into the spirit realm to check anytime soon.

His gaze briefly zoned out. "They're gone," he confirmed. "I didn't know you could fight both in this realm and the spirit realm at the same time."

"Are you shitting me?" So much for exorcising the problem. I might have taken control towards the end, but Evelyn had stepped into my body without my say-so, like, well, a vampire stealing another's undead vessel.

"If it's any consolation, your shade only attacked the enemies," he said. "Not me. I got in the way, but I wasn't who she was aiming at."

"You say that like it's a good thing."

He held his hand over his heart with a mockery of a sad expression. "I'm wounded, Jas."

"You're insufferable," I said, though his ridiculous antics helped me feel a little better. "How I am I to know you didn't coordinate the vampires' attack yourself?"

"You were outnumbered, Jas. If I'd been working with them, I could easily have taken you down while you were in the spirit realm."

"Not if she got to you first." I gave him a grim smile that had absolutely no humour in it. "You've seen what she can do. I doubt she knows friend from foe, so I can't say I know why she spared your life, but I think you should probably count yourself lucky."

He tilted his head on one side, a smile playing on his lips. "Threats, Jas?"

"More like a warning. Might have escaped your attention, but our exorcist is dead, and so is my shot at getting the shade out of my body. She's been in there a long time and I can't say I know what she's capable of, but I'd be on my guard."

His smile shifted, showing a hint of what might have been respect. I had the distinct impression that earning his respect was no easy feat, but it didn't make me want to thwack the smirk off his face any less.

"So now your exorcist is dead," I said. "What now, genius?"

"Mine? Not hardly. It was a long shot. He wasn't powerful… certainly not as powerful as your shade is."

"So you never planned to help me?" I said. "I thought you were a man of your word."

"I promised you an audience with the exorcist, and I apologise for not being able to follow up on that part of our bargain. However…" He paused. "I can't say I'm absolutely convinced it'd have worked. Shades are rare, and even rarer is a host who lives alongside the spirit for years without being aware. To undo the binding, you'd probably have to consult the spirit yourself and see if she remembers how she ended up bound to you."

Like it or not, he made total sense. Even the Hemlock witches couldn't possibly know what the spirit had been thinking while she'd been tied to me for twenty-two years, after all. Keir shouldn't know anything about my relationship with her, but it wasn't hard to guess, based on what he'd seen of me. I never had been a very good liar.

Keir himself, on the other hand? He could lie for a living. His too-handsome face was just a mask for a shadowy person who might be friend or foe. And he knew entirely too much about my coven for my liking. He might have helped me, but two of his fellow vampires had also known I was a Hemlock witch.

"How many people did you tell about me?" I asked. "I have literally never told a soul that I'm a Hemlock witch since I moved to this city, and now suddenly everyone knows."

"If you're accusing me of telling the other vampires, I didn't," he said. "Some of us may be friends and allies, but we're fairly independent of one another and don't share dangerous magical knowledge as easily as the guild does."

"Bashing the guild won't win you any favours," I said. "It's thanks to the magical laws set by the guild that people like you aren't running amok, sucking the souls out of innocent people. No wonder you give zero shits that the person you just fought off two vampires with carries the soul of a dead witch who hijacked my body without my permission."

"Don't mistake my pragmatism for indifference, Jas. I've been trying to work out how to handle this unfortunate development ever since I realised the shade wasn't you."

"Guess we're back to square one now your exorcist friend is deceased."

"I wouldn't call us friends," he said. "More acquaintances."

My hands curled into fists. "Are you incapable of taking this seriously? There are dead bodies here in broad daylight, and now I'm required by law to hand them over to the guild before a rogue reanimates them."

"Technically, they belong to the vampires, since they've already been used as hosts."

"You and I both know that so far I've met more vampires who want to kill me than not. Dispose of them."

Apparently he saw something in my expression that wasn't worth arguing with, because he pulled out his knife and hacked the nearest undead's head clean off.

"I meant with magic, you complete dingbat." How I had I ever thought this guy would actually help me out?

"I wanted to identify him first." He lifted the man's head, then put it back down. "From the smell of him, he's been near the witch market recently."

"What? Seriously?" Maybe it was the witches I should have spoken to after all. Isabel had yet to text me with an update on her progress with questioning people at the market, though I'd asked her to call me if I didn't return from my meeting with Keir within the hour. I felt in my pocket and found one of the spells Isabel had given me. "Watch out," I warned Keir, and threw it at the bodies, which instantly dissolved in a flash of flame.

"That's an impressive spell," he commented. "One of yours?"

"Nah, my mentor made it," I said. "It's not like it's much help in the spirit realm, with my witchy alter-ego piloting my body. So, if you hate the guild so much, who do you report rogues to? Or is it every vampire for themselves?"

"No, I'm planning to tell the king of the vampires in this city," he said. "He's no friend of the guild, but he's met with Lady Montgomery and is considered a trusted asset of your council. I'm sure he'd be willing to answer your questions. Provided you don't let on that you're from the guild."

"There's a king?" I raised an eyebrow. "And he'd believe I'm a rogue?"

Despite my reservations, I was through playing it safe. The spirit had taken control of my body without my permission, and if there was a vampire who might be able to help, even a little, it was worth a try.

"I think you can convince him," he responded.

I blinked, unsure whether he was making fun or not. "All right, then. I'll come and meet the vampire king."

12

Keir led me through the back streets for long enough that I wished I'd sketched a map as we walked. I was generally pretty good with directions and had purposefully got myself lost in different places each week when I'd first arrived in the city so I'd learn my way around quickly, but the vampires' haunts were an unknown territory. Especially the home of their king.

"It's more of a chosen title than a ceremonial one," Keir explained as we walked into a darkening street lit by a single street lamp. I'd be in the wrong job if I was scared of the dark, but today's encounter with the fury had made me edgy. Fighting in near-darkness was tricky at the best of times, but conventional necromancy didn't work on vampires the way it did on my usual opponents. And besides, I'd barely escaped a fight with two of them unscathed. I didn't want to go up against a horde.

"Relax," Keir said softly, apparently picking up on my tension. "They won't hurt you."

"Look, I literally just got attacked by two of you. I'm not optimistic."

"That's why we need to speak to the king. Rogues make the rest of us look bad. Even worse than normal," he added, having apparently caught my train of thought. "If you can believe that."

"I raise and lay the dead to rest for a living," I told him. "I'm in no position to question anyone else's life choices. Does vampirism run in the family in the same way as other magic types? I guess it does."

He shrugged. "In a way. Why?"

"Just curious if you follow the same rules as other supernaturals. You don't have council representatives…"

"Because while we might have a king, we're not an organised collective," he said, passing underneath the street lamp. Its light made his skin glow faintly ghostlike. "And there aren't enough of us."

I'd suspected there must be, otherwise I'd surely have run into a vampire or three in the spirit realm before. "Can a necromancer be born a vampire? I mean, you're related, right?"

"Only as superficially as a wolf shifter and a dragon shifter."

"With you as the dragon?"

Even white teeth showed as he grinned. "Naturally."

I gave him an eye-roll. "Is this vampire king a relation of yours, then?"

"No," he said. "My family is gone."

"Oh. Sorry." I looked away for a brief moment. "The invasion?"

"Mostly," he said, not elaborating further.

Okay. Sore topic—and none of my business. He didn't

need to know my history any more than I needed to know his. "So what do vampires do for a living? I take it you're not filthy rich like the mages are."

"No, I work as a freelancer," he said. "There are a lot of specialist jobs only a vampire can do."

I cast my mind around. "Spying on people? Pretending to be the recently dead? But you don't actually… kill the people you possess. That's illegal."

"Oh, I play by the rules." Another flash of teeth. "Mostly. I can use my zombies to get into places that it would be difficult for a living person to access."

"Useful," I commented. "Seems like a good fit for the guild. I take it you can use standard necromancy as well?"

"I can," he confirmed. "But I'm self-taught, for the most part. I had a somewhat unstable childhood. You haven't always worked for the guild? You're English."

"I grew up in a witch orphanage." I didn't add the part about Lady Harper taking me to live with the mages. He didn't seem to be particularly keen on supernatural authority figures, and besides, the less he knew about my coven, the better. "Then I moved here to train at the guild, since I was better at necromancy than witchcraft."

"And now you have both." His eyes gleamed with interest. "We do have more in common than I thought."

I didn't take his bait. "Yes, my relatives decided to make me into a host for an evil spirit, so I'm starting to think crazy attracts crazy."

His brow arched. "And there I was thinking you disliked my company."

Oh, shit. Bad choice of words there, Jas.

His steps halted beside a tall house with a high railing

around the front garden. Behind, a set of stone steps led to a basement flat. "The vampires' king lives down there."

"I expected a palace." I hesitated, then walked after him down the steep stone steps. "Unless there's a cave down here?"

"More of a tunnel."

Of course. Even the necromancers weren't *that* stereotypical. Okay, we did have an underground dungeon beneath the guild, but most of our activity was aboveground.

Keir rapped on the chipped black-painted door with his knuckles. His shoulders were a little tense, while his free hand twitched on the knife handle visible in his pocket. Maybe he wasn't as sold on their accepting a guild necromancer—not to mention a Hemlock witch—wandering into their territory as he'd claimed. If they all knew the Hemlocks, everyone in here might be a potential enemy.

The door opened, but nobody greeted us. Keir paused briefly, then walked into the darkness. It was so pitch-black that the room within might have been any size and I wouldn't have known. Stretching my hands out either side and finding walls made of cold plaster, I figured we must be in a hallway. "Why not buy electric lighting? He's a king, right? Nobody can see in here."

"Technically, we can, if we use the spirit realm," he said. "And on that note, he's been able to hear everything we've said ever since we reached the house."

"Wonderful." Any powerful necromancer could do the same, but if I checked into the spirit realm to sense whoever was in this room, I'd leave myself open to being taken over the person who shared my body again. If

Evelyn saw the vampires as a threat and lashed out, the consequences would land on my head, not hers.

We walked for several more metres before a ceiling light snapped on, revealing a room with earthen walls. I'd call it more of a cave than a tunnel, though several other openings branched off in places which might have contained doors before someone had torn them down and turned the basement into an underground lair.

I tensed as several people came out of those cave-like openings, all dressed in casual clothing and not visibly armed. I'd peg them as non-supernatural from the outside… if not for the shadowy outlines that appeared behind each of them when I risked a glimpse into the spirit realm. Needless to say, there wasn't a pair of fangs in sight.

"Why did you bring a guild necromancer here?" One of the vampires stepped towards me. He had a strong jawline peppered with light brown stubble, and muscles that would make a full-grown shifter whine with envy. What was with these people? Did they spend every moment they weren't vamping out tossing weights around?

And just how did he know I was from the guild? It wasn't like I wore the coat. *Dammit, Keir.*

"I brought her here," said Keir, "because both of us were attacked by rogue vampires. They murdered Nate and sent him to kill both of us."

"Nate?" The vampire sat down in an armchair as though it was a throne, his fellow vampires milling around him. "I never liked him."

Keir stiffened next to me. "Did you hear me? At least one rogue is still out there. He stole a group of undead from me and used them to attack several innocent people."

"Bring it to the summit on Thursday," said the vampire king, putting his feet up on a stool. "You can make your case then."

"That's too long," said Keir. "The rogues have tried to kill us multiple times in the last few days. They're risking our security."

The vampire king shrugged, accepting a drink from one of his fellow vampires. It looked blood-red in the light, but I'd bet it wasn't actually blood. "I hardly think we can keep track of every rogue. You're too good at making enemies, Keir."

"Does the guild know that?" I asked. "Because that's skirting awfully close to violating the necromancers' rulebook, if you let these vampires walk around unchecked while knowing they're likely to assault innocent people. Just saying."

Keir shot me a warning look.

"If they violate the laws, we take care of them ourselves," said the vampire king, removing his feet from the stool and rising smoothly to his feet. "As we will be doing, in our own time. You're responsible for your own safety, not us, guild lackey."

"What did you just call me?" Picking a fight with the vampire's king had *not* been on my plan, but this was the guy who'd met with Lady Montgomery, and I'd bet he'd never dream of speaking like that to *her*.

"That's not all we came to ask you," interjected Keir. "The vampires who attacked us might be working with someone from the witch markets."

The vampires' king scanned my face. "Witch, are you?"

"None of your business," I said. Considering his cavalier attitude to us being attacked by two of his fellow vampires, I didn't need everyone in this cave to know I had anything to do with the witches whatsoever. "We came here to ask if you were aware of any vampires going rogue. Since the answer is 'I don't give a shit,' I think we're done."

"The vampires in this room choose to be here," he said. "I don't require them to carry a membership card, which is more than I can say for your guild."

"Good for you," I said. "If you want to argue with guild representatives, you're welcome to speak to my supervisor instead. I'm sure she'll be interested to know some of your people attempted to murder the two of us. Like it or not, if she thinks you had anything to do with their actions, it's grounds for an arrest warrant."

His face reddened. "How dare you threaten me in my home?"

"I'm not threatening you, but I have every intention of reporting your rogues to the guild, and if I do, I have to tell them that you refused to help us. I just figured I'd warn you first."

The vampire king glared at Keir. "Get her out."

"Think about it," I said to him. "You can sit here in your mother's basement and refuse to take any action, or you can help us find the rogues and not have to watch your reputation burn to cinders." I didn't know the in-depth workings of vampire society, but with the mages at least, reputation was everything.

"Great-aunt's," growled the vampire king.

"I'm sorry, what?"

"Great-aunt's basement. And besides, I don't own

every vampire in the city. Take your little feud elsewhere. I'll have no part in it."

"With pleasure." I grabbed Keir's arm and hauled him after me. Once I was sure the others were out of hearing distance, I leaned over to hiss in his ear. "You brought me here so I'd hassle the king into taking action, didn't you? You can't threaten him on the guild's behalf on your own, so you decided to make use of your new contact. Me."

His pause lasted a second too long. Before he came out with an excuse, I said, "Are you trying to get me fired on top of fucking up my life? Because I'm legally required to send guild people down here to bang a few heads together if someone doesn't take some goddamn responsibility."

"Exactly," he said. "I can't argue for the guild myself, and besides, it's unlikely they would be able to pick up on a rogue vampire until someone's life was at risk. I wanted to handle the problem before it came to that."

"Well, it went swimmingly."

Between playing games with him, the vampires, the Hemlock witches, and Evelyn, I was in dire need of a nap. I texted Isabel and Lloyd telling them the evening was a bust, and Keir and I climbed the stone steps into near-darkness. Even the lone street lamp had gone out—and two heavyset figures blocked the road.

"Can I help you with something?" My hand inched towards my knife. "Or are you here to see the king?"

"You never should have come here, witch," said the vampire on the left, in a raspy voice.

"Seriously?" I reached for my own weapon. "You want to do this here, right next to your king's house?"

"He won't interfere."

Oh, wonderful.

I blocked his strike with my forearm, kicking him in the shins. I'd had enough training to be reasonably confident in taking down someone with no combat ability, but his punch had been too well-aimed to belong to someone who didn't know what he was doing. Unless I got lucky, I'd have to use my necromantic skills... which put me at risk of putting Evelyn in the driver's seat again.

Bloody vampires.

The second vampire grappled with Keir, so I focused my attention on the big guy in front of me. I'd never gone up against a *living* human in a to-the-death brawl, and he had about a hundred pounds of muscle on me. But while necromancy might be designed for the dead, it could still deal a hell of a blow to the living.

Kinetic energy burst from my hands, but the vampire shook it off as though I'd thrown a handful of glitter at him. His hands latched onto my shoulders—not in the physical world, but the spirit realm. Coldness spread throughout me, grey fog filling my vision. *Oh hell.*

He was draining me—fast. I could no longer feel my living body, only the coldness of death, paralysing me to the very soul. Through the blurred fog, I watched my body drop to the ground, the knife falling from my grip--

"Where the hell are you, Evelyn?" It didn't matter if he heard. I was going to die. No—both of us were.

No. I'm not.

I felt for that power—that relentless presence that I'd felt when the spirit took control of me the first time. The same magic that permeated the forest, a depthless force without end. My body glowed with it, and I wrenched myself free from the vampire's grip. His shadowy form recoiled, and as I raised my hands to strike, a second pair of hands rose beside mine.

I tilted my head to the side and looked into grey-blue eyes in a face with high cheekbones, full lips, blemish-free ghostly skin. Loose curls flowed in a non-existent breeze.

"Shade," growled the vampire, and I snapped my attention back onto him.

"He can only drain one of us," whispered Evelyn Hemlock.

It wasn't the first time I'd heard her speak, but now I saw her in person, it struck me that she wasn't much older than I was.

"He's in two places at once," I hissed, keeping one eye on his shadowy form, which he'd detached from his body to drain me without physically moving at all. "I need to take my body back."

"Then take it." Her hands lit up with blue light, and she blasted it at the vampire with all her might.

I closed my eyes and blinked out of Death back into my body, feeling ice crack on my hands as I clenched my fists. My knees smarted where I'd landed on the pavement, but the vampire's body stood rigid in front of me. The spirit was occupying all his attention. Maybe he wasn't such a powerful vampire after all.

I gripped my knife and stabbed upwards, but his hand caught mine. *Okay, I take that back.*

Magic burned my palms, lighting them up with white energy. Not necromancy, but a power that came from a deep well somewhere within me. Iron strength roared through my blood, and the vampire yelled in pain, dropping his hand. I'd snapped his wrist in my hand. Holy shit.

Note to self: do not use that power on necromancer missions, especially in front of novices.

I drew back and punched him in the ribs. Bones cracked beneath my knuckles. Magic surged in my fingertips, forming a whip that caught around his neck. I flung him to the earth, and his head cracked on the pavement.

Good job, whispered the voice, and I felt Evelyn's presence behind me once again. No... within me. Until I'd seen her face looking back at me, I hadn't truly believed we were two separate entities. Separate, and yet—I'd used her power.

Now I understood what soul-bonded meant. I couldn't separate myself from her. Which meant any notions of using an exorcism were well and truly wiped out. Her magic was mine, and I was her... vessel. Yet despite that, she'd looked human. Maybe having her soul lie dormant inside my body hadn't damaged either of us at all.

Dammit. I'm not telling Cordelia she was right.

Keir staggered across my path. Blood drenched his shirt, but the second vampire was bleeding, too. I moved in to help, but he got there first. Grabbing the other vampire by the shoulders, he locked his grip tight, and I shivered at the sensation as his magic brushed against mine. Despite myself, I tapped into Death once again, seeing the blurred shapes of the two vampires who at first appeared to be in an embrace.

Threads of blue energy surged from one shadow to the other, and while one grew brighter, the other dimmed.

I blinked, the greyness cleared, and the vampire's limp body fell to the earth. Keir had literally drained the life out of the guy right through the spirit realm.

He turned to me, his whole body glowing with blue-white energy, and glanced down at his arm. "Fucker. I liked this jacket."

"Ouch," I said, seeing the deep cut through the torn sleeve. "You need a healing spell on that."

"Are you hurt?" He eyed me, his brow crinkled, the blue glow fading a little.

"Alive, pissed off, ready to get out of here. You?"

"All of the above." He picked up his knife from where he'd dropped it. "Leave the vampires there. That ought to convince the king to take some action."

He began to walk away. Blood streamed down his arm, and he walked a little unsteadily.

"If you go anywhere near the guild like that, they'll mistake you for an undead," I said.

"Whoever said I was going to the guild?"

"You're bleeding," I said. "I'm taking a wild guess that you don't have a healing spell on you. My friend has some, but otherwise, the guild's the only option. Unless there's a place on your territory where people won't try to kill us?"

"Territory?" he echoed. "I wouldn't say it's mine, any more than it's the vampire king's. He's likely not to last long in the position, besides." He attempted to clean the wound on the ripped sleeve of his jacket and succeeded only in getting blood everywhere.

"Considering he didn't lift a finger to help us, he's on my eternal shit list," I said. "Come on. I'll introduce you to my mentor. It's lucky she's nicer than I am."

13

"You have got to be joking," said Isabel, folding her arms in the doorway of her hotel room. "You want me to help a vampire—one of the people trying to wipe out your coven?"

"Two other vampires tried to kill both of us," I said. "He's not the one we're after. And if he dies, I lose my only lead on the actual killer."

She muttered something under her breath, before stepping aside to let us in. I didn't know the witches who owned the hotel, but Isabel classified them as safe. I suspected Keir would have put up more of an argument if he didn't have an open wound.

Lloyd had been waiting outside when Keir and I had reached the hotel. Apparently he and Isabel had devised various plans to get the guild involved for backup if need be after they hadn't heard from me for a while. It was very thoughtful of them, and a welcome change from dealing with vampires who wouldn't intervene to stop someone attacking one of their own people.

"I take it the exorcism didn't go as planned?" added Isabel, heading to the small desk built into the wall, where she'd put what looked like a month's supply of spell ingredients.

"Nope," I said, removing my jacket to check on the damage. I'd been lucky to escape with a few scratches. Given that I'd nearly had my soul sucked out, the evening might easily have ended very differently. "The guy we met with turned out to be dead, controlled by another vampire. Then two more vampires ambushed us after our meeting with the vampire king."

"I think the question is, who *is* the vampire king?" asked Lloyd, picking up a band-shaped spell to examine it. "Since when *was* there one, for that matter?"

I shot Keir a look. He'd sat on the free chair, easing his jacket off to expose the wound.

"There's always been a designated leader," he said. "It's a requirement, so the Mage Lords have someone to speak to if there's a serious problem, but we don't all answer to the same person."

"If he's as rude to the Mage Lords as he was to us, I take it there's never been a serious problem."

Light flashed from the floor, where Isabel was in the process of tossing ingredients into a chalk circle.

"No, I can't say there has," said Keir, stretching out his injured arm and wincing a little. The cut was even deeper than it'd looked before. "If it's any consolation, you needn't worry about retaliation if you report the attack to the guild. They attacked you because you're a Hemlock witch, not because of your guild status."

"I don't give a shit why they attacked me," I said. "They

can join the poisoners on my list of enemies. Might they be working together?"

"I assume they are," he said.

"How'd you figure that one out?" asked Lloyd, replacing Isabel's spell on the desk and digging in his pocket for his phone. Like me, he'd left his necromancer coat behind and dressed in simple jeans and T-shirt, so nobody would ask questions about a necromancer hanging out at a hotel which belonged to the witches.

Keir turned in my direction. "The person who tried to poison you worked out your identity, and your friendship with him—" he eyed Lloyd—"without ever meeting you in person. That suggests they got that information via the spirit world."

"That wouldn't explain how they knew I was a Hemlock witch," I said. "I'm not kidding—I never even told Lloyd."

"Which you still owe me for," Lloyd interjected. "Not to mention the crap we're going to be in if Lady Montgomery finds out."

"Oh, I'm telling her about the vampires." I walked to the bathroom and ran a cloth under the tap to dab at the blood on my face. "Including their lazy arse of a king."

Keir didn't say anything. I might have won this round, but we still had no way of knowing how the enemy had got wind of my existence, short of seeing the spirit looking through my eyes and somehow working out she was a Hemlock witch.

"She's not wrong," Isabel commented. "Want me to look at that arm?"

Keir offered her his injured arm. "It's up to you, Jas,

but remember that these people already want you dead. Do you really want them to learn of all your allies?"

"Might make them think twice about attacking me again, knowing I have the whole guild at my back," I answered. "Since the presence of one of their own didn't stop them trying to wipe you out, too."

"Ouch," he said. Then, as Isabel dabbed at the wound, "*Ouch.*" Light flared up around his injury, and he hissed in pain, yanking his arm away from Isabel.

"Keep still or it's going to get a lot more painful." She reached for another spell. "That cleansing spell got most of the crap out of the wound, but let me know if you want a second round."

"You put salt in it on purpose, didn't you?" he said accusingly.

"I can if you want to," offered Lloyd. "We could have left you to die."

"Keir, stop being a dick," I said, attempting to defuse the situation before it blew up. "You got us attacked by your allies—twice, I might add. If I were you, I'd be seriously re-evaluating my friendship choices."

"I wouldn't call Nate a friend. Nor any of the other vampires we encountered today, come to that." Keir held his arm steady so Isabel could put the salve on the open wound. I had the impression he didn't like surrendering control. "But now you have me here, I suppose I owe you. What do you want to know?"

"For a start," I said, "you never told me who summoned that fury to begin with, let alone how you knew it was underground."

Isabel's hands slipped and brushed the wound,

resulting in another exclamation of pain from Keir. "Did you say fury?"

"You're not saying you've met them, too?" I asked.

"A few times." She gave Keir a wary look. "They haven't been seen anywhere in this realm in over a year, as far as I know."

"What the bloody hell is a fury?" Lloyd wanted to know.

"Big evil thing with wings and talons that's ridiculously difficult to kill," I said. "It came from… *where* did it come from?"

"Nobody's exactly sure on that one," Keir said. "But it was summoned using a ritual formerly known only to a few, including the Hemlock Coven."

"Not just them," Isabel added. "Someone tried to do the same thing over a year ago, back at home. That's how Ivy and I wound up meeting the Hemlock witches to begin with. The person who killed Francine—my last coven leader—worked with a bunch of wannabe anti-supernatural assassins who thought it was fun to summon those monsters. They all died, but I guess their ideas lived on. I don't know how *he* found out." She shot Keir a look.

I shook my head. "But—how are my coven's secrets spreading everywhere when nobody else is supposed to know? I don't suppose Cordelia or Lady Harper told you?"

"We have worse problems if it *is* the same ritual," she said. "Believe me. Ivy and I barely defeated the furies, but I didn't think anyone lived to tell tales."

"Damn." That setup in the warehouse… had it been an attempt at a similar ritual? There was a thin line between necromantic blood magic and forbidden witch rituals, enough that they were pretty much the same, because both involved summoning things from dark dimensions.

So much for keeping the necromancers' guild out of my problems.

Lloyd groaned. "More enemies?"

"Same ones," I said. "I think it's safe to say they're all working together. Clearly, they want the Hemlock witches out of the picture, but I don't know if that's their endgame. Was either of those vampires who attacked us the one who stole your zombies?"

Keir shook his head. "I never did manage to track the person responsible."

"So he might still be out there," I said. "Can you try to track him? The same way I did to you?"

"Not if the zombies were destroyed," he answered. "There are a lot of us, and we know all the tricks for hiding ourselves in the spirit realm. But I might be able to find a way." He eyed Isabel. "I owe you for your help."

Isabel glowered at him. "I'm helping you because Jas said so, and for no other reason. If you even think about turning on us, you'll find yourself on the receiving end of my coven's magic, and believe me, you won't like it."

"No, you won't," Lloyd confirmed. "She took seven zombies apart earlier without even touching them."

"The other reason is that I've encountered those furies before," Isabel added. "And since you fought against them, you're not on the same side as the dicks who want Jas dead."

He grinned. "I'm honoured."

"Don't let it get to your head," I said to him. "If you want to return the favour, you'll tell us everything you know about the rogues and why they might be plotting against the witches. I wouldn't have thought there'd be any real reason for a vampire to turn on the guild if they wanted to keep their head, but who knows."

"The traitors must have decided it was worth the risk," said Keir. "Maybe they were offered power, maybe not. But a rogue vampire isn't capable of enacting a summoning ritual."

"A witch is," I said. "There's a witch—more than one—behind this. Right?"

He inclined his head.

"Then I have to report this to the guild." I gave Lloyd a sideways glance. "The other day, we were on a mission, and we found evidence of what appeared to be some kind of illegal summoning. It involved chalk symbols and witch props. Might it have been the same?"

Keir rose to his feet. "You didn't mention that before."

"That's because I didn't know rituals were involved until you mentioned the furies were summoned using one," I said. "And we were dealing with a real bastard of a half-faerie ghost the other day, beside what looked like a witch symbol and a chalk circle. He was way too strong. I thought the spell might be amplifying his power, but the evidence is gone."

Keir picked up his ruined jacket and moved towards the door. "If that's the case... I need to look into this a little more. Thank you for the spells, Isabel."

"You're leaving?" I said.

"Before a witch with spirit sensitivity realises there's a vampire in the hotel? Yes."

It was unlikely that any of the witches here were necromancers on the side, but I didn't have any real argument to make him stay, especially when I needed to leave soon if I wanted to report the evening's events to the guild. "Let me know if you come up with any theories."

"I will." He gave me a smile—so fast, I might have imagined it—and then he was gone.

"Charming, isn't he?" said Lloyd, the moment the door closed behind him.

"He has his moments."

Lloyd snorted. "On his deathbed, maybe. *Vampires.* I knew the senior necromancers were sitting on some major secrets, but I wish I'd got to meet the vampires' king."

"You don't. He was a slob living in his great-aunt's basement surrounded by willing servants."

"Wait, that's a career option?"

I rolled my eyes. "Look, can you back me up when I report to the guild? I don't want them to throw Keir into a cell, considering we're short on allies, but the vamps have some serious management issues."

"That's a major understatement," said Isabel, tipping a bunch of used spells into the bin.

"Not that he didn't deserve being yelled at, but did something happen?" I asked. "Aside from the obvious?"

"Lady Harper," she said. "She called and read me the riot act for letting you run around unsupervised. Apparently she found out about your last trip into the forest. I think it was you she wanted to yell at, but she couldn't get through to your phone."

I pulled my mobile phone out of my pocket. Seven missed calls, including some from numbers I didn't know. "Ah. Shit. Sorry."

"That's Ivy," said Isabel, indicating one of the numbers.

"It's true that we should be further in training than we are."

"Actually, I might have had a breakthrough," I said. "Near-death experiences are good for something. I used Evelyn's magic, on purpose this time, and I even saw her."

Her eyes widened. "You saw the witch? When?"

"When I fought the vampires," I said. "One of them tried to drain me, and my souls… split. I saw and spoke to her."

Lloyd's jaw hit the floor. "Uh. You spoke to the weird spirit living in your head? About what?"

"We were in the middle of fighting a vampire. It wasn't an in-depth conversation. But I did use her magic." I turned to Isabel. "Lady Harper shouldn't be giving you grief. I won't hold it against you if you want to get out of this madness while you can."

"Oh, no, I'm not about to leave town when there's a witch breaking the rules," she said. "Not to mention I've dealt with the furies before. It's possible that some of the witches who used the ritual the first time around passed on the knowledge to others."

"Witches?" asked Lloyd. "Er, no offence, but aren't witches the least power-hungry supernaturals there are?"

"Aside from my coven?" I said. "Yes, but every supernatural group has its defectors."

"The Hemlock coven wants power?" Isabel crouched down to dab at the chalk on the carpet with a damp cloth. "I thought they gave it up when they got stuck in the forest."

I shrugged. "Yes, they did, but they must have wanted the power to have it in the first place."

The image of that giant eye came to mind, and I firmly

shoved it down. I knew, deep in my bones, that it was real, and that their magic—*my* magic—kept that beast caged. *Don't think about that. It won't help.*

The sound of shattering glass came from somewhere close by, followed by screaming.

Lloyd grabbed the back of the chair. "What the—?"

A moment later, a blast shook the room. Bright spells sprang to life on the door, walls and floor, filling the room with grey light.

Isabel sprang to her feet. "Someone attacked the hotel."

"What *is* that?" Lloyd stared at the shimmering lines on the wall.

"A shield," answered Isabel, hands stretched towards the wall as though checking for gaps in the defensive spell. "The hotel's protected, but the attacker struck from outside."

"Shit." I sprinted to the window, but it showed only an empty car park, and we were four floors up. The attacker would be long gone by the time I got downstairs. "Right. Back in a second."

I tapped into the spirit realm. Faint shimmering marked the presence of a couple of hundred souls, but it took several long moments before I found the vampire's shadowy outline.

"Keir, did you see that?"

No response.

"Keir?"

"I'm following the attacker," he said, his voice slightly breathless. "Get back to your friends."

I checked out of the spirit realm, to find myself face to face with Lloyd. "Did you catch him?" he asked.

"No. Keir is chasing him." I moved towards Isabel,

who'd opened the hotel room door. A commotion came from the corridor, where it sounded like everyone had come out of their rooms to see what was going on.

"The hotel's shields blocked the attack before it did any damage," she said, letting the door close behind her. "Unfortunately, they also short-circuited the elevators."

I swore. Unless I learned to fly in the next ten seconds, there was no chance of pursuing the enemy on foot. I tapped into the spirit realm again. "Keir?"

"I lost him." It never ceased to be weird hearing his voice coming from a human-shaped shadow. "I think he's using one of our tricks to hide himself. I'll keep looking out for him."

"Damn. Keep me updated." I blinked back into the waking world.

"Any luck?" asked Isabel.

"Keir lost the guy," I said to the others. "Tracking through the spirit realm is hard even for us." There were a handful of people I knew of in the guild—Morgan and Ilsa Lynn, for a start—who could find anyone in the city just through the spirit realm, but it was easier to find people whose spirit sight was stronger, giving them a more permanent presence in Death. That ought to include vampires, but if they had tricks to hide themselves, I'd likely only been able to find Keir because he wanted to be found.

Maybe that explained why I'd been easy to track, once the enemy knew who they were looking for. The hotel might be well-protected, but it didn't have iron and hundreds of necromancers defending the place. I had no intention of anyone innocent getting injured or killed on my watch. No way in hell.

"I need to leave," I said. "If I'm the target—"

"Help me with this," said Isabel, scattering herbs into a hastily drawn chalk circle. "You used the witch's magic, right? Can you use it to help me redo the defences on the room?"

"The wards? I can try." Wariness rose within me. I'd managed to use Evelyn's magic independently against the vampires, but I'd only used it to kill, not protect. Given the nature of the spells on the forest, though, I knew my coven was capable of powerful defensive spells.

"Thanks," she said. "I should probably mention that Lady Harper didn't actually tell me you were possessed by a living person when she asked me to do this. She just said your magic was dormant. When I confronted her over that, she didn't take it well."

"Seriously?" I stared at her. "She's such a snake. She played both of us."

Isabel started sorting ingredients into piles. "On the coven's orders. She knows what's in that forest. She and the other Hemlocks are on the same page, and they're willing to do anything to make sure they don't die out without an heir."

"That is some next level creepy shit," Lloyd commented. "What was this witch like when you spoke to her?"

"Not very talkative, but we were kind of occupied. She gave me permission to use her magic to fight."

"But is she evil, though?" asked Lloyd. "That's the key question."

"I don't know about 'evil'. But there's something off about her."

"She's been living in your head for twenty-something

years. She's probably dying to get away from you. I mean, if she wasn't already dead."

I gave him the finger. "Behave. Are you sure about this, Isabel? I don't want to knock the building down."

"That won't happen," she said. "Let's see what you can do."

14

Isabel cleared the floor around a fresh chalk circle. "Try the basic warding spell again first. If that works, go for something stronger."

"Got it." I took the ingredients and placed them in the circle in front of me. My hands tingled with power, though that might have been a reaction to the wards shimmering at the room's edges.

The edges of the chalk circle lit up white-green. I held my hands steady, energy continuing to rush into the circle. Its glow expanded. "Whoa. That's not supposed to—"

Tremors ran through the room, and through me. Light spun from my fingertips, a weave of magic that lit up the whole room, and kept spreading, through the walls, as though they weren't there. I heard exclamations from the other rooms as though their inhabitants were right next to me—as though I was in the spirit realm and the waking world at the same time.

My hands dropped, the light dimming. "Holy shit. What was that?"

"That was *not* a basic ward," said Isabel. "I think you just tapped into the Hemlocks' power. Those symbols look just like the ones in their forest."

I jumped away from the circle, which did indeed look like a webbed replica of the spell keeping the beast caged. When I squinted, an overlay of the same glyphs covered the whole room.

"Is that a good thing?" I asked uncertainly.

"It would be if we weren't in a hotel full of witches who all just felt the forces of the universe rearrange themselves," said Isabel.

"So did I," said Lloyd, hanging onto the back of the chair as though afraid he'd be blown away. "Don't do it at the guild."

"I think the guild can take it." I pushed to my feet. "The good news is that someone could drop a nuclear bomb on this building and it'd probably do no damage."

"That's not just good news, that's fucking amazing," said Lloyd. "I want to hire you as my bodyguard."

"Are you forgetting I have the power on loan?" I turned to Isabel. "I don't know if you want to come to the guild with us, but I don't want people coming after you asking who put up that ward."

"They won't know it came from this room," she said. "But you should probably leave before someone comes knocking. It's a good job most of the witches in here are hedge witch level and have no idea just how powerful that spell was."

"Jesus." I wiped my sweaty palms on my jeans. "Note to self: work on toning it down."

"You're telling me," said Isabel. "Is it safe for you to go to the guild, or would you rather stay here tonight?"

"The guild is made out of iron." I nodded to Lloyd. "About as safe as you can get. Lloyd and I need to tell them about the vampires, and while I'm at it, I'll give Lady Harper a call. I'd like to know her reasoning for not telling any of us a damn thing before throwing me to the wolves."

Lady Harper picked up after the first ring. I'd opted to make the call while walking back, so I could interrogate her without anyone except Lloyd hearing.

"Hello, Lady Harper," I said.

"So nice to hear you from you, Jas."

Her sarcasm practically seared me through the phone. "Isn't it just?" I said. "Thanks for duping me. Oh, and thanks for tricking Isabel into helping me without telling any of us there was a massively overpowered spirit possessing me."

My hands still trembled with the aftermath of handling all that power. Not least because Evelyn's magic was the same as Cordelia and the others'. If they expected me to take their place, to give up my life… I had no argument to prove my magic wasn't strong enough to do it.

I'd never wished so badly that I'd been born a dud, with no magic at all.

Lady Harper gave a laugh that sounded way too evil-witchy for someone who was more of a mage than a witch. "I take it there have been some new developments. Care to discuss them in person?"

I'd rather eat dirt. "I have an apprenticeship and a job, so no. None of us are getting paid for this crap, you know."

"Actually, I offered Isabel's coven a substantial bonus," said Lady Harper. "And I will do the same for the guild if you decide to embrace your rightful position and leave to help your birth coven. You'll have free accommodation, everything you could ever want…"

"That, Lady Harper, is known as *blackmail*." She'd been spending way too much time in that forest. "And having zero morals. What did they promise *you*, then?"

"The continued safety and security of our magical community."

"And the entire planet." I rolled my eyes. "Would be a great deal, if not for the fact that I don't know if the person living in my head actually wants to work for the common good."

As lucid as she'd seemed when I'd looked into her eyes, witches with the interests of humanity at heart didn't snap a man's ribs with a single blow or lash out and nearly hit my allies. And as much as it might be a necessity for us to work together, I couldn't forget that Evelyn didn't always ask my permission before taking the wheel. She could take over whenever she wanted to, and people would think she was me.

"What would give you that idea?" she enquired. "Evelyn was devoted to her cause."

"You knew her." I'd forgotten, ridiculously, that Lady Harper was eighty-something years old and had known every member of the coven in the last three generations. Alive or otherwise. "What was she like as a person?"

"Devoted. Skilled. Understanding of our cause."

"A willing lapdog, then. Isabel and I just tried to access her help to make a basic ward, and she unleashed so much magic she put every witch within a mile on high alert."

"So you've managed to harness her magic. Excellent."

"Nothing is *excellent* about bringing more enemies on our tail," I said, through gritted teeth. "Someone tried to attack me at Isabel's hotel. We all have targets on our backs, and if anyone gets hurt, so help me—"

"Isabel knew what she was getting into, and she has the resources and defences to protect herself. As for you, you've seen what her magic can do. Nothing will happen to you, provided you don't do anything foolish."

Lloyd elbowed me, alerting me that the guild was just ahead. "Yeah, that's a load of bullshit. Over half a dozen people have tried to kill me this week and it's only Tuesday."

I hung up. So much for getting answers. If anything, I had a shit-ton more questions, not least about who in hell Evelyn Hemlock actually was.

"Evil old hag," I muttered, walking after Lloyd into the lobby.

"I hope you don't mean the boss," said a passing novice. "She's in a top-secret meeting, by the way, but she told you to add yourself to the rota tomorrow."

"Great." I pocketed my phone. "Guess I'll have to tell her in the morning."

And then? Most necromancers probably couldn't track the vampires down—not the ones who'd tried to kill me, anyway, assuming any had survived. And then there was the person who'd tried to attack the hotel. I hoped Keir was having better luck.

"Tracking," I said to Lloyd, as we reached the stairs. "Who here can track people over a distance and isn't likely to report us to the boss?"

"Ilsa Lynn," he said immediately. "Pretty sure even the boss doesn't know how often she does it, but she gets an exception, being Gatekeeper."

"She won't be here now. She lives over the other side of the bridge." Which meant we had until morning to form a plan.

"Oh, yeah," said Lloyd. "Are vampires typically something the Gatekeeper deals with?"

"Precisely what I wanted to find out.'

Ilsa Lynn's title of Gatekeeper referred to the gates between the first layer of the spirit realm and the true afterlife. I wasn't sure if she'd ever met a vampire before, but her spirit sight went a mile further than mine. It was worth asking her for help finding the rogues, so I could hunt them down before they hurt anyone else.

No ghostly appearances disturbed me in the night, and I woke surprisingly well-rested. I texted Isabel and found that nobody else had tried to attack the hotel—probably because I'd inadvertently warded it against almost anything. The witches hadn't yet guessed who was responsible, but if the Mage Lords found out, I could say goodbye to any semblance of stealth. I also hadn't thought to get Keir's number so I could check whether he'd had any luck tracking the person who'd attacked the hotel, and though he was just a trip into the spirit realm away, I hadn't seen him when I'd checked in there. Maybe he was hiding himself, too.

Lady Montgomery was nowhere to be seen and didn't answer when I'd knocked on her office door, so I was left with the next best option: ask the Gatekeeper's advice. It didn't hurt that Ilsa Lynn happened to be dating the boss's son, River. Not to mention her family was sworn into a secret vow to the faerie courts, so she'd know all about family secrets and obligations.

"Hey, Jas," asked Ilsa, who I found checking the rota pinned to the noticeboard in the lobby. "Did you make some embellishments here, by any chance? You and Lloyd are always on the same patrols."

"Guilty." I'd put both of us on the same patrol as her, in the hope of having a legitimate excuse to talk to the Gatekeeper without ending up in even more trouble than I already was. "I actually need to talk to you, away from the guild."

"Aren't you supposed to be laying low?" she asked.

"What would give you that idea?" Maybe her brother had told her I'd run off with the book of advanced magic. Or perhaps she'd talked to the boss.

"There are stories spreading about you, Jas," Ilsa said, giving me a serious look.

"Probably," I said. "I might need your help with something a little off-book."

Ilsa stepped away from the rota. "Does it have to do with vampires, by any chance?" she asked. "Morgan decided to enlighten me on that one."

"And you asked Lady Montgomery?" I guessed. "Good, because I don't have a lot of time. Long story short, there are rogue vampires out there in the spirit realm who tried to kill me, and I have no clue where they went. I know your spirit sight goes further than anyone else's, so I wondered if you could help."

"Normally, I could," Ilsa said. "But since I've never seen the vampires in person, I wouldn't know where to start. They might be miles away, as far as the spirit realm goes."

Damn. I'd suspected, but it would be nice to have some direction. "You know, I'm pretty sure my own spirit sight goes pretty far. I've just never tested it." But I'd detached from my body and survived, thanks to the spirit. Maybe having two souls made me less likely to fall victim to the downsides of going too deep into the spirit realm. On the other hand, giving Evelyn the ability to possess my body at will came with its own set of downsides.

"If it goes wrong, you might get dragged through the gates of death," said Lloyd. "Can't our not-so-fanged friend do it instead?"

"I don't think he can tell people's locations from within the spirit realm," I said. "Otherwise he'd have found me sooner."

"Most people can't," said Ilsa. "But Morgan and I can."

"Someone say my name?" Her brother walked up behind us. "I'm not on duty."

"We are," I said. *Damn. I didn't want to bring half the guild into it.* "Ilsa—it's up to you if you want to help out. I'm on thin ice with the boss already. Morgan, feel free to tag along." Maybe having a psychic on board would be useful, and I'd learned through experience that forbidding one of the Lynn siblings to do something was a great way to ensure they came along whether you liked it or not. At least neither of them was likely to tell on us to the boss.

"Looking for vampires? I'm in." Morgan dug his hands into the pockets of his slightly oversized necromancer coat. He and his sister shared the same dark brown hair and eyes, but Ilsa was tall and curvy, while Morgan was as pale as a weeks-old corpse and almost as skinny. I hadn't wanted to drag too many people into my shit show of a life, but I could do worse than ask for the help of two of the guild's most powerful necromancers.

"So how did you wind up being attacked by a vampire?" Ilsa asked, as we walked out of the guild's headquarters onto the cobbled street.

"An accident," I said. "Most of them abide by the rules, but there are a few rogues who've set their sights on me. I'm sure at least one of them escaped."

"Why would they target you to begin with?" she asked. "I read their entry in Morgan's book, but it didn't say why they might fixate on one individual." Knowing Ilsa, she'd probably taken out every book on vampires the guild had out of academic interest. Her curiosity knew no bounds, and I'd hoped her endless thirst for knowledge would be enough to encourage her to help us.

"I'm kind of sworn not to tell anyone," I said, glancing sideways to gauge her reaction. Ilsa had been carrying secrets of her own ever since she'd first entered the guild, after all.

"Sounds familiar," she said. *I knew I picked the right person to ask.* "I might be able to help you learn to extend your spirit sight, but can vampires really suck out your soul through the spirit realm?"

"Only if they get hold of you, spiritually speaking," I said. "They aren't working alone, though. There are witches involved, too. I don't suppose anyone's found anything... odd, when patrolling? You went out yesterday, right?"

She nodded. "No. Zombies, ghosts, pretty standard. What do you mean by 'odd'?"

I debated, then said, "Rituals."

Her body stiffened. "No. Why?"

"Lloyd and I found something weird on our last mission," I said. "We're pretty sure there's someone in the city messing with dark magic, and it might be linked to the vampires."

"Dark as in blood magic?" asked Morgan, and Ilsa shot him a warning look.

"Yes," said Lloyd. "*Someone* didn't believe me at first. Chalk symbols and weird stains are always dodgy. I knew that faerie ghost was more than just a lost spirit."

"No need to rub it in," I said, at the same time as Ilsa said, "Faerie ghost?"

"Just a poltergeist," I said. "But we think he had a boost from some kind of witch magic." I spotted a nearby alley that looked promising. "There's definitely a witch after me as well, but I can probably only track the vampires."

"If you're certain," said Ilsa, walking after me into the alley. "I shouldn't be lecturing anyone on safety, considering, but—Morgan, don't you even think about going in there to chase vampires without candles."

Her brother had stopped walking, wearing the vacant expression of a necromancer deep in the spirit world. With a blink, his gaze cleared, and he scowled at his sister. "I wouldn't know what they looked like, anyway."

"Shadows," I said, setting the first candle down at the alley entrance and beckoning to Lloyd. "I'll go in. I might not find anyone… I never did see what the vampire who stole the zombies looked like, and Keir might have caught him."

"Who stole whose zombies?" Morgan frowned.

"As I said—long story." I resumed setting up the circle, while Lloyd moved in to help me.

"Are you certain about this?" he asked, in a low voice.

"Positive. It's necromancy I'm using, not… the other thing."

Not that I trusted the spirit in the slightest, but she'd only used magic to defend my life. It might mean she was an ally, or not, but I wasn't ready to start using her power in front of strangers in a non-life-or-death scenario. Definitely not until I'd learned to tone it all the way down.

I stood in the completed candle circle and turned to Ilsa. "Any tips for finding a particular spirit?"

"Picture what they look like," she said. "Clearly, in your mind's eye. You know how to recognise people you know well in the spirit realm, right? Even when you can't see them. It's like that. I can guide you, but I never actually saw the vampires, so you'll have to do most of the work."

"Good enough." I tapped into the spirit realm. Grey fog filled the space, while the others resembled vague white shapes. I did know how to recognise people I knew well, even without using my physical senses. I sensed Lloyd close by, a familiar presence. In front of me, Ilsa's spirit was a very strong presence, almost covering Morgan's, but he was there, too. And…

No sign of Keir at all.

Unease fluttered through me. Had he disconnected from the spirit realm? Surely not. It had seemed like he was in there all the time, and I'd been around him long enough that I should be able to track if he was near. Even when he'd been talking to me in the waking world, he was always there. Why would he pick now to hide himself?

"Anything?" asked Ilsa, her spirit glowing even brighter than mine. "What do vampires look like, anyway?"

"Shadowy," I said. "If you see what looks like a silhouette cut-out of a person, it's a vampire. When they're draining you, though... it's like they're infused with a bluish white glow, and you have to break the connection using necromancy."

Unless you have an extra soul.

"Nice," said Ilsa, as I blinked the fog away. "So they can control undead from a distance? Most necromancers can only operate within a few feet. That makes catching rogues trickier, for sure."

"If Lady Montgomery knows, hopefully she has a plan to find the bastards," I said. "Let's just say our allies are in short supply."

Keir's absence shouldn't bother me. Maybe he'd only appeared so close in the spirit realm before because he'd been stalking me, if not in the real-world sense. But still...

"Can I go further than the city from here?" I asked. "That's what you two can do, right?"

"You don't wanna do that," said Morgan. "There are side effects, if you go that deep in the spirit world."

"And you'd know?" asked Lloyd, who looked a little miffed at being left out of our jaunt into Death.

"Yes, I would," Morgan said. "I spent two years there and I still can't walk in a straight line."

Ah. It made sense that Death would come with some serious downsides, aside from the constant danger of drifting beyond the gates and permanently disconnecting from your body. Ilsa, being Gatekeeper, probably didn't need to worry as much, but if taken unawares, maybe even she'd have trouble fighting off a vampire.

"What other side effects are we talking about?" said Lloyd.

"For a start, you're completely unaware of what's happening in the real world if you go deep enough," Morgan said. "A person could sneak up and steal the clothes off your back and you wouldn't know it. Not that it's ever happened to me."

"Uh-huh," I said. "Aside from that?"

"Imagine being in a coma for months and you've pretty much got it," said Ilsa.

"It doesn't help that Death is fucking freezing," Morgan added. "I've permanently lost all feeling in part of my hand."

Ilsa whirled on him. "What? You never told me that."

"I 'spose not." He shrugged.

Ilsa gave an exasperated sigh. "No wonder Lady Montgomery took you off the rota."

I tuned out their bickering and tapped into the spirit realm again. With my spirit sight amplified by the circle, there was no reason I shouldn't be able to find Keir, or at least sense him. He'd always been there before, and his absence made me edgy.

Familiarity pinged on my vision, then disappeared just as quickly, like a flicker of movement in the corner of my eye.

Keir. It was definitely him I'd sensed, for a moment. Then he'd vanished.

I blinked back to alertness, moving so fast I accidentally kicked one of the candles over.

"What is it?" asked Lloyd.

"I think Keir might be in trouble," I said. "Our... vampire ally. He's sort of there, in the spirit realm, but I can't figure out where, exactly. I did say I'd meet him in person today."

Morgan yelled without warning, dropping to his knees and clutching his head.

"Morgan!" said Ilsa. "What happened this time?"

He pressed his hands to his forehead. "Someone is making a real racket over there in the spirit world."

My heart lurched. "What do you mean?" I hadn't heard or seen anything aside from the weird flickering of Keir's presence.

"He can 'hear' anyone with a particularly strong presence," said Ilsa. "Particularly if they're in distress."

"Oh. Shit." I tapped into the spirit realm again, focusing fiercely on Keir. A bolt of light shot through the spirit realm, then vanished. *What was that?*

"I can probably track him," said Morgan, who appeared to have forgotten all about warnings.

"No chance." Ilsa grabbed his arm. "We're reporting this, and you're getting back to the guild before you pass out cold like last time. Are you two coming back?"

I shook my head. "I need to find my ally... I can't tell where he is." He must be close, but aside from that brief flicker, he'd barely been there at all. What could cause that effect on a vampire?

"What's going on?" Lloyd asked.

"Haven't a clue. Keir... it's like he's half there, half not." Crap. Was someone draining him? Or—he did say vampires needed to frequently feed on others' souls, otherwise they'd die.

My stomach turned over. Something was seriously wrong, and while it seemed a bad idea not to have the Lynn siblings with me when I confronted the problem, neither of them had ever faced a vampire before. Maybe I should have checked up on Keir after he'd chased the person who'd attacked the hotel, but it wasn't like I had any way to contact him outside of the spirit realm.

"Hey. Evelyn. I need some help," I said. "I think I'm going to need your magic."

Evelyn's ghostly form appeared before me, so suddenly that I jumped—as much as a ghost could, anyway. She appeared less transparent than before, her hair tumbling over her shoulders, and clear enough for me to see we were more or less the same height. Her high cheekbones, greyish eyes and full lips with a slight cleft might have been a mirror of my own face, though my jet-black hair and lip piercing hid some of my Hemlock features.

"Yes?" asked Evelyn, her voice calm.

"I might need to borrow your magic again. I think my ally has been kidnapped. I thought I'd ask nicely."

I also wished we had time for an actual conversation, so I could figure out if we were remotely on the same page as far as our goals for the Hemlock magic went.

Her semi-transparent face flickered, making it hard to read her expression. "You have my magic. It's yours."

Okay... was there something in her tone that suggested resentment, or anger? With her voice so faint, it was hard to tell. But another flicker caught my eye. I looked down, sensing Keir's presence grow stronger. And closer.

I dropped the spirit sight and looked at a bewildered Lloyd.

"Underground," I said. "The enemy—that's where they're operating from. No wonder nobody has managed to find them."

15

Going back into the tunnels seemed a foolish move, but the spirit realm didn't lie. Keir was somewhere close by, and, given the way his spirit kept flickering in and out of existence, he was on the verge of disappearing.

"Any tunnel entrances around here?" I walked down the alley, Lloyd behind me, and headed down another cobbled street. "He's close… he must have come this way right after leaving the hotel."

Which meant there was a strong chance the person who'd attacked us was somewhere near, assuming Keir hadn't killed them.

"If I knew that, we'd have found them when patrolling," said Lloyd. "What's he doing underground?"

"I think he was attacked by another vampire," I said. "Based on the way his spirit keeps fading in and out. But it wouldn't surprise me if there were more of those fury monsters around."

"Summoned by a ritual?" he asked. "You don't think

that's what that setup in the warehouse was meant for, do you?"

"Nah, we'd have known if there was one of those monsters in there." I shuddered at the thought. I'd been completely unprepared, not knowing just how many people had been hunting me. Lloyd or I might easily have died back then.

"What's the difference between a witch ritual and a necromancer's summoning, then?" he asked. "They always say not to put blood anywhere near a summoning circle. I guess it's the same for witches' chalk circles, right?"

"Yes, but... it's worse. Witch magic isn't drawn to death, not the way necromancy is. Our magic comes from life, not the dead."

"That sounds like witchcraft is supposed to be good and necromancy is evil," he commented. "Which you know, isn't true. I mean, I suppose there are more rogue necromancers than power-hungry witches, when it comes down to it."

"The Hemlocks would beg to differ." I paused midway down the street, opposite a café which didn't look like it'd been open since before the invasion, and checked the spirit realm again. Once more, there was a flicker of life from Keir. "He's close."

I looked at the wall. Part of it was bricked up, a long stretch between abandoned, empty shops with shattered glass windows. The wall shimmered when I tilted my head. I pressed my palm to it and a stinging pain shot to my elbow.

Ow. I winced and yanked my hand away. "That was a ward." Not a Hemlock one, and no indication as to whether it belonged to friend or foe.

We're wasting time. I paced the street, but didn't find so much as a sewer entrance with a ladder like last time.

"Nothing," said Lloyd, meeting me in front of the wall again. "I reckon that's the only way in, Jas, but it has 'trap' written all over it."

"I know." Frustration burned beneath my skin. I checked the spirit realm again, searching for Keir's presence. His spirit flickered, then went out. My heart lurched. "Damn. I have to get in there."

Hoping I wasn't too late, I held my hands over the wall, magic humming against my palms. The ward only covered the bare stretch of wall. I tilted my head, seeing the weaving glyphs around the edges. Clever. The person who'd set it up was more technically gifted than I was, but not perfect. There were gaps in the spell that a skilled witch could undo. Evelyn's magic, ever below the surface, flowed from my hands as I held them out. I knew the reversal spell that would undo a protective ward, but I'd never managed to use it without props before. With Evelyn guiding my hand, though, I felt like I could grab the threads of magic and undo them with a single tug.

Power surged from my fingertips, rippling along the wall's surface. Lloyd whispered, "Damn."

In one wave, the wards dissolved, and the wall went entirely blank before a door handle appeared. *Whoa there.* I'd only intended to temporarily undo the wards and reveal what was below the surface, not switch them off altogether.

"Really hope I haven't set anything nasty free," I said. "But I'm about to go and kill it anyway."

"You're bonkers," said Lloyd. "Those witches have finally driven you mad."

I grabbed the door handle and yanked it open. A tunnel yawned ahead, sloping downhill.

A hoarse cry came from within. *Keir.*

Lloyd's eyes widened. "Should I call Isabel for backup? Or the guild?"

"Isabel," I said. "I'll get Keir out first." From the flickering of his presence, I didn't have long until I was too late.

I ran through the door, following his faint presence. He was so close—and it was pitch black in here. I grabbed a candle from my pocket, and there was a thud as the door closed behind me.

"Oh, come on."

A bone-chilling scream cut off my words. Furies.

Too late to turn back. I continued into the dark, cursing under my breath. So much for sneaking up on the enemy.

My feet caught on fabric, and I tripped headlong over a human-shaped body. "Oh, shit." I crawled to my knees, my candle reflecting on Keir's face.

"Nice of you to drop in, Jas," he said.

Light trickled in from somewhere ahead. I backed away, checking the spirit realm, but it was definitely him. "Jesus. How long have you been down here?"

"A while." Blood streaked his face, and his wrists and ankles were bound with thick ropes.

"Why not call and ask for my help?"

"I don't recall getting your phone number. And I was rather short on resources." He twitched his bound hands, his face alarmingly pale under the blood. "Luckily, the furies seem more intent on devouring their summoner."

"Hang on. Let me get those off you."

I hadn't brought the tools to undo bonds, but with witchcraft, maybe I didn't need them. I drew on the same magic I'd use to melt the wards and directed it at the ropes.

To my shock as much as his, white light poured from my hands, and the ropes dissolved into nothing.

Keir blinked in confusion, turning his freed hands over. "New trick?" He shifted into a sitting position, tugging at the ropes on his legs.

"Let me try." I grabbed the ropes, getting mud and slime on me in the process. "You're absolutely filthy."

He gave a choked laugh. "You have no idea how hard it is not to make an inappropriate comment here, Jas."

My hands slipped on the rope knots. "You're not helping me decide whether it was a good idea to get myself locked in here with you or not."

He chuckled under his breath. "Damned vampire."

"A vampire did this?"

"I reckon he planned on saving me for whoever summoned those furies, but I don't think it ended well for him."

"Shit." No wonder I hadn't been able to sense any other vampires in the spirit realm, if he'd been devoured by winged monsters.

The ropes dissolved like the others, and Keir climbed to his feet, wincing as he stretched out his arms. He must have been stuck here for hours.

"Where *are* the furies?" I asked. "And who summoned them?"

"I didn't see," he said, in a low voice. "I wasn't their priority. Let's put it that way."

I shuddered, digging in my pockets for another candle. "Can vampires see in the dark?"

"No, but I can sense anyone living or otherwise through the spirit realm. There's nobody alive in the next room."

"I think…" I trailed off. A faint thrumming sensation in my fingertips indicated witchcraft, but it wasn't from me. *More dark witch magic?* I shone the candle light ahead, wishing I could cast a spell to light the whole place up. But that would bring all the bad guys straight to me, and while Evelyn seemed to be cooperating with me at the moment, Keir was in bad enough shape already.

"Jas?" He walked alongside me, towards the humming sensation. The tunnel opened into a chamber whose walls dripped with water, and…

I moved closer and my stomach flipped. Blood oozed between the cracks on the walls—recently shed blood—between crudely drawn symbols. A body lay at the foot of the wall. Human. *Vampire? Or witch?*

"Jesus," I said. "This is dark magic. A witch did it."

Bile rose in my throat. Even as a nonentity of a witch, I'd known that witches had far less of a propensity towards dark magic than any other kind of supernatural. Yet beneath the sick horror, something inside me—in the power that had brought down the wards—wanted to touch the walls and feel that magic mingling with mine. *Mine,* whispered Evelyn's voice.

No, it bloody well isn't, I told her.

I side-stepped the man's body, and pressed my hands to the glyphs on the wall. Focusing hard, I used the same spell I'd used to undo the wards on the door. It was too late to stop whatever the blood spilled here had summoned, but I could at least deal with the aftermath.

White light flared from my palms, and the glyphs vanished, leaving droplets of blood trickling down the walls like condensation.

Keir stiffened. "They know we're here. They can smell us."

"Bring it." I stepped back from the wall, my hands shaking, wishing I could squash Evelyn's sick fascination with the dark magic. Turning to the sloping tunnel, I called, "Are you too much of a coward to attack me in person?" My voice echoed back at me, Evelyn's magic humming in tune with the echoes.

Rustling sounded, and a fury crashed into me from above in an explosion of talons. I gripped the bloodstained wall for balance, pain tearing through my arm as its claw ripped into the skin. Shit. My spirit sight hadn't warned me the bastards were right above me, and apparently, neither had Keir's.

Releasing a cry, a second fury flew at us with its talons outstretched, and the candle fell from my hand as I grabbed my knife.

I sank the knife into the first fury's side as Keir engaged the second one, dealing a blow with his own knife. One-handedly, I worked one of the bracelets Isabel had given me down my injured wrist. The wound was deep, rendering my left hand almost useless. At least I was right-handed.

"Duck," I warned Keir, and threw one of Isabel's explosives.

A blast went off, sending the fury careening sideways into its neighbour, and the two of them hit the wall hard enough to shake the whole tunnel. The fury I'd hit recovered quickly, detaching itself from the wall with eyes like dark glowing pits, a chunk of flesh missing from its face. Damn. The spell hadn't killed it? Its scaly skin must be made of cement. My arm throbbed with pain, and I'd used my best explosive.

The beast dived at me, another cry ripping from its lungs. *Should have aimed for the talons, Jas.* I dove to the bloodstained stone floor, and its claws narrowly missed taking a slice out of my face. Keir stabbed it in the side, but his long knife barely dented its scales.

Sudden bolts of white energy burst from my palms, crashing into the furies with more force than an explosive spell. Scales scattered as the blast tore into their concrete skin, and I ducked to avoid getting hit. *Might want to give me a warning next time, Evelyn.*

Keir shot me a dumbfounded look, then went in for the kill, sinking his knife into the nearest fury's neck and slicing off its head. I ran to his side, stabbing the other fury in the eye. The beast's flailing stilled as the knife reached its mark.

"Ugh." The blue-tinged blood staining my clothes shimmered, showing me the candle I'd dropped. I carefully picked it up, both hands still soaked in the blood from the wall. It'd need a serious hosing down before being used in necromancy again—heaven knew what those monsters' blood would do if allowed anywhere near a summoning circle.

"We're not alone," Keir murmured, his face pale under the blood.

My hands tingled, and a faint breeze stirred my hair. "The summoner," I whispered. "They're close."

Magic hummed in my skin, burning in my bones, filling every shadow. Keir tensed beside me, and he raised his knife, its gleam reflecting his bloody face.

"Show yourself," he said.

A woman with filthy, matted blond hair staggered into view. She'd have been quite pretty if not for the mud caking her face and the unnatural grin stretching her cheeks. "There you are, Jacinda Hemlock."

"How the hell do you know my name?" I'd never told my real full name to anyone. Not even Keir.

She laughed, a deep, rattling sound that echoed off the glyph-covered walls. "Who doesn't?"

"Really creepy," I told her. "Seriously, you should star in low-budget horror movies rather than screwing around with the dark dimensions."

She pushed her hair from her face, still grinning. "It's an *honour* to meet you, Jacinda. Are you ready to die?"

"I'm a necromancer. Always ready to die, never keen to make it permanent. Which coven are you from?"

The witch's hands glowed white-blue, and a wave of energy blasted Keir and me off our feet. I threw out my hands to break my fall, the impact jolting my injured arm. I gritted my teeth, my vision swimming. She'd hit us with kinetic energy—necromancy. She must be part witch, part necromancer. Not a combination I wanted to face while incapacitated—but unlike the furies, she wouldn't be immune to necromancy herself.

I raised my hand and sent my own kinetic attack at her, but she barely flinched. An alarming amount of blood soaked my arm, and Keir didn't look to be in spectacular condition, either. *Now would be a fine time, Evelyn.*

The spirit realm unfolded without warning, sending

me plunging into the grey. I floated above my body, looking down on the cave as I—Jas—rose to my feet.

I wasn't inside my body at all. She'd shoved me out.

"What the hell, Evelyn?" I yelled.

I floated, watching helplessly as my body moved of its own accord, aglow with necromantic power. Through the grey, the witch's body shifted. And in the spot where her spirit should be was a gaping hole, and threads of blue magic.

She's a vampire. No—there's one controlling her. Her body wasn't alive at all, and someone was using her as a mouthpiece. That meant the only way to kill the enemy was through the spirit realm.

"She's a vampire!" I shouted at Keir, wincing as another blast of necromantic power took my body off its feet. Pain shot through my skull, drawing me back into my own skin again. I grimaced and crawled to my knees, a bolt of pain in my leg making my eyes water. The witch-zombie had thrown me into my own knife, and Evelyn had helpfully withdrawn to leave me to suffer the pain alone. *We're supposed to be a team, dammit.*

"There will be no running for you, Jacinda," whispered the witch, grabbing me by the throat.

Cold hands gripped me through both the waking and spirit world, and my body numbed. *Shit.* Evelyn was nowhere in sight. Maybe she'd *let* the enemy drain my soul, leaving her to take my place.

Keir collided with the witch from the side, delivering an impressive right hook to her jaw. She flew backwards off me, and I crawled away, pain shooting up my leg again.

"Thanks," I gasped to him.

"Don't mention it," he said. "Banish her, Jas. She's stronger than the others."

He didn't need to tell me twice.

I shifted into Death, reaching for the blue threads connecting the vampire to the witch's body, and pulled as hard as I could. Banishing words rose to my mouth, and Keir shouted a warning as she hit out at my vulnerable, mortal body.

Bolts of magical energy surged from my hands. Evelyn's magical attack tore through the witch's body, ripping through skin and bone, and the threads of the vampire's control began to slip away. *Don't you dare.*

In the spirit world, I gripped the vampire's trace with my fingers, and he appeared before me as a shadowy outline.

"Go through the gates of hell," I said, then shouted the words of banishing.

The vampire's presence slipped away as the gates of death loomed above me, and I blinked back into my body. The witch-zombie lay sprawled, shredded by magic beyond mortal hands.

I crawled over to Keir, biting pain reminding me of the stab wound in my leg. "Can you walk?"

He exhaled in a noise that probably meant yes but didn't sound optimistic. He managed to push himself upright with one hand, the other bleeding heavily. Blood dripped down my leg, while my left arm was all but useless. We more or less leaned on each other to retrace our steps. His harsh breathing echoed my own.

"Some use I am as a defender of this realm, if I couldn't even stop an oversized chicken from cutting me up," I said, between breaths.

He choked on a laugh, then swore. "Don't make me laugh. I think I might have cracked a few ribs when they threw me in here."

"Knew I packed two healing spells for a reason. Better get away from the ritual before using them."

"I need more than a healing spell." He staggered forwards another few steps. "The vampire drained me dry before he met his unfortunate end."

"What, you mean... he sucked out your soul?" No wonder I hadn't been able to sense him in the spirit realm from outside. "You need to feed on someone. Right?"

"You have a spare soul." He half leaned against me to walk uphill.

"She wouldn't take kindly to you taking a bite out of her."

"And would you?"

I didn't spare him the dignity of a response, mostly because he was leaning so heavily on my shoulder that I worried he'd actually collapse on me.

Once we'd left the ritual room behind, I paused and dug in my pocket for the two healing spells. As I activated my own, the pain disappeared from my arm and leg. While I was still dizzy from the blood loss and adrenaline, I could stand upright without keeling over.

"You okay?" I asked Keir.

"Better." He pressed a hand to his forehead. "I haven't been drained like that in years."

"Is the only way to recover for you to drain someone else's spirit?"

"They do call it a curse for a reason," he said, with a chuckle. "I think I can make it home, but anyone unfortunate enough to run into me is likely to have an unpleasant experience."

"Can you even walk home in that state?" False bravado aside, we were both covered in blood, and if I went to Isabel for a cleansing spell, the last thing I needed was him offering to drain my friends' souls. "All right, I'll do it. No messing around."

He faced me. "You or her."

"Hmm." I bit my lip. After the stunt Evelyn had pulled, I was kind of tempted to offer her to him as bait, even if she had saved our lives. "Best not risk her magic cutting you to pieces like that witch. What exactly do I have to do?"

"Just keep still." He moved closer to me, his breathing harsh and ragged despite his lack of visible injuries. "You feel... different, to other spirits. I think it's the shade. I'll only draw from you, not her."

"Go on," I said.

His hands grasped my shoulders, and a tickling sensation ran down the back of my neck, sparking shudders down the length of my spine. Pleasant tingles sparked in my fingertips, unexpectedly. *Oh. This isn't so bad.*

Then, coldness. My body locked to the spot, my fingers numbing, then my hands. My pulse slowed, and the pressure lifted from my shoulders. He spoke into my ear, but I didn't quite catch the words. His lips were inches from my neck, and a wild impulse urged me to arch my neck and cover that last inch between us, but he got there first. His lips trailed down my neck, his hands gripping me—but not my physical body. He might be feeding on my soul, but it felt more like he was giving something to me.

And I wanted more.

Uh. Jas. What the hell are you doing?

I tugged myself free and pulled back from him. "Done? Now we need to get out of his hellhole."

Keir caught his breath. The colour had come back to his cheeks—if anything, he was flushed more than usual, and the glint in his eyes sparked an inexplicable rush of heat deep inside me. No wonder humans let vampires drain them without screaming and panicking. I hadn't known it felt that… intimate.

"Didn't you enjoy yourself?" His mouth quirked, and I found myself wondering if kissing those lips would feel quite as good as letting him feed on my spirit. Then I mentally slapped myself. He might be fairly attractive, but I'd like to think I had a little more self-respect than to make out with a vampire inside a den belonging to someone who'd used a witch as a puppet to summon horrible monsters. It wasn't like we'd ever see one another again after this whole sorry business was over.

It only felt so good because he sucked part of my soul out. Think about that, Jas, not his lips on your neck. He'd probably done the same to a thousand people. I highly doubted it'd been a notable experience for him—just another day as a vampire.

"Let's keep this purely business," I said to him. "Also, you should probably know the door might have locked itself behind me."

"I imagine that magic of yours can get us out, Jas." Under the blood and dirt on his face, I detected a trace of… disappointment? That couldn't be right.

"Better hope it can." I turned to walk up the last stretch of tunnel.

"By the way," he added. "I wanted to thank you for not leaving me to die down here. I doubt I could have made it out without your help."

Well, well. He had some humility after all.

"No problem." I turned back to him. "Just shout a little louder next time. I almost missed you. Or you know, give me your phone number."

He grinned. "All right. Do I put you under 'Jas Lyons' or 'Jacinda Hemlock'?"

"Too soon," I muttered. "Way too soon, mate. Come on. Lloyd's probably called half the guild by now."

16

Isabel rolled her eyes at Keir and me as we walked up to the café to meet her. "You're as bad as Ivy. Both of you. Please tell me you haven't been walking around human-friendly places covered in all that blood."

"We walked through the mercenaries' district," I said, pulling out a chair next to the same table as before. "Nobody batted an eyelid. They've seen worse shit from their own windows." I'd spent the walk back bringing Lloyd up to speed, and texted Isabel with brief details asking her to meet us at Cassandra's Café.

Isabel passed me a cleansing spell. "Jas, does some of that blood belong to the witch who attacked you?"

"Yes, but most of it's the furies'. And mine. Oh, and the vampire who was unlucky enough to turn into a human sacrifice."

"You need to stop getting attacked when I'm not around to help," said Isabel.

"It wasn't exactly planned. Why did you ask about the witch's blood?"

"I might be able to use it to identify the witch's coven. Then I can find out pretty quickly whether she was in on the enemy's plan or an innocent bystander."

My gaze snapped up. "Seriously?" I inwardly shuddered at the memory of the bloodstained glyphs on the cave wall. Blood magic... dark magic. And entirely too similar to the raw power that had blasted from my hands, ripping the witch to shreds.

Keir accepted another cleansing spell from Isabel and took a seat on my right. While unlocking the tunnel door using magic had gone a way towards ridding me of the echo of his touch, his closeness stirred a spark to my hands again. Considering thinking of Evelyn's magic made my skin feel slimy, I'd rather focus on the vampire's touch instead, but he was distracting in a different way. Not an unpleasant one, but the last thing I needed was a diversion.

Lloyd scowled at him. "You're staying with us, too?"

"I'm intrigued to see what your friend does with that blood," he answered. "Witch magic has never interested me before, but now..."

"If you think about drinking *my* blood, vampire, you're out."

Keir gave him a cold look. "That's not how vampirism works. Pity the guild neglected to keep you up to speed."

"Whoa," I said. "Stop bickering, you two, and order some damn food so the people in the café stop staring at us." I didn't blame Lloyd for being pissed off that I'd run into the tunnel to rescue Keir and nearly died for it, but still.

Keir climbed to his feet. "It's clear I'm not welcome here, so I'll leave. Jas, you can catch up with your friends. Or, if you'd prefer, you're welcome to come with me, and we can continue our conversation from the tunnel."

Did he just hit on me in front of my friends, in public? Yes, he did. "No thanks," I said. "I'll stay."

"If you're sure," said Keir. "Stay safe, Jas."

I jumped when his fingers brushed the back of my chair, lingering just inches from my neck. He couldn't possibly know the effect his touch had had on me, right? A smile played on his mouth, but he turned away before my gaze could linger for long.

Bloody vampires.

"Leaving?" asked Lloyd. "Some ally he turned out to be."

"He was chasing the person who tried to attack the hotel when he got captured," I said. "Lloyd, sorry I ditched you. Isabel, sorry I didn't invite you along for the ride, too. What do you need to do with this blood? Because I can't say it's... clean." Especially the blood that had been on my hands when Evelyn had unleashed her magic. Blood was a source of power, so did that mean it'd given her a boost? *No way. Witches use blood in tracking spells all the time.* Okay, they didn't normally use it to tear people to ribbons, but nobody said my coven was remotely conventional.

"An identifying spell will do." Isabel held out a hand as I pulled off my necromancer coat and handed it to her, before applying a cleansing spell to my skin.

"I forgive you," Lloyd said, "but you owe me. I have a zombie shark movie marathon planned for the weekend and you're going to be there."

"Done," I said. "I didn't mean to run in there alone. I wasn't sure if I was actually picking up on Keir or not. They nearly killed him."

"Would that be such a tragedy, though?"

I elbowed him in the ribs. "Knock it off."

He poked me in the arm in retaliation. "What's so great about him?"

I dropped my gaze. "He saved my life at least twice, for a start. Also, he stopped Evelyn from taking over my mind."

And he probably kisses like the devil, supplied a voice in the back of my head, which I studiously ignored.

"Right." Lloyd rolled his eyes. "Never underestimate the skill of stopping a mad spirit. He kind of *is* one, technically."

"Vampires aren't the same," I said. "I know it *looks* like they're all villains, but that wouldn't be giving Lady Montgomery much credit for keeping the peace. Keir had a point when he said knowledge passes quickly in Death. That's how they found me. Someone said my name in the wrong place, and the next thing you know, hemlock poison."

Isabel looked up from where she was in the process of extracting the witch's blood from my coat. "The witch was definitely dead? And her ghost wasn't around?"

"Definitely dead," I said. "And no, her ghost was long gone."

"Got it," she said. "I don't like using blood spells when the person's still living, but it's not like she can do anything now she's dead."

"Don't speak too soon," said Lloyd. "We have the dead on our tail every day—or we did, before we started getting mobbed by vampires. Sure seems convenient that it happened right after you met that dude."

"It wasn't him," I said. "The ritual... the vampire piloted a witch's body to do it, but there's got to be another witch behind this. The vampires couldn't have figured out the coven's secrets without someone betraying us."

"Bastards." Isabel sketched chalk symbols on the table. While I didn't *think* the café had a policy against using magic on the premises, I hoped nobody walked out of the door while she was working her witchcraft.

"Any luck, Isabel?"

She put down the chalk, holding her coat at an angle that concealed the spell from anyone who passed by. "No. I'll need a more complex setup to get any real answers." Her phone buzzed on the table, and she picked it up. "Ivy said Lady Harper is throwing a fit."

"Shit, did you tell her what Evelyn did?"

"No, but I should." She looked at me. "At this rate, she's going to get you killed, assuming you don't do it yourself by running into tunnels after vampires in distress."

"I'm not going to die," I said. "I have the extra spirit as insurance. Unfortunately."

"What did she even do in there?" asked Lloyd. "You came out of that tunnel looking kind of... crazed. Unless it was that vampire. You looked all hot and bothered..."

"Don't be absurd."

Occasionally, Lloyd tried to play matchmaker. Whenever someone asked if we were an item, he always said, hell, no, and then insisted on setting me up with someone. Keir would not fall into the category of suitable dates, within the limited supernatural circles who didn't ask awkward questions. Seductive vampire abilities or not, I was not the quick fling type, and he didn't strike me as the sort of person into long-term relationships. Now, with another person sharing my body, normal things like dating had never seemed further away.

"Then what happened?" He leaned forward. "I'm the last person who'd judge you."

"Evelyn Hemlock used blood magic." I spoke as quietly and clearly as I could. "She made me use blood magic, and tore the witch to pieces."

Was that the Hemlocks' speciality? Power over life and death? No wonder I'd turned out to be a necromancer as well.

"She... what?" said Lloyd. "Okay, that's bad. Really bad. Tell the boss."

"You think she'd let me stay at the guild if she knew? Possessing people is illegal, let alone using *that* type of magic."

"It's not like she can arrest the Hemlock Coven's heir."

A flash of light from Isabel's chalk circle drew my eyes. She shook her head over it. "It's not giving me a conclusive answer. Also, Lady Harper is threatening to come and see us."

"Please, no." I cast my mind around in an attempt to find an excuse that would stop the angry old mage from steamrollering into what was left of my life here. "Tell her we're close to answers, and the guild is already at our back. You know what she's like, she probably has some kind of grudge against Lady Montgomery like she does against everyone else she runs into."

Isabel grimaced. "Yes, she probably does. Maybe she

can help deal with your little spirit problem, but she's a mage, not a witch."

"And bonkers," I put in. "She'd come into the guild and start making unreasonable demands. It's not like even her mage magic can find hidden vampires, stop witch rituals, or tear out unwanted spirits. Must be why she's so dead set on making *me* be her stand-in."

"Right. I'll set Ivy on her… that'll keep her busy for a while." She began putting her spell ingredients away. "I'll have to take this spell back to the hotel with me, I think."

"Question," said Lloyd. "You said the spirit went out of hand, right? How? Did she take total control?"

"More than once," I said. "It wasn't an accident like last time. I don't know if she just didn't trust me or whatever, but it was scary as fuck, and I'm not sure she has an 'off' switch."

Where was an exorcist when I needed one? Finding an independent one was all but impossible, short of taking the case to the upper levels of the guild and getting jailed for my trouble. Lady Montgomery might trust me, but the guild's upper department tended to see things in black and white. I'd used blood magic while under control of a shade. I could be the leader of the Mage Guild and still be executed for that. Not even my Hemlock blood status would save my neck, whatever Lloyd seemed to think.

I'd see just how far the conspiracy stretched before I threw myself on the boss's mercy. The sooner I got the spirit out of me, the better—and that meant getting the guild on my side.

17

I knocked on Lady Montgomery's office door, steeling myself. While I wasn't sure how much I could actually tell her, maybe dropping some hints about the spirit's powers would ease the blow when it finally fell.

Who was I kidding? The best-case scenario was that I'd lose my apprenticeship and end up having to flee the mortal realm to that creepy forest for the rest of my life. No, thanks.

The door opened and the woman herself looked expectantly at me.

"Lady Montgomery," I said. "Hi."

"Mind telling me where you've been today, Jas?"

"Not in a council meeting." Oops. I probably shouldn't have said that aloud. "I mean, my vampire friend got kidnapped by a vampire possessing a witch, and it all went downhill from there."

The boss listened with slightly raised eyebrows as I sketched out the series of events. I didn't care if she knew about the tunnels, even if Keir might kick up a fuss if a bunch of necromancers decided to wander onto his turf. Worryingly, however, when I tried to mention the furies, I found myself skipping over the details and just saying that it looked like blood magic had taken place in the tunnel. So they fit into the same category as the Hemlock witches as far as the confidentiality agreement went. I also left out Evelyn's decision to hijack my body, for obvious reasons, but made it clear the vampires and the rogue witches were working in conjunction.

Lady Montgomery was silent for a moment after I'd finished, drumming two fingers on the desk. "This vampire king... I don't believe I've spoken to the latest. Thurston."

"That's his name?" I asked. "I didn't realise they switched leaders so often. It seems pretty informal compared to the guild."

"They do have a significant amount of disdain for ceremony," she said. "I will assemble an envoy and send them to speak to the king tomorrow. If he fails to provide an adequate explanation as to why some of his people are working against guild law, we'll take further steps."

You could always count on Lady Montgomery to have the final word. "What about the witches, though?" I asked. "They don't fall under guild laws. And they've managed to evade attention until now."

"I will inform the Mage Lords," she said. "They'll send an envoy of their own, to the covens, to find out who is responsible for enacting illegal blood magic rituals."

A shiver trailed down my back. Her tone left little doubt that I couldn't count on the guild's protection if word got out that I had a witch who casually used blood magic sharing my body. "Er, but what if the person responsible isn't part of a coven? Or not a local one?"

Isabel hadn't found any more leads on whoever had sold the hemlock, nor where the witch who'd died in the cave had come from, but in order for word of the Hemlock Coven's existence to spread, someone had to have learned about them to begin with. Since I hadn't told a soul since my arrival and the knowledge of the furies' ritual had apparently made it here from England, maybe the covens' secrets had come from the same place.

Lady Montgomery picked up a pen and scribbled a note. "What makes you say that?"

"My friend—she's a witch, and none of her spells have managed to track the enemy yet. I don't think the vampire king himself knows, and if he did, he might do a runner."

"Then he will face the law. Like psychics, vampires are capable of living as legal members of supernatural society, but the moment they stray outside the boundaries of guild law, they will face the same punishment as any transgressor."

That would be perfectly reasonable, if not for the fact that my entire existence is against guild law. Crap on a stick. Did the Hemlocks assume the laws didn't apply to them, or did they simply not care?

"As for you, Jas," she said, "I'd suggest you stay here at the guild's headquarters while we get to the bottom of this."

Damn. She believed she was making the right move, and who knew, maybe she was. The vampire king needed to answer for his people, but in the meantime, our real enemy was sneaking around under our feet, undetected.

And what if she was sending my fellow necromancers into a deadly trap?

Lloyd waited in the corridor outside her office, looking uncharacteristically grim. "What's the verdict?"

"She's sending people to talk to the vampires tomorrow."

"And by talk, you mean..."

"Play judge, jury and executioner?" I grimaced. "It depends how much evidence they find, but if that vampire king broke the law, he'll probably spend the rest of his life in the cells. Meanwhile, the real enemy is hiding."

"Maybe a group of necromancers visiting the king will draw them out," he said. "Hand the case over to senior management. The Mage Lords, too. Bet they can take out these witches. They must be wimps if they're hiding behind vampires."

"Have you forgotten the part where they keep summoning furies?" I whispered. "And for the record, I tried to tell the boss about those monsters and I couldn't. They're under the same geas as my coven."

He blinked, befuddlement spreading across his face. "What? How can those monsters be linked to your coven?"

"Because—" *They're from the same place as the Ancients. A realm only my coven knows about, and I bloody hope it stays that way.*

Except it wasn't true. Keir knew, and maybe he did know how the other vampires had found out. We might have had a couple of shared near-death experiences, but that didn't make him a hundred percent trustworthy.

Lloyd shook his head. "I don't think we should just lie down and give up, but what exactly are the survival rates for summoning things using blood magic? Every cautionary tale they tell novices begins with blood magic and ends with a massacre."

"Today nearly ended the same way," I added. "Isabel never managed to track the witches responsible."

"Why not let her handle the witches?" he asked. "She has way more experience than you do."

I folded my arms. "You know it's not her job, right?"

"It sure as hell isn't yours." He met my eyes and we glared at one another. "Don't fight me on this, Jas. Did you at least tell the boss about the extra person squatting in your body?"

"I couldn't tell her," I said. "I told you, I'm under a geas that prevents me from talking about the Hemlock Coven except to people already in the know. Isabel knows because they elected to tell her. *You* know because... I have no idea."

"Because I saw you die," he said quietly. "I keep thinking about the other night, at the cemetery, when... I'm sure I saw her, looking at me through your eyes. Evelyn. At the time, I thought it was a trick of the light. I mean, you were dying."

"Don't say that." I dropped my arms to my sides, my skin crawling. How many times had people looked at me and seen another person staring back? Maybe she'd been trying to take control all along, and I was better off running into the forest after all. I was violating the guild's safety rules just by living here.

"Jas, you nearly died today, too," said Lloyd. "You're acting like you have to handle everything alone because your coven said so, but you're messing with things that are way too dangerous."

"That's not the only reason," I said. "Look, you know me, and I know you. You own every obscure zombie film from the eighties, you have a younger sister at university, and you use your guild salary to pay her tuition."

He frowned. "Yeah, so?"

"I know more about you than I do about Evelyn Hemlock. We exchanged a few words, but she's basically a stranger. Living inside my *body*. Would you freak out if someone started shooting lightning bolts from your hands randomly?"

"Doesn't sound all that different from a mage ability, to be honest."

"Bad example." We reached the corridor's end, far out of earshot of Lady Montgomery' office. "Okay. What if, whenever you were under stress, you defaulted to dark magic?"

"Jas, you know I discovered my talent when I accidentally reanimated my sister's dead cat, don't you? Necromancy pretty much *is* dark magic."

I groaned and rested my head against the wall. "Blood magic," I said to the plaster. "Like weaponised blood magic. That's what it felt like. The ritual was similar to my magic. The *fury-summoning, human sacrificial* ritual. I mean she was bound to me using a blood sacrifice to begin with, so I suppose it's not really a surprise."

I turned to see him staring at me, mouth slightly agape. "Does the boss know *that?*"

"Hell, no. The mages don't distinguish between being in control of your own mind and being possessed when you use dark magic—if anything, the possession makes it worse. They usually execute people who do what I did— what *she* did—on the spot. No trial."

The Mage Lords were ruthless. They had to be. And while I'd known that my coven had a dodgy history, I'd never for a moment believed myself to be swayed towards dark magic, even for a second.

Lloyd shook his head. "You're more than her, and I don't think you need her at all. You used the magic yourself at least once, right? If you get her out of your body, exorcise her, you might get to be the Hemlock heir without the weird side effects."

"I don't think it's that simple," I said. "Besides, the exorcist is dead, and I'm not so sure even a vampire can get rid of her entirely. Have you ever heard of a case of possession where the host didn't end up dead?"

"Who's possessed?" asked a female voice.

"Nobody." I turned to face Ilsa Lynn, hoping she hadn't heard the rest of our conversation. Though if she had, it was likely the geas would lift as it had with Lloyd. But who knew if she'd report me to the boss or not? Even the Gatekeeper couldn't perform an exorcism.

"Never mind," said Lloyd. "I'm going to check something out in the archives, okay? You two catch up."

And he headed downstairs. What was with him? Okay, he had reason to be concerned about me, and he and I had always played by the rulebook before, but events were too far off script to stick within the guidelines now. The witch's soul was already bound with mine. I'd broken the rules from the second I'd stepped through the guild's doors seven years ago.

"I take it you and Morgan made it back okay?" I asked Ilsa.

"Yeah. I don't know what set Morgan off. He heard

something odd, in the spirit realm. Said it didn't sound human."

The fury? They weren't spirit creatures, right? I'd thought they were corporeal, if evil incarnate, but I'd assumed it was the vampire he'd heard.

"Did you manage to find your friend?" she asked.

"Yes," I said. "But we found and killed another rogue vampire, possessing a witch. Lady Montgomery is sending an envoy to their king tomorrow."

"She is?" asked Ilsa. "I was on my way to speak to her. Maybe I'll try to get in on that."

"They need powerful necromancers, for sure. But I'm not sure the guild's is the best approach. Suppose this is beyond the rulebook…"

"In what way?"

I shrugged. What could I say? Under the geas—not a whole lot. And in the end, the vampires weren't the guild's main concern.

No… there was a witch masterminding this plot against my coven. I'd known it in my bones the moment I'd seen those glyphs on the walls of the tunnel.

My phone buzzed with a call. Isabel's name appeared on the screen as I answered.

"I found where that witch came from," she said. "I'm at the guild, now."

Isabel waited outside the oak doors, hovering on the balls of her feet. I'd have been concerned about talking about the threat in public view, but there were few people around. Whatever Lloyd had gone into the archives for, he didn't answer my text message, so I'd made my way down through the lobby alone.

"You found the witch?" I asked.

"I found the one who bought the hemlock," she said. "She wasn't part of an official coven. More of a loosely connected group of witches who meet up occasionally or pass on their messages through non-conventional means."

"That sounds like a coven to me."

"It would be," Isabel said, "but when I traced that witch's blood to her home, I ran into her family. They didn't know she was a witch at all, but they hadn't seen her in months. Same with the person who bought the hemlock. I asked around the market."

"Seriously? How's it possible not to know?"

Isabel shook her head. "It's rare, especially now. But it paints an ugly picture. From the questioning I did at the market, there are stories of other disappearances. Witches who've stopped showing up to meetings. Young, or unsupported ones. Relatives of other witches who didn't belong to a coven. I wish I could pin the blame on one coven, but this is the best I could do."

"You did better than me," I said. "I should have questioned the vampires before Evelyn killed them. But what I don't get is their fixation on the Hemlock Coven."

"I do," said Isabel. "Hemlock magic is powerful enough to decimate any other witch's power. I don't know how they found out you existed, but now they know what your magic can do, they'll want you out of the picture one way or another."

"Because they think I'm a guild lackey, except with more power than they have." I might not have spent my entire life living with the mages, but I'd lived among them long enough to see how cut-throat the upper echelons of the supernatural community were. If you had power, you had to expect to defend it on a constant basis. The reason the most powerful often ended up as leaders was because being in charge meant having more allies—and because if they already had a target on their backs, they might as well make use of it. That's what Lady Harper had always claimed was the reason she'd served on the mage council twice.

I'd never wanted power, much less to have to fight to defend it. Sure, I'd met a few people—Ilsa and Morgan being two of them—who had shit-loads of power but didn't want to wield a position of authority. But they'd both nearly died for it several times. And I was in way over my head.

My phone buzzed. Lloyd. "Yes?" I asked. "Lloyd, I'm literally outside the guild's doors. Why not come and talk to me face to face? What did you need to run to the archives for?"

"I found something, Jas," he said, in a low voice. "I looked up the ritual we found, afterwards. Out of curiosity. And I found..."

I beckoned Isabel to follow me inside. "Look, I'll come and find you. I'm with Isabel, and she has an update on the witches—"

"Your coven was involved with the guild," he said. "It took some digging, but... the guild arrested someone with the surname 'Hemlock' for practising blood magic. She was put on trial and executed."

Coldness spread through my chest, to my bones. "Seriously?"

Pain bolted across my forehead, sharp and sudden, I

braced myself against the wall, my eyes watering, as a resounding scream echoed through my head, bringing the grey haze of the spirit world.

"What the—?"

Another scream echoed in my head like the cry of a fury, so close, it was like it came from right next to me— on and on, like a relentless howl of anguish.

Evelyn was screaming, too. The noise, the awful howling through the spirit realm, was hurting her.

"Evelyn!" I tapped into my spirit sight, the lobby swaying before my eyes, but the greyness was too blurred even to sense Isabel next to me. "What the hell is going on?"

Isabel shook her head, clutching her forehead. "Not witch magic. It's coming from—everywhere."

"No," I said. "It's coming from inside the spirit realm."

The front doors flew open, and a blast of necromantic power roared through the lobby, sending me flying onto my back. Three people ran in. All were male, and none wore necromancers' cloaks.

"Hey!" I yelled, rolling to my feet and running at the intruders. One of them raised his hands and hit me with another kinetic blast. I dodged, reaching for the witch's magic—and nothing happened. The blast struck me in the chest, knocking the breath from my lungs, and my back slammed into the marble floor once again.

Whatever they'd done had hit Evelyn twice as hard as it'd hit me, and I couldn't reach her.

Or her magic.

18

A second later, the vampire's hands were on my shoulders. I twisted out of his hands and gave him a sharp kick in the fork of his legs, reaching into my pocket. Without Evelyn's magic, all I had were spells, and not enough of them. My vision swam with the haze of the spirit realm, but worse than that—the wards on the building ought to have stopped them from getting inside. How had they brought down the security?

I kicked the vampire in the gut while he was down, glimpsing Isabel grappling with the second. Presumably due to her coven's defensive magic, he couldn't get a grip on her, but the third had vanished from my line of sight.

Damn. I had to stop the bastards before they got their soul-sucking hands on anyone in the guild.

My attacker lunged at me again, and this time my boot connected with his nose. Cartilage cracked beneath my toes and he fell back, swearing. Injuries in this realm wouldn't impede his spirit sight, but why had the screaming attack in the spirit realm affected us and not the vampires?

I left the vampire bleeding and scanned the lobby for his friend. *There.* The third vampire sprinted in the direction of the stairs, and I threw a trapping spell at him. Lines of red light pinned him to the ground, and two cloaked necromancers climbed down the stairs and stumbled over his body, eyes wide with shock. Several others followed. *Backup. Thank god for that.*

"Someone raise the alarm!" I shouted. "Get the senior necromancers in here. *Now.*"

Whatever the vampires had done to the spirit realm was beyond any novice necromancer. The settings around the building were fixed so that no dark magic could be used inside, nor any summoning that wasn't under the control of a guild member—but the wards were at least partly responsible for that, and the enemy had already bypassed them. If the vampires had the chance to unleash the extent of their powers, people would die.

The vampire I'd trapped twisted onto his back. *Oh crap.* The spell wasn't designed to trap a person, certainly not one as strong as him. He lunged for one of the novices, who screamed.

"Stop!"

I threw another spell at him. The impact blasted him into the stairwell, causing him to let go of the novice—but as he hit the stairs, he slammed his palms into the floor. A shimmering line appeared, blocking the stairs.

Shit. I wasn't the only one carrying witch spells.

"Nobody's coming to save you now, witch," hissed the vampire I'd kicked in the face. His arms locked around my ankles, sending me sprawling onto my back. I kicked out, determined not to let him get a grip on me.

"I always wanted to feed on a necromancer," he said, his smile bloody where his broken nose dripped down his face.

"Ew. No thanks." I wrenched my legs free from him, and the front doors flew wide, allowing another group of intruders in. *Goddammit.*

I worked another explosive spell off my wrist and threw it at the intruders, blasting three of them through the half-open door. The spell blocking the stairs wouldn't be permanent, but novices were no match for one vampire, let alone five.

I swept the vampire's legs out from underneath him and sprinted towards the stairs, but a second resounding scream rocked the spirit realm. An anguished howl from the depths of Death tore through the air, making even the waking world shimmer, distorted. More, quieter screams came from closer in the spirit realm—the sound of necromancers in horrible pain. My head pounded, my knees giving out, while blood trickled from my nose. I gasped, tasting copper on my lips, the vampire blurring before me as he reached for my spirit.

"Get... back."

I lashed out wildly. By some small miracle, my hand actually grasped him, despite the tremors shaking both my body and spirit alike. I pushed with one hand, the banishing words flying from my tongue.

He merely laughed, and a blurred shadow appeared behind the man.

Dead. He's dead.

The vampires were piloting these bodies from a

distance. No matter how much damage I dealt, they'd stay alive, and the guild's own defences would prevent me from banishing them.

The still-bleeding vampire's vessel lunged in my direction, and I threw a trapping spell. Red lights expanded to cover him and the neighbouring vampire, giving Isabel the chance to kick away her attacker, dual-wielding spells of her own. Even she wouldn't have a limitless supply, but unlike me, she wasn't dependent on someone who'd gone awfully quiet.

How had they made my connection to Evelyn disappear?

There was only one explanation: they must have known about the shade and attacked her directly on purpose. That, or they'd aimed their attack at the spirit realm in general, to take the entire guild out of commission. Despite the barrier on the stairs, no noise came from the staircase at the lobby's other side, and even the other necromancers' screams had died down. Lady Montgomery and Ilsa had been upstairs, but there was no sign of a single higher ranked necromancer. Only novices, who would never have seen a vampire before in their lives.

"Watch out!" I yelled at the nearest cloaked necromancer. "They're like overpowered zombies. Someone is controlling all of them at once."

The vampire I'd used the trapping spell on broke through the lines of red light, crashing into me and knocking me onto my back again. Of course, not using his real body meant he could do as much damage to himself as he liked and he wouldn't feel any pain. I could fend off an attacker using hand-to-hand, but only a banishing would force the vamp to let go of his vessel, and the bastards had short-circuited my spirit sight. Nobody else was using necromancy at all.

Looked like my second guess was right—they hadn't been aiming to take out Evelyn, but the entire spirit realm. *No. It can't be permanently broken.* Otherwise, we'd have ghosts materialising at every corner.

I ducked his grabbing hands and caught his wrist, twisting hard. Then I hit him again in his broken nose, for all the good it did. Even if I destroyed this body, the vampire would just send another one after me.

Grey fog filled the room, and I grabbed for the shadowy shape of his spirit in front of me. It was like trying to grab a rocking boat while tossed about in the tides, and while the threads of blue light gradually became visible, they kept slipping through my grasp. How could he have a strong grip on his vessel when nobody else could use necromancy at all?

Pain exploded through my skull as he threw me to the floor, right in my own trapping spell. Blood dripped onto my face and I blinked the grey away. The vampire leaned over me, teeth bared in a bloody smile. "Surrender, little witch."

"No chance." I rolled to the side, fetching up against the red lines of the spell. Witch magic. Lloyd was right—I didn't *need* the spirit to use it. I was as much a Hemlock witch as she was.

The power came in a faint trickle at first as I gripped the threads holding me captive. My fingertips lit up, white-blue, and the vampire's eyes widened as the trapping spell's lines vanished. A whipcord of magic caught him around the ankles and slammed him to the ground again. Whoa. There was the cranky spirit I knew. *Calm down, Evelyn. You can't go mad in here. People will get hurt.*

People were already hurt. Bodies—black-cloaked bodies, some of them teenage novices—lay inert, drained dry, as the vampires' spirits pulsed with more power. I'd been too late to save them.

I forgot all about keeping the spirit's magic under control and leapt at the nearest vampire with a hoarse scream, my hands seeking his spirit. He growled and tried to buck me off, but this time, my grip held true. I screamed the banishing words, and the vessel's body grew limp, falling to the ground. I climbed off him, looking for Isabel. She'd backed against the wall, cornered by two vessels.

"Two on one isn't fair," I said, but the words didn't come from my mouth, and the spirit that moved my limbs wasn't mine.

White-hot energy lanced through the nearest vampire. He screamed, his legs folding at the knee, blood pouring from lacerations in his skin.

Another vampire ran at me, and the whip-like thread of magic caught his legs, sending him flying into the wall. He slid to the ground, leaving a vampire-shaped bloodstain behind.

Whoa. Good job blood magic *didn't* work inside the building. Evelyn didn't care how much damage she did, only that she revenged herself on whoever had knocked her out.

Right now, I was pretty much in agreement.

Isabel threw a spell at the last standing vessel. He collapsed onto his front, and through the spirit realm, I felt the vampire's grip on the vessel slip. With a roar of rage, I lunged towards him, reaching for the threads of blue light before they faded. "Tell me where you are. Tell me."

"It's worth more than my life to tell you, Hemlock... I hope you all burn."

Evelyn's magic sizzled through the connection, and the vampire's grip on the vessel cut out. He was gone.

I released a breath. "Evelyn, you are deep in the shit."

"Was that her?" Isabel asked, staring at the bodies. I didn't need to check into the spirit realm to tell which were dead, and which weren't.

"Yes." I swore. "How am I supposed to explain how I did that?" I pointed at the vampire-shaped bloodstain halfway up the wall.

"Cleansing spell. I'll do it. Are the wards still on?"

"I'm guessing not." I looked down at my bloody hands. I'd been intending to grab a weapon, but I took back every thought I'd ever had about witch magic not naturally being designed for combat. Evelyn had a real bloodthirsty streak, and she'd taken total control—again. I grabbed a cleansing spell from my pocket to clean off the blood before running to check the wards outside the front doors. Something had gone horribly wrong.

Outside the front doors, the walls shimmered with light, faintly. Even before I touched the walls, I knew there was a gap in the defences, a spot where the inbuilt protective spells had begun to unravel.

A witch had done this.

Okay, now you're going to behave yourself, Evelyn. Help me fix this.

I pulled her magic under my control, focused on the

same warding I'd used in the hotel room, and pushed it into the wards already on the building's exterior.

Isabel moved alongside me, her hands moving, whispering under her breath. The walls shimmered, and I released a breath, breaking the connection. "I think it'll hold."

"It will," Isabel confirmed. "I need to help the injured."

"I'll undo the barrier on the stairs."

We re-entered the lobby. Isabel ran to a stirring novice, pulling a healing spell from her pocket. "I'll handle things down here. You get that spell undone and check upstairs."

"Will do." I ran to the stairs, Evelyn's magic already springing to my hands, cutting through the barrier spell like paper. Someone had made an advanced witch spell to bind the place, but whoever had attacked the spirit realm had been no witch. But since when could vampires do that kind of damage?

I dragged the body of a fallen vessel aside and scrambled up the stairs, finding myself face to face with Morgan Lynn lying half-conscious on the steps. He groaned faintly.

"Hey. Do you need a healing spell?"

"No," he said, scrunching his face up. Blood streamed from his nose. "I need to know who the rogue psychic is so I can knock them in the face."

"Rogue... psychic?" That scream... oh, god. "Did a psychic attack the spirit realm? Is that who screamed?"

He lifted his head. "Yeah. Must've been. Nothing else is that strong."

Shit. The enemy had a psychic. No wonder they'd known my name. Psychics, I'd heard, had the ability to read thoughts and impressions from powerful necromancers... and I'd bet my second soul that included vampires. But I hadn't known they could unleash a psychic scream that shook the whole spirit realm and prevented anyone from using necromancy at all.

"How in hell did it not affect the vampires?" I asked, climbing past him to see the whole stairway was blocked by passed-out necromancers. "Those vessels were under tight control. Unless the vamps were wearing the equivalent of noise-cancelling headphones or something, they shouldn't have been able to interact with the spirit world at all."

"Iron," Morgan said immediately. "Iron dampens psychic powers and makes you less open to spiritual attacks whether you're a psychic or not."

I stared at him as he pushed to his knees. "Iron? Seriously? This whole building's made of it."

"Yes, but the spirit realm's still accessible on the inside. They blew the wards out, I guess, so the attack got inside here."

I fixed it. But for how long? The attack had even been strong enough to affect non-necromancers, though it explained why Isabel had recovered faster.

"The boss needs to know," I said, half to myself. "If there's a psychic out there—someone has to find them before they strike again."

"The boss?" said Morgan. "Any high-ranked necromancer who got hit will be out cold. For sure."

Having two spirits had saved me. Again. "Shit a brick. Nobody should be that powerful." I stared at the bodies in the lobby. With a psychic on their side, the enemy could take out any necromancer who opposed them.

Isabel appeared at the foot of the stairs. "I've helped everyone I can down here, but I don't know how many people got hurt upstairs. Does the guild have enough healing spells?"

"They do," said Morgan, half leaning on the wall. "Most senior necromancers will be out for the count, but I can find them."

"Good, because we need to find that psychic." I turned to Isabel. "That's what the blast was—a psychic, screaming loud enough to crack the spirit realm. Every necromancer above a certain degree of power is going to be pretty much catatonic for hours at least."

Isabel swore, pulling out her phone. "If every necromancer is out, how did those vampires get in?"

"Iron." I spotted a discarded knife and picked it up. "It blocks psychics from your mind. It helps that you're not a necromancer, but—" My phone buzzed in my pocket and I pulled it out. "Lloyd?"

Silence. Nothing more than ragged breathing.

"Lloyd?" My heart jumped into my throat. "Lloyd. Answer me. Are you in the archive room? I'll send—"

"Not the guild," he gasped. "Don't come—"

The call cut out.

I met Isabel's eyes. "They took him."

19

Keir picked up his phone after one ring. "Jas," he said. "I'm outside. The wards won't let me in."

"I redid them after the vampires attacked us. I guess you probably sensed them when you were running to the guild, right?" I moved in the direction of the doors, my fist clenching around my phone. "It had better really be you."

"You're welcome to check." His voice sounded breathless, like he'd sprinted here.

I tapped into the spirit realm and sensed Keir behind the doors, alone. *Good.*

"They took Lloyd," I said, hurrying out to meet him. "So I'm going after them."

Keir eyed the wards flickering on either side of the entrance. "This is the best place for you to stay. It's protected."

"Because I redid the protections using Evelyn's magic. It might not last. They have Lloyd, and they also have a psychic. That's who attacked the spirit realm. You felt it, right? The screaming."

He nodded, his face pale. "Yes... a psychic. That must be our missing link."

"They're not using the psychic to get info on me anymore, since they have everything they need," I said. "Instead, they can attack the guild without setting foot near the place. If not for Evelyn, I'd be passed out or worse. The vampires made themselves immune, by carrying iron."

Keir's eyes widened. "I carry an iron knife. That must be why it didn't affect me as strongly."

"Speaking of weapons." I scanned the bodies in the lobby. "I need to arm myself. Hang on a moment."

"So you didn't know?" Isabel asked him. "You're not working with the enemy? This was more than an attack on the guild: it was a diversion, too."

Keir walked into the lobby behind me, warily glancing at the wards as though expecting them to block his path. "You still don't trust me."

"Nobody is supposed to be able to get in here, Keir," I said. "Let alone break the wards. You seriously didn't know the vampires might be planning this?" I turned over the nearest vessel's body and retrieved a knife from his pocket. He didn't just have weapons, but an iron wristband, too. *I'll take that.* It was a little loose on my wrist, but I slid it halfway up my arm.

"Of course not." Keir's gaze skimmed the fallen vampires and necromancers, and the bloodstains on the polished floor. "I have all the weapons I need. I assume you have some idea where your friend is?"

"Yes," said Isabel, to my surprise. "I have a few

addresses the rogue witches might have used, gathered from the market."

"Too vague," said Keir. "Are you capable of searching for your friend through the spirit realm, Jas?"

"Possibly." I moved to the next vessel, grabbing as many weapons as I could conceivably fit into my pockets without accidentally stabbing myself. "I'll do it now."

The grey fog of the spirit realm still looked distorted, odd, and no ghosts appeared to be within sight. I should use candles, but if I ran to get some, I'd get waylaid, and I didn't have time to deal with the senior necromancers demanding an explanation. Lloyd's life might depend on it.

My actions had led the enemy to our doorstep. If they hadn't known I worked for the guild… *No. it's not my fault.* They'd been one step ahead of me all along, but they'd taken Lloyd because they couldn't beat me on my own turf. Instead, they wanted to lure me to theirs.

I'd better give them a fight to remember, then.

"Lloyd." The greyness swallowed up my voice. I reached for the ghostly trace of his presence—even if he was dead, there'd be something, given that it'd been mere minutes since our phone call. Then I drove my consciousness in his direction.

I bounced off something solid, like my ghost had run full-tilt into a spiritual wall. I winced, hovering on the spot, and tried again. The same barrier blocked my path.

"Ow." I returned to my body, rubbing my forehead. "They have some kind of spirit barrier, I think. But he's alive. I'd know if he wasn't."

"Can you tell where the barrier is?" asked Keir.

I shook my head. "I'd be able to if we were close to it,

in the real world. If there are a number of vampires close together, it'll point us to the spirit barrier's location."

"I doubt they'll make it that easy," said Keir, his eyes on Isabel. "Do you have a definite address for these rogue witches?"

"Only the place where the witch you fought underground used to live," said Isabel. "It's probably cleared out by now, but if Jas knows the general direction of the barrier…"

"I'll be able to sense if we get close to it, too," Keir put in. "I can't project far, but I'll know another vampire when I sense them. Unless they attack the spirit realm again."

"Then we'd better move fast," I said. "If it helps, I know the general direction of the barrier. I'll know if it's our enemy's hideout as soon as we get close. If not, assume it's a trap and act accordingly."

We had little choice. Lady Montgomery was incapacitated. So was Ilsa, and every other powerful necromancer in the guild. Any witches might be working for the enemy. That left three of us against an unknown foe with a psychic powerful enough to blast out the defences on the whole guild. I didn't like the odds.

Isabel took the lead, walking down the darkening street. I didn't hold out much hope that the witches had left any clues behind, but Lloyd didn't deserve to get wrapped up in this.

"I can't believe they took out the guild," I whispered to Isabel. Then I shot Keir a sideways look. "Not permanently. They're probably pissed and planning revenge right now, and I can expect to be fired by the morning, assuming I survive this."

"You think I'd take advantage of the guild being incapacitated?" he asked. "I thought you'd revised your opinion of me."

"I'm having a little difficulty telling friend from foe at the moment. But no, I don't think you would. Having said that, the enemy has a psychic who can read any thought from anyone's head, if they're a strong enough necromancer. I guess that includes vampires, too."

"That's how they knew your coven," said Keir. "I should have guessed. If you never told a soul, and there's nobody in town who knows your family…"

"There is," I said. "The Briar Coven. Lady Harper sent them to spy on me."

Isabel swore under her breath. "Damn her. I don't believe for a minute anyone would betray Lady Harper and get away with it, but that psychic… can they read anyone's thoughts at any given time?"

"According to Morgan Lynn, just powerful necromancers. I don't know. Maybe it wasn't the witches' fault. I just wanted to be angry with Lady Harper for leaving me completely underprepared for this crap."

"You're prepared as anyone might possibly be," Keir said, his eyes faintly glowing with white light as he tapped out of the spirit realm. "Now isn't the time for second guessing."

"Why are you coming with us?" asked Isabel.

"Isn't it obvious? I owe you."

His tone didn't sound entirely sincere, but there was no time for an interrogation. Isabel led us down a cobbled side street, and Keir paused to check the spirit realm once again. "I can't sense any vampires close by."

"Maybe the iron stops them being traced, too," said Isabel. "I don't know, I'm not an expert."

"Maybe it does," I said. "I really need to look into this when I'm back at the guild. That psychic blast even knocked Evelyn out of commission. And she's really, really pissed. If she goes off the rails again—both of you should keep your distance."

Keir turned to me. "Are you sure she's uncontrollable? She might share your body, but you can exert control over other spirits, using necromancy. Why not do the same to her?"

"What, like a vampire?" I shook my head. "She's overpowered, and we're not exactly separate, besides. We're bonded. I can stop her taking the reins, to some degree, but when that blast hit me, it knocked out both of us. And we're about to go up against a psychic, more vampires and potentially a whole witch coven."

"It's not a big coven," Isabel put in. "More like a small group of misinformed individuals pulled into a scheme they likely don't understand. I—I have no idea how they got so many witches involved at all. This type of magic is antithetical to nature. And you know, when you use witch magic against nature, there are side effects. There's a reason the Mage Lords banned it."

I thought of the carnage Evelyn had wreaked. Maybe it was my coven we should be worried about, not the enemy. What did Cordelia really want me to do with the spirit in my head? Even if I'd been willing to give my body up to Evelyn for their cause, she was far from coven leader material. Slicing people to ribbons while revelling in the bloodshed was not a stellar requirement for leadership even if I'd had a real coven to rule over. But who knew, maybe the Hemlocks had planned things that way. They also cared for my safety considerably less than hers. I'd literally died for her already. I was nothing more than insurance. As long as she was attached to me, she couldn't die.

"The question is," said Keir, "why would they choose now to strike? They've had the tools in place for quite a while, if this psychic of theirs is an informant."

"Who knows." Isabel picked up speed, standing on tiptoe to peer past the houses. "Maybe they realised just how powerful Jas is and decided to take her out of commission along with the guild."

"You told the guild about the vampires?" Keir asked. I didn't miss the accusatory undertone to his words.

"Yes, I did," I said. "You know perfectly well the vampire king was letting people work against the law right in front of him without reporting them to the guild. If they did that, who knows what other laws they broke? Some innocent people are dead in there, Keir, and this week, I've met way more bad vampires than good ones."

Not that I was celebrating being right, considering said vampires had orchestrated a massacre. I hadn't counted the dead, but at least half a dozen people had died. Maybe the enemy had heard I'd warned the guild, or maybe they were incensed that I'd outsmarted the vampire in the cave. Either way, this was the endgame, and there was no room for doubts.

"What *is* your problem with the guild?" I asked, when he didn't respond.

"I have no problem with the guild," he said, through

gritted teeth. "I have a lot of problems with self-proclaimed authority figures hoarding knowledge and then acting surprised when that knowledge is used against them by those they betray."

"Come again? The guild betrayed you?"

"The Mage Lords," he corrected. "The guild's number one allies."

"Uh, that'd be because they're the leaders of the entire supernatural community," I said to him. "What did they do to you?"

"Now isn't the time for a discussion."

"It's important," I said. "If you're going to claim I'm exempt from your weird vendetta despite being a Hemlock witch and a guild lackey, I should tell you I was raised by mages for half my life. My foster mother—"

"I have no issue with your family."

"You know half the mages are related, right? Including me. I'm part mage. So chances are, you do have an issue with me."

He shook his head. "You didn't make the laws. It doesn't matter. Are we close to the witches?"

"Don't change the subject." I scanned the stone buildings and the cobbled street winding downhill. "Isabel?"

"We're close," she said. "Check the spirit realm. I can only sense spells when I'm too near to block them."

I touched into the spirit realm, looking carefully for any signs of a trap. None... and no sign of any visible spirit barrier, either. "This isn't our place," I said. "You're right—they must have evacuated. Maybe we should be searching underground..." But the way the attack had hit, I'd felt it come from a certain direction. "Oh, damn."

"Jas?" queried Keir. "What is it?"

"Spirit lines," I said. "The guild's on a spirit line. That psychic attack hit dead on. It must have come from—"

"A key point," finished Keir. "You're right. I don't have a map on me, but—"

"You don't need one," I said. "I know where it is."

Spirit lines criss-crossed the whole country, and they all amplified magic to some degree. Every witch knew that—and they also knew that where one spirit line crossed another, it formed a key point where gaps into other realms, liminal spaces, could open. Like the forest.

Isabel's wide eyes met mine. "They wouldn't."

"They would," I answered. "But—they shouldn't know. They shouldn't…"

"They have a psychic," said Keir. "There's nothing they can't know. Which key point?"

"There's one over the train station." *And it's where the Hemlocks are.*

"But—" Isabel broke off. "Even if they did know, they'd be risking their own necks to try anything there. It's no better than the Ley Line."

"I think both of you are underestimating what our enemies will do to win," Keir said. "Where's your coven?"

Oh god. If I told him—but what did it matter, now? Whatever his problem was with the Hemlocks, odds were, we'd all be dead by the end of the night anyway.

"They're in a liminal space," I said. "On the spirit line that goes through—hell, I've no idea of the limits, I don't have a map on me. Except it connects to the disused railway tracks."

"Then we'll go there," he said. "Even if the enemy isn't there, they're likely on the same spirit line, and it's easier to track from a key point."

"It's also easier to get hit," I pointed out. "The Hemlock witches are protected. They've been there for over thirty years and even outlasted the faerie invasion."

But with other witches, armed with blood magic, working against them? Now the enemy knew the Hemlocks' location, if there was the slightest chance that they might be able to break into the forest, we'd have worse than furies on our hands. We'd have a full-blown supernatural war.

20

Several frantic minutes later, we reached Waverley Bridge. Looking down at the faerie-infested shattered glass that had once covered the train station, there was no way to tell if any nefarious rituals were taking place in there. It was a downright risky place to try any dodgy magic. Fae nested in the walls, zombies rose from the carcasses of broken-down trains, and the tangled spirit lines amplified any magic nearby almost as much as the Ley Line did. But unlike the Ley Line, a path to my own coven lay somewhere under our feet.

"How did you get in there?" Keir indicated the mass of broken concrete and the gutted shells of old cars blocking the road down into the station.

"The Hemlocks' magic kind of tossed me onto the rails down there." I pointed. "But if you can really use the spirit realm to figure out their location, you can probably do it from here on the bridge. God only knows what nasties are lurking in there. Even the necromancers aren't sent in unless we can get a guarantee there's only undead, not wild fae."

"Aren't you capable of killing them?" He eyed my knife, which I kept clenched in my hand. "The guild uses iron weapons."

"Yes, we do," I said. "But faeries don't play fair. It's not like we have the Sight. Besides, I think we have worse than faeries on our hands."

"You're not wrong." He scanned the blockade. "I can't get a reading on the spirit realm here. I think the key point is messing with my vision."

I tapped into the spirit realm. If the barrier was close, I couldn't tell. Everything was blurred, like seeing through a fogged window.

"I guess there's a bunch of iron in the place blocking our spirit sight," I observed. "It always surprised me that the fae moved in, considering, but the spirit lines act as a magical amplifier. No wonder the psychic reached so far."

While the spirit realm might be eerily quiet, I knew the psychic must be close. The scream had hit the guild directly. I scanned the greyness, looking for familiarity.

The cold presence of a barrier was all the confirmation I needed. "Lloyd's in there." I jerked my chin at the ruins. "This way."

I walked slowly down the sloping road, occasionally having to climb onto the walls or clamber over debris to avoid the broken-down vehicles blocking the path. Stone balconies overlooked the train tracks, and darkness gathered below, hiding predators from sight.

Even the mercenaries avoided this place. So did half-faeries, and they *had* the Sight. Faeries which managed to exist around iron were not to be trifled with. The vampires and witches must have cleared them out, though too much darkness shrouded the place for me to be able to tell whereabouts the enemy might be hiding.

Inside the station, the shattered glass fronts of shops and cafés waited ahead below a collapsed bridge, while on the right, the carcass of a train exuded a stench that suggested it was a minefield of undead.

"Hello, Jacinda," said a male voice from next to me, in the spirit realm.

I turned my head, letting the grey fog filter in, but not enough to completely mask my sight. "Hey. Are you the enemy, or just another gormless lackey?"

The touch of his spirit on mine was unmistakable: vampire.

I recoiled, readying myself to fight. Shuffling movements came from all around. Isabel's hands rose, her skin glowing faintly with the spells on her wrists. Keir clenched his knife, his knuckles whitening. Heads popped up, and my vision flickered with threads of blue light. Vampires. No—a vampire-controlled zombie army.

Here we go.

"Ready?" I said, and all hell broke loose.

The dead poured down the broken-down escalators, clambered over the collapsed bridge and leaped down to land on the fractured ground in clumsy rows. If one vampire controlled them, they'd be less coordinated than your average zombie. The bad news was that like zombies, they got the upper hand by swarming. And swarm, they did.

Isabel hurled an explosive at the escalator. The resulting blast sent severed limbs flying and toppling bodies blocked the stairs, but the other zombies just climbed over their fallen companions. I reached for a spell, then stopped. The enemy probably wanted us to waste our entire arsenal on this zombie plague, but the witches and vampires waited somewhere out of sight—not to mention the psychic.

Time to make use of my necromancy training.

I threw up a barrier spell in front of me. The spirit realm overlaid my vision, showing Keir next to me, Isabel on my right, and zombies, connected to their hosts by visible threads of blue energy. The bastards weren't even directly involved in the fight. They must be hiding elsewhere inside the station. My spirit sight was still blurred, but I reached out ghostly hands and grabbed onto the nearest thread of blue light. Chanting the required words of control, I kept my grip strong, while Isabel threw spells left and right, creating a ruckus that kept the vampire's attention in several places at once. He'd set most of the zombies on autopilot, but that made them vulnerable. Beside me, I sensed Keir attempting to override their control, too.

I let go of the first zombie and grabbed for another, jumping to a third the instant the vampire noticed. With his attention split between the three of us, his army wouldn't be nearly as effective. I reached out, threads of blue energy connecting my hands to the zombies, and yanked them out of his grip. The vampire's frustrated howl ripped through my mind, though muted, and less painful than the psychic's scream.

I pulled, hard. *You're mine.*

"Go on," I growled, ignoring the vampire's furious presence attempting to tug the zombies free from my grip. "Attack the others."

Chaos erupted as the zombies turned on one another, offering me the chance to scan the spirit realm again. The barrier blocked me from sensing Lloyd, but a shadowy form that wasn't Keir caught my eye. A vampire was hiding, close by. The person controlling the army.

The barrier spell faded as it hit its limit, but the vampires were too busy fighting one another to notice Isabel close in and blast them to pieces.

Keir, meanwhile, had grabbed hold of his own battalion from the group of zombies who hadn't been taken to bits, and was directing them to turn on their fellow undead. Shooting him a nod, I moved to the side, searching for our hidden adversary.

Figures moved within a coffee shop's shattered ruins. *Aha.* I sprinted across the debris and ran inside, leaping over broken glass. The faint smell of coffee still permeated the air, even as the interior lay in ruins, and shadowy figures stirred at the back.

"I can sense you, arsehole," I said. "You should have picked on someone else."

A zombie lunged at me. I reached for the blue threads of the vampire's control and pulled the undead under my spell. "Go on. Fight your master."

"You bitch," snarled a voice through the zombie's mouth.

"You caught me on a bad day," I said, and sent my new puppet staggering towards the vampire hiding at the back, behind two more zombies. "Come on, at least put some effort in. Did you really sign up to this of your own free will? What're you getting out of helping a creepy cult kidnap my friend?"

"To stay alive," said the vampire. "Or else perish when they wake the spirit lines."

"Doesn't sound like much of a choice." I directed the zombie with a wave of my hand, and the vampire yelped as the zombie punched out his two companions. "I like this guy. Maybe I'll keep him when we storm the place. But I'll be honest, I don't really want to stay here all night. Care to tell me where your master is?"

"No." He waved a hand, and his zombies recovered. Mine got there first, and a scuffle of clumsy punches broke out. *Now I've got you.*

The vampire ducked around the zombies, running towards the door. I tackled him, and we crashed onto a table. Evelyn's magic buzzed in my hands, threatening to break through, but I grabbed hold of his spirit with my fingertips. "Tell me where your master is hiding."

He yelled aloud, fighting to escape my grip, but I could tell that his spirit was depleted. Someone had already drained him, maybe a more powerful vampire.

"Last chance," I said. "Tell me. Now."

He shuddered. "Here, and everywhere, all at the same time. They're... torturing her..." His voice stuttered to silence, and his spirit vanished.

Damn. I hadn't even needed to finish him. Someone on his own side had done that for me. He must have used whatever was left of his power to direct those zombies at me. But who was *she,* and who was doing the torturing?

I grabbed control of the surviving zombies and directed them to leave the café and re-join the battle, while I headed in the direction the vampire had pointed. Ahead were the shattered screens which used to show the train times, some of them still intermittently flickering with orange light. Words chased each other across one of them—*Come and find me, Jacinda Hemlock.*

"Seriously?" I said. "Is this a joke?"

Come and find me, Jacinda Hemlock.

It was no joke, more of a twisted game. The witches must be seriously pissed off that I'd used Evelyn's power to undo their spells and make a mockery of them. What'd started as an attempt to get the Hemlocks out of the picture had turned into a challenge I couldn't afford to lose.

I sprinted back to the battle, where one of Keir's zombies ripped into another. "Hey, those are mine," I told him. "I think we got them all."

"Good." He looked unhurt, his eyes glittering with blue light and his spirit glowing as it did when he'd just fed. "Did you find the vampire?"

"One of them. I think another attacked him, and he died before he could give me a clear answer on where the enemy is. He said *here, and everywhere, all at the same time.* Did he mean the psychic, or…?"

"The liminal space."

"*A* liminal space," I corrected. "There might be a dozen here for all we know."

They weren't in the Hemlocks' forest. I'd know—Evelyn would know—if they were. Our magic would react. So where *were* they? Since we were on top of a key point, the spirit lines were tangled enough that an army of zombies could hide in plain sight, let alone a witch. She might be hiding anywhere.

Keir indicated the zombie. "None of them will talk. The vampires. I think they were led here against their will."

"They still worked for the enemy. The one I just spoke to said that he picked their side because they're going to wake the spirit lines. Any idea what he meant by that?"

"No, but it can't be good."

Isabel ran up to us, climbing over fallen zombies. "I'm the only one of the three of us without the spirit sight, Jas. Can either of you two pick up on anything?"

"Well, they definitely know we're here," I said. "They're messing with us. If we find the spirit barrier, that'll be where the cowardly witches are hiding. Their vampires, they don't seem to mind leaving around to be collateral damage."

"That's because they can only control their zombies from within the same dimension," Keir said. "The psychic, though... I'm assuming they aren't behind the spirit barrier, unless they were taken there after attacking."

I swore. "Of course, why make it easy." Crossing realms must be somewhere in the Hemlocks' skillset, otherwise the forest wouldn't be able to exist the way it did, but Evelyn hadn't shared that particular talent with me yet.

"I can make her sing for you again, Jacinda," whispered a female voice.

I jumped, while Keir swore loudly. "Who are you?"

A soft laugh tickled my ear. "I can make her sing ..."

Well, that answered the question about whether or not the psychic was a willing participant. "Kidnapping people isn't nice," I told the disembodied voice. "Neither is breaking every law in the supernatural rulebook. Also, even necromancers know not to mess with the spirit lines if you want to keep your soul attached to your body."

"That would require having a body, Jas," whispered the voice.

Huh. The person behind this was dead. Should have figured. Who else would be able to use necromancy skills to find vampires?

"Have it your way," I said. "You should know that being dead makes you even less of a threat to me than before. I banish ghosts in my sleep. Show me Lloyd, and I'll talk."

"Jas!" yelled Keir.

White noise exploded in my skull, and power roared to my fingertips. Keir and Isabel shouted my name, but I'd already floated out of my body into the greyness.

Evelyn was at the wheel. Again.

"Stop that!" I shouted, but it was too late. The world turned to black.

21

I floated in the blackness, unable to see anything. Not even the spirit realm.

Had the witch drawn out Evelyn's power on purpose? Where *was* I? Not the wreckage of the train station, but the spirit realm looked the same no matter where you were. Which meant I must still be in the waking world, even if I wasn't on earth at all.

Lights snapped on. Twelve lights. Candles.

A body lay between the candles, inert on the floor of a room so dark I could barely make out the floor between the candles. Even from above, I knew the body was mine. Beside me floated a second spirit, both of us as transparent as ghosts, trapped in the spirit circle.

The ghost turned on the spot to narrow her eyes at me. "Oh, for fuck's sake," said Evelyn.

She looked much the same as before. Long, flowing hair, full lips, eyes that would have been grey-blue in life but now looked more grey-black. Behind her was darkness. We must have fallen into a liminal space—or rather, been dragged into one, the instant she'd used her magic.

"If your magic hurt my friends," I said to her, "I'll take my body back and leave you here to rot."

"Neither of us is getting out of this circle," Evelyn said. "I didn't hurt your friends, Jacinda. But this spirit circle is too powerful to break from the inside."

I thought so. As long as the candles burned, we'd remain trapped—which gave more than long enough for the witches and their army to go after the Hemlock Coven.

Whether the witches could actually get through to them was a different story, but if the psychic kept attacking the spirit line, the whole country would feel the aftershocks, and worse than furies would escape onto earth. And the two of us would remain trapped here, helpless to stop it.

Some Hemlock heir I'd turned out to be.

"It was your magic that set her off," I said. "Did you see that coming?"

"No." Evelyn scowled. "Aren't you a necromancer? Can't you switch the candles off?"

"Not from here, no. I thought you knew all about magic."

Evelyn's lips pursed. "I've spent twenty years barely existing, Jacinda. My memory isn't what it used to be. But if the candles go out, the power holding us captive will dissipate, and we'll be back in your body again."

Yeah, I'm not so sure I want that. But never mind the spirit and her weird Jekyll and Hyde act. Normally a spirit circle took so much power that a high-ranked necromancer would be in severe danger of losing their life if it kept running too long. But there were no necromancers here, and we weren't on earth at all.

"Gotta hand it to her," I muttered. "There I was thinking she wanted to spill *my* blood to fuel her damned ritual, but I guess her plans are more sophisticated than 'set a bunch of angry pterodactyl-like bird monsters loose in the city.'"

"The furies were never more than a means to an end," said Evelyn. "They might have answered the call when she tried contacting the dark dimensions, but her fixation is on more than that. She wants the power in the liminal spaces, where my magic lies buried."

"Your magic?" I asked. "You have plenty of power."

"Not that magic," she said. "Most of it resides in the forest. I possess a mere echo."

"Uh, because the Hemlocks are kind of using their power to stop a giant monster from devouring the world. That's the real reason they got stuck in the forest—right?"

"That creature is called the Devourer. The Hemlocks gave up their magic to keep it imprisoned a long time ago, but it won't last. They may have defeated the Ancients, but they knew all along that it was a temporary victory, nothing more."

"I have absolutely no idea what you're talking about," I said. "But if you think stopping that giant monster from devouring the world is a bad thing, we're not on the same page."

"There's still so much you don't understand, Jacinda."

A shiver trembled through my ghostly form, and I felt the echo of her magic, when her rage had overwhelmed me. Jekyll and Hyde indeed. Maybe leaving her here wouldn't be such a bad idea—if I ever got out.

"If I don't understand," I said, "it's because nobody decided to explain this to me before they put your spirit in my body as a child."

"That's not what they did," she said. "Our souls are one. I'm not in your body, I'm you, as much as you are. We're fused, Jas. I know you *think* we can be separated, like a spirit removed from a body it's possessing, but I'm not possessing you, Jas. I've been you since my rebirth, and especially since I awakened upon your arrival here."

Ah. Shit. She'd guessed my plan. And I'd had my doubts a simple exorcism would work for a while. But there was absolutely no chance I'd let her take the reins again, not knowing she wanted *more* power.

"Why did they do it?" I asked. "Why did they need to bind us? You were still alive."

"I was close to death," she said. "The only way they could ensure an heir survived to adulthood was to bind us. The remaining Hemlocks were trapped in the forest, doomed to destruction. You were whole."

"I was a baby. I had no choice," I said. "You volunteered to save your own neck, is that what you're saying? Just because they decided that sticking around in their forest was more important than ensuring their own bloodline survived through any means other than trapping an innocent child?"

"You're heir because the others died," said the spirit. "They killed us, before the faeries ever came here. And they want you dead because you're the only one left."

Oh, shit. "They died. There were others."

Of course. The Hemlock witches would have wanted to ensure their magic passed on to someone after death. The ritual... it'd been a last resort after all. We'd both been used, but if the alternative was letting that monster loose—the Hemlocks had faced a difficult choice.

I had limited sympathy for them, regardless. They had enough magic that they ought to have found another way than binding two souls permanently, especially one with a major screw loose. And if we both died today, it'd have all been for nothing.

"There were others," she said. "My brothers and sisters and cousins. All of them—dead."

"And now I'm going to join them." I looked down at my inert body lying in the middle of the circle. Even in the best-case scenario, if the others managed to stop the enemy before she could break the spirit line, they could search for days and never find whichever liminal space I'd been taken into. My body would die of dehydration or starvation, or the spirit circle would implode and kill me. Maybe, if I managed to call on the little necromantic power I had in this place, I might get to choose my own method of death. A cheerful thought. *They don't teach you that at the guild.*

I gritted my teeth. *Dammit. I* do *have some magic left.* Blue light sparked to my hands. Necromancy.

Evelyn's eyes gleamed as she watched me, hunger stirring in her expression. "Interesting. Maybe there was another reason they picked you. I have the power of life. You have the power of death."

"And you have delusions of grandeur." The light grew brighter. "I'm not *that* powerful a necromancer. Not even as much as a vampire…" Wait a moment.

Blue light lit up my palms—like the light connecting me with an undead. Then I held out my hands over my own limp body. Evelyn watched me with an eager light burning in her eyes. I still felt her magic, distantly, the echo of its power. Considering part of her was in me, and vice versa, maybe there was no way to separate the two.

"All right." I flexed my fingers. "Now for a little bit of necromancy..."

My body jumped to its feet, swaying with the unsteadiness of the recently dead.

"Aha." I grinned. "That's more like it."

"You do have power," she said, hunger permeating her words. "Strong. I wonder... can I use that, too?"

"Try it and you're never leaving this place."

The circle's edge shimmered as my body walked like a puppet on strings, towards the candles, and my hands pressed against the boundary. An invisible shield kept us caged, fuelled by the candles, but the source of power wasn't limitless. It was weird watching my body move without feeling a thing. Zombies couldn't use magic. But my body was alive, and my magic remained active. I gripped tighter, moving until I was right behind my reanimated body. As I moved my hand, so did she. I had witch spells in my pocket. Explosives.

It took several attempts to make my clumsy zombie hands pull the band off my wrist and throw it into the air, but my aim was dead on. As the witch explosive went off, the nearest candle toppled, and I crashed back into my body so hard, my knees hit the floor. "Hell, yeah."

Problem: now I needed to find the way *out*. Pitch black darkness surrounded us, and when I tapped into the spirit realm, a familiar blurriness blocked my vision. Blurriness that ended, abruptly, at the back of the circle.

A roaring noise came from behind, and a gust of wind

swept into me. Oh, bloody hell. They must have booby-trapped the circle.

The candles began to slide backwards into a yawning gulf, blackness so dark I couldn't see the bottom. The blackness grew, swallowing the next two candles, and at the same moment, the psychic's screaming began anew.

I flew from my body, crashing into Evelyn as though she was a solid person and not a ghost. I hardly noticed I was clinging to her until she let go, having been doing the same to me. She spoke, her words lost beneath the screaming, but I heard her warning loud and clear. If I didn't get my body out of that circle, asap, I'd be sucked into the void. The dimension was collapsing right behind us.

With shaking hands, I gripped hold of the tenuous connection between me and my body and made her walk forwards—one step, two—until we were outside the circle. The screaming kicked up a notch, and Evelyn screamed, too, the racket throbbing in my skull. I floated in and out of my body, forcing myself to walk—another step, then another. Gods, it was so dark in here.

"She meant to destroy us," whispered Evelyn. "If we'd stayed in the circle…"

The scream would have sent both of us flying into the collapsing void. The endless wailing continued, but I did my best to tune it out. Wind whispered at my heels, telling me the rest of the circle was being pulled into the void, too, and the room would follow.

No. I can't die here.

With each step, I fused within my body until I was running outright, outracing the blackness, my breath coming in sharp gasps. The room, whatever it was, was ice-cold, and everything was so pitch-black, I might have been on the edge of a cliff and I wouldn't have known it.

"Use the magic," whispered Evelyn in my ear.

"What would that achieve?" I hissed back, breathlessly. "It's as dark as Satan's armpit in here. Less talking, more running."

Even if using Evelyn's magic didn't do the enemy's job for her, it was too volatile for me to risk unleashing that power here. All magic affected the spirit lines. And if it was true, and more of it was sealed beneath the surface of this line than even the forest—there was absolutely no way I could let the witch get her hands on it.

And that went double for the one sharing my body.

The noise grew louder, a relentless scream of pain and anger rolled into one. Wait—had they left the psychic in the same liminal space we were in?

Evelyn's magic writhed beneath the surface, and one of the remaining shielding spells on my wrist hissed and sparked. Cold air whipped at my ankles. The entire room with the candles had gone, sucked into emptiness. If I didn't slow down whatever spell was causing the floor to collapse, we'd be pulled into darkness one way or another.

I pushed the shield spell down my wrist, Evelyn's magic sparking from my fingertips, and threw the shield behind us. A shimmering barrier extended, flowing beneath our feet. I didn't know for sure it would hold, but it bought us more time to run.

My vision blurred as the wailing noise grew more insistent, but now I knew for certain—the psychic was here, in the same dimension as us. Tracking her was possible just by following the noise, and surely even the witch's ghost would be too disorientated from the shaking spirit realm to realise we'd survived our escape.

A growing light appeared ahead and I flat-out sprinted towards it, skidding to a halt at the figure lying prone on the floor, trapped beneath shimmering glyphs and surrounded by chalk symbols. So many layers of magic pinned her down, she couldn't move. All she could do was scream, endlessly, a wail of pain and terror. They hadn't just used the psychic—they'd left her to die here.

And if we didn't get her out, we'd be next.

22

The psychic was a young woman, from what I could see, and despite the spells' tight grip on her, she struggled against the bonds with tenacity. Her scream ebbed and flowed, not coming from her mouth but from her soul. And I'd bet anything those chalk symbols amplified her magic, like the symbol Lloyd and I had found at the warehouse the other day.

Not only the Hemlocks laid claim to this power.

"The magic will be ours again when we kill them," Evelyn helpfully supplied.

Wonderful. Psycho witch and I were in agreement once again.

I took another step and collided with a solid barrier. Two shadowy figures appeared on either side of the psychic, hands aglow with spell-light. Witches. Behind them, more human-shaped shadows rose into view as the spells' lights spread, lighting the gloom.

"Easy way or hard way," I told them. "Step away from

the girl, or I'll turn your magic inside out and let it eat you alive."

I wasn't sure whether it was me who said that or the spirit, to be perfectly honest.

Evelyn's magic sprang to my palms. The witches screamed, flung back as my power tore into their bodies and spirits alike. The rippling white light struck the barrier around the psychic, and I ran forwards, ignoring the spirit's insistent pushing against my skull. *You can't take the reins. Not yet.*

My hands pressed against the spell-barrier. No spell couldn't be undone, and this wasn't a powerful one. The enemy hadn't really expected me to make it in here. I was supposed to die the instant she started screaming.

Magic poured from my hands, undoing the binding spell pinning her down, nullifying the amplifying spells, swamping the other witches' magic with my own. As the light faded, it took me a moment to realise the weird humming in my head wasn't the magic, but the absence of pain. The psychic had stopped screaming, and lay limp on the floor, surrounded by the bodies of the witches Evelyn's power had torn to shreds.

The last part of the binding spell unravelled, and the psychic rolled onto her back, gasping for air. "I'm so sorry."

Her eyes rolled back in her skull and she collapsed.

"Oh, bloody hell."

The psychic looked like a kid, probably untrained, and it'd be cruel to leave her behind. But if the enemy got hold of her again, the guild might not be so lucky this time.

"Leave her," whispered Evelyn.

"Shut up," I muttered. "Yes, I know you're pissed, but we need protection, not violence. She's on our side."

"Are you quite sure?" said another voice.

A female ghost floated above the floor just a few feet away. Not the spirit, though they shared the same flowing curls and grey-blue eyes. And her voice... I knew it. She was the person who'd taunted me in the station and dragged me into this hellhole to die. The person who'd claimed to no longer be living.

"That was a cheap trick," I said to her, moving in front of the psychic.

"Hardly worse than the crimes the Hemlocks have committed." The ghost eyed the witches' fallen bodies. "Poor souls. They were just like you, Jas."

"I never signed up to kidnap an innocent girl as part of a nasty death cult hell-bent on destruction."

"Innocent? Nothing is innocent about the guild. They have as much blood on their hands as the rest of us."

"Because they executed people for practising blood magic? You're a Hemlock, aren't you?"

Her mouth twisted. "Your friend couldn't resist nosing into our history, could he?"

"If you hurt him in any way, I'll pull your eyeballs out through your throat." Beside me, the psychic stirred, but I kept my gaze on the witch's ghost. "What's the point in all this? You want the Hemlocks' power, right?"

"We Hemlocks are predisposed to want what is ours."

"Yes, we are," whispered Evelyn.

"You don't have magic," I said loudly, more to drown out Evelyn than anything. "You couldn't be heir even if you were alive, but you wanted it, didn't you?"

"Quiet," she said, soft and sharp.

"Did I hit a nerve? Sorry, my ancestor is feeling a little restless."

"What did they do to you?" she hissed. "Why do you have our power? You're nobody."

My body froze, and Evelyn spoke through my mouth. "It's been a while, Leila."

"Evelyn," said the witch. "I should have known you'd find a way to cling to power. Sharing the body of another, though?"

"It worked, didn't it?" said Evelyn. "I survived. And so did my power."

"It should have been mine," said Leila. "I'm as much a Hemlock as you are."

"Not according to the laws of succession," Evelyn responded. "The magic passes on when one person takes over from the other, and you weren't chosen. I was."

"Because you bound yourself to a child." Her lip curled.

"Guys!" I spoke, with difficulty. "Listen, I don't give a shit what argument you two have. I'm not all that thrilled at sharing headspace with Evelyn either, but it's my problem now, not yours."

"The coven," said the ghost, "is mine."

I took a step forwards, and candles sprang to life at my feet. Another rippling spirit barrier separated me from the witch's ghost. "I got out of one of your circles. I can do it again."

"You'll stay there until my witches kill you," she said. "You and the psychic, too. And I'll take care of your friends myself."

"Get back here," I warned. "If you lay a finger on them—"

Cold hands grabbed my shoulders, and the psychic

whimpered. A dozen witches rose to their feet, their mutilated bodies reanimated.

Let me out, whispered Evelyn. *You can leave the circle as a ghost. Find your friends.*

As another candle light flared, I lost my grip on my body and floated upwards. My body continued to move, Evelyn in control once more. Her hands glowed with the light of the Hemlocks' magic, and the candles shifted, leaving a slight gap which closed almost instantly.

She was giving me the chance to escape… if I was willing to leave my body behind. If I flew out the circle, Evelyn would stop the reanimated witches from killing the psychic, while I went to find my friends and chased down Leila Hemlock. There was no other way to end it.

With the last of my power, I floated back into my body, threw a shield spell over the psychic, then floated upwards once more.

Evelyn's magic struck the candle, a gap appeared in the circle, and I flew out in a blur of light.

I'll destroy you before you get to my friends.

23

Leila's eyes widened as I shot at her with the force of a bullet. She'd never expected me to attack her in the spirit realm, let alone abandon my body. I gripped her spirit, shouted the banishing words—and she disappeared.

"Oh, come on." She hadn't gone into Death, but skipped out of the liminal space altogether.

I *should* be able to cross dimensions, especially as a ghost. I really hoped I'd remember the way back, because I did *not* want to leave Evelyn in charge of controlling my body indefinitely.

I closed my eyes and opened them again, reaching for my spirit sight. The world faded, going transparent, but instead of Death, a forest path appeared, flickering beneath my feet.

"Hey. Cordelia." Anger sparked beneath my fear, catching alight. "Thanks a bunch for telling me you left Leila Hemlock alive."

"She wasn't supposed to live," hissed Cordelia's voice.

"She must have hidden herself away, between worlds. Destroy her, before she takes our power and dooms us all."

"Maybe I'll let her kick you around for a bit." I turned away from the forest path. From her tone, the witch hadn't gone after the Hemlocks yet. The magic kept her out. So she'd stuck to her word and gone after my friends. "How in hell do I cross dimensions from here?"

"Feel your way," Cordelia's voice said, ringing through the trees. "Our magic is everywhere at once."

"Because that explains a lot." I felt the forest's magic humming through me, and the ever-present spirit realm, but the real world remained beyond reach. Multiple worlds overlapped here. There must be a dozen liminal spaces folded into this key point, because of the tangle of spirit lines. No wonder the witch had managed to stay hidden from sight. I could still sense my own magic, though muted, as Evelyn used it on my behalf. I couldn't see her, thanks to the spirit barrier, and if ever I had proof that we were two separate people, this was it.

I searched for Keir instead, seeking his familiar form in the spirit realm, and spotted his shadowy outline. I reached out, sensing another spirit near him. *Lloyd?*

The forest vanished, and I appeared in the train station again. Keir leaned against a pile of rubble in a darkened room, the dimly flickering light of a torch illuminating his exhausted features.

"Keir!"

His eyes widened. "Jas. You're…"

"More or less alive. Where's—"

"Isabel found your friend. They're fine."

My shoulders slumped with relief. "I thought I was too

late. The witch—I don't know if you saw her, but she's a ghost, and she threatened to come after you and the others. She's a Hemlock."

"A ghost?" he echoed. "Are you sure?"

"She's floating around making threats." But if she and Evelyn knew each other, she'd either died recently or she'd been a ghost for over twenty years. Even the most powerful spirits didn't last that long. "Shit. I bet she lied. She must have detached from her body…"

So I wouldn't be able to kill her until I found where she'd hidden herself. Clever. Of course, I could still banish her beyond the gates of Death, but I'd bet she'd prepared for that, too.

"Then we need to find it," said Keir. "I think your friend needs help."

I spun around on the spot, seeing Isabel crouched beside a familiar figure.

"Lloyd!" I zipped over to him, and stopped. He was trapped in a similar web to the one that'd held the psychic, while Isabel worked on undoing the spell holding him captive. "Thank god you're alive. I thought I was too late."

"I'm fairly glad of that, too," he muttered. "Bloody ghost."

Isabel glanced over her shoulder at me, then returned to working on the spell. "The psychic's screaming wiped out the vampires. Why would she knock out her own army?"

"To kill me," I said. "It almost worked. The psychic is okay, but I left Evelyn in control of my body. We need to get Lloyd out of here. The enemy is coming—"

A shadow stirred in the corner of my vision, and Isabel

reached for her spells. I floated on the spot, bracing myself.

The world flickered, but instead of the fog of the spirit realm appearing, the room I'd left behind overlaid my vision. Burning candles at my feet, witches revived by vampire magic, the psychic cowering behind the shield I'd conjured... and in the middle of it all, her.

Evelyn Hemlock.

It was creepy to see my own mouth smiling so nastily —almost as much as it was to see the gleam of triumph in her eyes.

Thanks for giving me your body, that smile said.

For an instant, she disappeared, to be replaced with a yawning gulf of whiteness, with a pair of glowing grey-black eyes within. *Oh,* said the part of me not numb with horror. *That's what she looks like in the spirit realm. No wonder that ghost ran screaming.*

The spirit circle broke open, and the vampire-controlled witches swarmed into the real world.

Isabel reacted first, a spell flying from her hand and striking down one of the witches. At least the shielding spell I'd thrown at the psychic remained functioning, but Lloyd was still trapped in the web, and Keir's spirit was almost depleted.

Oh, yeah, and Evelyn had *stolen my body.*

I flew at her, only to collide with Leila's ghostly form. She bared her teeth, her hands locking around my throat. I glimpsed Keir running towards us, grabbing her spirit with his vampire's touch, trying to pull her off me.

Lloyd yelled from behind me. I recognised the words he shouted as a necromancer's banishing spell, but the ghost hung on, tenacious. She was too powerful.

A witch-zombie slammed into Keir, but he got there first, ripping the spirit controlling her out with both hands. His own spirit glowed, satiated, and he turned his back and ran towards Evelyn.

What is he doing?

"Don't!" I shouted, struggling to break free from Leila's grip. "You can't kill me," I snarled at her. "You're no necromancer."

"But I am." Lloyd staggered away from the wall, still half-covered in the witch's trapping spell. "Next time you kidnap the Hemlock heir's best friend, you might want to try checking he isn't a necromancer."

He raised a hand, which glowed with white-blue light. The witch-zombies halted mid-assault, now under his command. Leila yelled in anger, briefly relaxing her hold on me, and I broke free, spinning above the chaos. The witches' mutilated bodies remained still, under Lloyd's control—except for one.

I halted above the witch nearest to the back. The glow above her body was different to the others. Leila was piloting her own body. *Of course.* She'd been hiding right in front of us, biding her time.

Our eyes met as I dived at her, and she came upright with a knife pressed to the psychic's throat. "I can make her break your spell," she said. "And then, the spirit line."

Despite the words coming from the witch's mouth, the glow told me she hadn't reconnected with her body yet, but was still controlling it from a distance. Which gave me an opening.

I reached for the threads of magic connecting the witch with her body. I'd had enough practise wresting control from the spirit, but she fought hard, the knife threatening to cut the psychic's throat. Carefully, I wrenched, hard, and the knife dropped in her hand. "Run!" I yelled at the psychic as the witch's spirit's hands closed around my throat again. Despite her rage, she couldn't really harm me as a ghost. She hadn't practised—been forced to practise—as I had.

At least there was one thing I could thank Evelyn Hemlock for.

I gripped hard on the threads controlling her body, jerking her hands like a puppet. Driving the knife towards her own heart.

"That won't work, Jacinda," she hissed. "I'm a coven leader. I can't be harmed."

Shit. She had the same protections as Isabel?

"Nice try." The psychic lifted her head and looked the ghostly form of the witch in the eyes. "I can read your mind as well as anyone's. You're not a real coven leader. Your magic can easily be undone."

"You will die for that." Leila let go of my throat, grabbing the reins and diving into her own body. But before she could strike, Evelyn Hemlock blocked her way.

"Are you on my side or not?" I demanded. "Come on, now's not the time to throw a tantrum. Let me back in."

"Why would I let you do that? It's been so long." Her hands glowed. "And this magic is rightfully mine."

Leila screamed. A knife protruded from her back, gripped in the psychic's hand. The moment she'd dropped her guard, the psychic had struck, and blood flowed freely from the wound.

Leila let out an enraged cry, throwing the psychic to the side and yanking the knife free. "It's a fine evening for blood magic," she said, spitting out blood. "Let my blood open the veil. Speak the words, Evelyn. Let us mend this rift between us and use the Hemlocks' magic for its *real* purpose."

"With pleasure," said Evelyn.

No.

Light glowed at my palms as her magic rose to the surface. I felt its echo inside me, even here.

I can still use it.

I raised my own transparent hands, and drew on the magic myself. It was as much mine as hers, and I wouldn't let her win this.

Threads of sheer white magic poured from my hands, clashing with Evelyn's. In the spirit realm, she glared at me, two grey-black eyes staring from a void of white chaos and terror. A shade. I couldn't rid myself of her—but I could bind her.

I cast the binding spell, pouring every inch of power I could conjure into it. Like the ward on the hotel, every second made it stronger, and I felt its resonant hum through the spirit realm, the mortal realm, and every world in between. Even a ghost could be bound, if you had enough magic. And the Hemlocks' power was limitless.

Evelyn's ghostly form hovered behind my body, trapped in a web of shimmering glyphs. She screamed in rage, but all I heard was blessed silence. Leila lay dead below, her spirit gone, snuffed out by Evelyn's power.

Then I floated down, and blinked awake in my body again. *It's over.*

24

The Hemlock magic faded as I lowered my hands. Being able to feel the aches and pains of battle brought a rush of relief so giddying, I could have danced.

The psychic stirred beside Leila's dead body, trembling all over, while Keir, Isabel and Lloyd all stared at me.

"Is that you, Jas?" Lloyd asked uncertainly.

I managed a nod. "Yeah. It's me. I locked her out."

"Thank god." He stumbled forwards, and Isabel moved in to catch his arm before he fell on his face.

"Let me get the rest of that spell off you," she said to him. "It was a tricky one."

"Hang on, I can help." I walked to her side, tapping into the Hemlocks' power. "Sorry, Lloyd. I didn't know the vampires would take you from the guild."

"Actually, it wasn't them," he said, shaking one leg as I freed it. "I got away from the vampires, but then I ran into another trap because of that damned girl."

"Who?" My hands stilled on the spell. "You mean the

girl you've been 'seeing' on the side, against the guild's rules?"

"I know, I know. I hardly thought she'd have made friends with a bunch of masochistic vampires, did I?"

I finished the spell and his other leg broke free. "Don't trust the dead. *Any* of them."

"You really think I'll ever trust any of them after this? Forget it." He ran forwards and hugged me. "You're covered in blood."

"I know. We should destroy these bodies. Burn the whole place, even. Right, Isabel?"

"Is the witch definitely gone?" Keir wanted to know.

I nodded. "Yep. Permanently dead. She didn't see that one coming."

Neither had Evelyn. How long had she been planning to seize control over my body? Probably from the moment she'd awakened. And the forgotten Hemlock had almost given her that chance.

I'd never trust a single one of them again. Cordelia included.

Once we'd thoroughly destroyed the bodies of the fallen witches, I approached the psychic. She was smaller than she'd seemed in battle, barely five feet tall. Her features suggested Asian heritage, and I'd guess she was in her late teens at most. "What's your name?"

"Mackie," she whispered.

"Okay. You're going to have to come with us. Don't worry. You're safe now."

"Not to the guild," she said. "Absolutely not. They'll have me locked up. I attacked them."

You're not the only one with that worry, believe me.

Wait. She knew my secrets—she'd read every one of

them from my mind. Everything, from Cordelia's ultimatum down to Evelyn's betrayal.

"You saved me," Mackie said, her dark eyes meeting mine. "I won't betray you. But the guild—"

"They know you exist," I said. "If you turn yourself in first, they'll see you were used against your will and they'll spare you from punishment. If not, they'll keep hunting you. Trust me, it's better this way."

"I can back you up," Lloyd added.

She looked at the floor, mumbling, "I'm not great at following rules."

"Look at Lloyd and me," I said. "Do we look like we're following the rules? Really?"

A smile tugged at her mouth, briefly. "All right."

The five of us limped up the road to the guild twenty minutes later. I'd spoken for most of the walk back, while the others had listened in slack-jawed silence as I'd told them what Evelyn had done.

"So the spirit was bound to yours to fulfil the role as heir, only to decide she wanted to steal the power for herself?" asked Lloyd.

"Yep," I said. "I can't destroy her, because we're permanently bonded. If one of us dies, so does the other."

"That is fucked up."

Isabel looked like she agreed, and while Keir didn't meet my eyes, I was sure he must be thinking the same. As for Mackie, it didn't matter if she heard our conversation or not. There wasn't any point in keeping secrets from someone who could read minds.

"But she's gone now, right?" asked Isabel.

I shook my head. "I still have her magic, but I bound her, somewhere in the spirit realm. She'll be pissed if she ever gets out, but I'm not planning on leaving this body unattended for the foreseeable future."

Until I figured out how to sever the connection without ending up dead myself, keeping her locked away was the next best thing.

Keir paused outside the guild's doors. "I don't think it's a good idea for me to go in there with you."

"Why not?" I said. "Trust me, they're going to pin at least some of the blame for this on the vampires."

"They have bigger concerns than me," he said, with a glance at Mackie. "I'll come and talk to you tomorrow, if you need me."

I was far too tired to take in the double meaning in his words until Lloyd nudged me, once we'd passed through the guild's doors.

"What?" I said.

"Just ask him out if you want to."

"Look, we've a potential catastrophe to avert. Where's Lady Montgomery?"

I really hoped the senior necromancers would be merciful. Mackie looked terrified, staring at the cloaked figures huddled around the bodies laid out in the lobby. The necromancers had recovered for long enough to gather the dead, led by a tall figure in robes adorned with badges. Lady Montgomery caught my gaze and turned in our direction. Ah. Maybe I wouldn't get to rehearse my piece after all.

Leaving the novices, she swept towards us. "I already sent out two rescue parties looking for you, and I have people scouting the spirit realm as we speak. I take it you caught the person responsible?"

Mackie shifted next to me. Lady Montgomery turned to her with a questioning look in her eyes.

"They kidnapped her," I said quickly. "The enemy attacked the guild by forcing her to use her power."

"So you're the one responsible," Lady Montgomery said, giving Mackie an appraising look. "You must be a high grade psychic. Who trained you?"

Mackie's fists clenched at her sides. "I trained myself."

"Take her to Ilsa Lynn," Lady Montgomery said to Lloyd. "We only have one resident psychic at the moment, and I wouldn't say he's particularly ready to be a mentor."

"Morgan?" I said. "Ah. Yeah. She's seriously powerful. She needs guidance. None of this was her fault, though."

"Lady Montgomery!" said a frantic voice, and a group of novices waylaid her. "We need you upstairs—urgently."

"I'll be with you shortly." She turned back to me. "You're to come to my office as soon as I finish dealing with this. That's an order."

"I'll be there," I said.

"I'll go back to the hotel," Isabel said quietly. "Your defences are still active, and it's nowhere near the spirit line."

"If you're sure." I walked back to the guild's door, and to my intense surprise, found Keir standing outside. "I thought you were leaving."

"I just wanted to make sure you were safe," he said.

"I should leave," said Isabel, getting the vibe that he wanted to talk to me alone. "Thanks for your help in the fight, Keir."

He blinked in surprise. "You, too. You fight well."

"I'm going to speak to the Hemlocks first thing tomorrow," I said to Isabel. "They have a lot to answer for."

"They do," she said. "I'll see you then, okay?"

"Take care." I waved her off, then I faced Keir. "What did you want to talk to me about?"

"The Hemlocks," he said. "I figured I owe you an explanation."

"You mean... how you heard of my coven." *Please, no.* I didn't have the energy to deal with another betrayal, not after Evelyn.

"The Ancients were the ones who took my brother."

My mouth dropped open. "What? I thought your family died."

"They did. Except him." His words were calm, but laced with an undercurrent of anger. "They took him, and I've never been able to track him down. Not even through the spirit realm. I'd know if he died. He's alive, and he's with the Ancients, wherever they are."

"But... that's impossible. The Ancients... they can't come to earth." Not if they were all like that monstrous beast the Hemlocks' magic kept contained. Right?

"I only know what I saw," he said. "I wasn't at home when they took him, but he warned me through the spirit realm. He said, 'the Ancients are coming'. Then he vanished."

"How—how long ago was this?"

"Eight years ago," he said. "I've been searching for him since then, and the only clue I ever found was that the Hemlocks knew the Ancients. I assumed that if I found a Hemlock, I'd be able to find them. But now I've seen those dimensions..."

"I don't know how to find them," I admitted, an inexplicable rush of sadness constricting my throat. "The only Ancient I've ever seen, if you don't count the furies, is a monster imprisoned inside a void. Nobody could survive there."

"My brother wouldn't lie, Jas."

I shook my head. "The Hemlock Coven—their magic, our magic, is used to protect the world against these... Ancients. I don't know how to get into their dimension, if it's even possible. The other Hemlocks have been holding that dimensional rift closed for years."

"I only know what he told me," Keir said. "As for why I'm not the biggest fan of the mages, they dismissed me when I went to them to help. Knowing what I do now, about the Hemlocks, I suppose I'm correct in assuming the mages don't know of your coven's existence?"

"Not that I'm aware of." I said. "Except Lady Harper, and I've no idea what she *or* the Hemlock witches are going to say when I tell them. I don't think even they knew she'd turn against their own cause." My phone buzzed. "I'm gonna ignore that."

"Wise idea." His hand closed over mine. Despite the coldness of his touch, I wanted to lean in and forget the horrors I'd witnessed tonight, just for a moment.

The buzzing continued, insistently. "Right. I'll just see who it is."

Lady Harper. She didn't waste any time.

I took in a breath. "Best get this over with. Fair warning: there might be shouting involved."

"I'll keep my distance," he said, not moving.

I raised the phone to my ear. "Lady Harper."

"What in the Sidhe's name was that?" she demanded. "I

felt the spirit line—*your* spirit line. Every necromancer in town is shouting about it."

"Just the usual," I said. "A witch calling herself a Hemlock joined forces with Evelyn and tried to break into the forest through the spirit line. I stopped them."

A long pause followed. "Excuse me?"

"Talk to Cordelia. Does the name Leila Hemlock ring a bell?"

There was another pause, a shorter one. "She died."

"Unfortunately not," I said. "She hid in a liminal space, recruiting witches and vampires on the fringes, and finally kidnapped a psychic and forced her to break into people's minds until she found out who I was. Then I got to witness a lovely family reunion. If there are any other family members I should know about, then I swear—"

"None should be alive," she said. "Jas, are you sure you didn't misunderstand Evelyn's intentions?"

"The part when she told me she wanted more power, not just the Hemlocks', or the part where she shoved me out of my own body and started to help Leila open the spirit line?" My fist clenched over my phone. "She would happily have booted me out for good while she used my magic to break through the spirit line along with Leila, her supposed enemy. I have every right to bind her where she can't hurt anyone." I hung up without waiting for a response, breathing heavily.

Keir remained where he stood, inches away from me. "Feel better?"

"Not really. Guess I won't be welcome home anytime soon."

"I thought this was your home," said Keir. "Unless you don't want to stay at the guild?"

"I need the law on my side. You know why."

His fingertips trailed along my cheek—cold, but not unpleasantly so. "Are you sure I can't change your mind?"

I shivered, leaning into his touch—both physically and otherwise. "What, be a rogue like you? Tempting offer, but no thanks." Despite my words, I tilted my head to meet his, and shivered when his lips teased mine.

"Sure?" he murmured against my lips.

"Positive." I kissed him back, warmth spreading straight to my core as his hands, chill to touch, gripped my shoulders. "That doesn't mean I don't want to see you again."

"Let me get back to you on that." His lips lingered over mine, his hands slow to release me. "I only had a taste of you, and I want more."

The feeling was mutual. Unfortunately. Why couldn't I like normal, steady guys who didn't have entirely too lax a relationship between the dead and the living.?

Probably because of that extra soul of yours.

I booted the thought clean out of my head and kissed him again. "You're making it really difficult to leave," he murmured.

"Unless you want an all-night interrogation from Lady Montgomery, you should probably go. But I'll text you later." At least something good had come out of tonight.

"See you around, Jas." He released me as Lloyd pushed the guild door open behind me.

"Are you done?" he asked.

"For now," said Keir, and gave me a wave before walking off.

Lloyd crossed his arms, propping the door open with

his shoulder. "Really? You nag me about ghosts, and then make out with a vampire?"

"He's still one of the living," I said. "Relatively speaking, anyway. And didn't you say you were swearing off ghosts for life?"

"Being stuck in there with that witch kind of put me off lost spirits, to be honest, even if that girl hadn't tried to get me killed."

"I'd be worried if it didn't." I followed him back into the lobby. "Let's go and deal with the boss. Then… we'll have our zombie film night tomorrow?"

"I wouldn't miss it."

Isabel and I walked back to the train station first thing the next morning. The ruins looked no different to last night, though the witches took pity on us this time around. Within seconds of stepping onto the bridge, the world faded out, to be replaced by the Hemlocks' cave.

"Jacinda," said Cordelia. "We owe you our thanks for defending the spirit line."

"And I owe you no thanks for leaving me at Evelyn's mercy."

There was no need to explain the battle. The forest would have read it from my mind the instant I'd entered. The witches couldn't fake ignorance. They knew exactly what she'd done.

"You sealed her away?" Cordelia asked me.

"Yes, I'm unhurt. Thanks for asking." My nails bit into my palms. "Lady Harper says she didn't know Leila Hemlock was still alive. Did you?"

"No," she said. "We haven't left this forest in over thirty years, and there's nothing any of us could have done without leaving, and thus damning the world to destruction."

"That's precisely what just happened, or close enough." My voice shook with anger. "The spirit lines are vulnerable, and she just exploited a major weakness. People died."

"I offer my sincere condolences. Casualties are an unfortunate side effect of this war of ours."

"Of yours," I corrected. "I didn't ask for any part in this."

Instead of offering a response, she turned her pitch-dark eyes on Isabel. "Have you anything to add?"

"No," said Isabel. "Jas pretty much said it all. And if I was her, I'd be figuring out a way to permanently get rid of that spirit."

"Believe me, I am," I said. "I didn't want to be right, Cordelia. I tried to believe she wasn't unstable, but she's been trapped in a dormant state for decades. She's not the person you knew when she was alive."

Cordelia leaned forwards. "Isabel. You go, while I talk with Jacinda alone."

Isabel hesitated, but I turned away from Cordelia to speak to her. "It's okay. You should get back to your coven."

"I'll keep looking for more information on who found out the Hemlocks' secrets," she said. "I get the feeling we only scratched the surface."

"I really hope not," I said, accompanying her to the cave door. "Say hi to Ivy for me."

"I will. You did great back there." Isabel lowered her

voice. "You're better than they are. You don't have to do anything they say."

"Watch it," I whispered. "You don't want them to throw you into the middle of a faerie's nest."

"Even they wouldn't dare attack another coven leader." She grinned. "You're welcome to come and visit me at any time."

She waved at me, and the door closed behind her. I turned back to Cordelia, waiting for an apology that never came.

"Someday, Jacinda, you will come to understand why we made the decisions we did," said Cordelia.

"I understand why you did it," I said. "That doesn't change the fact that you broke every rule in the book in binding the two of us and left me to face the consequences."

"The rulebook was created for humans, not for us," said Cordelia.

"You're still human." *That* was her takeaway from all this? No apology, no admission of wrongdoing… just the usual righteous declaration that whatever they did was beyond reproach just because they happened to have the word 'Hemlock' attached to them. I swallowed down my rage and disgust, shaking my head. "Look. I get that Evelyn was supposed to be your saviour. It won't kill you to admit you might have been wrong about her, and find a solution that doesn't involve the magical law enforcement coming down on all our heads. I'm not the one who has the power here, Cordelia. I happen to like my soul still attached to my body—that's *my* soul, not Evelyn's. So if you don't mind, I'd like to get back to my job."

As far as I was concerned, I was through with the

Hemlocks until they saw some sense. Maybe Evelyn hadn't come by her power-mad tendencies through being stuck inside my body, but had learned it directly from the others. This was my legacy. Ancient and terrifying magic that warped the mind and tore dimensions to pieces.

Give me tame, ordinary necromancy any day of the week. Necromancy had saved my neck as much as witchcraft in the end, and I had some serious catching up to do on my apprenticeship. Besides, I'd always felt more at home among the dead than the living.

The instant I turned my back, the cave disappeared, leaving me on the bridge. I'd half expected them to dump me in the middle of the ruins as a last act of defiance, though in fairness, there were a few necromancers running around down there on the guild's orders, in case the enemy had left any more dangerous spells or zombies behind.

I'd won this round—for now. I knew the spirit was likely hiding a thousand more secrets, and I doubted she'd consent to being imprisoned forever. But I'd find a way to get rid of her for good, without letting that monster out into the world.

For now, I had some ghosts to banish, and a zombie movie marathon had never sounded so good.

ABOUT THE AUTHOR

Emma is the New York Times and USA Today Bestselling author of the Changeling Chronicles urban fantasy series.

Emma spent her childhood creating imaginary worlds to compensate for a disappointingly average reality, so it was probably inevitable that she ended up writing fantasy novels. When she's not immersed in her own fictional universes, Emma can be found with her head in a book or wandering around the world in search of adventure.

Find out more about Emma's books at
www.emmaladams.com.

www.ingramcontent.com/pod-product-compliance
Lightning Source LLC
LaVergne TN
LVHW041624060526
838200LV00040B/1427